FINDING NOWHERE:
The barefoot chronicles

JS Brough

JS BROUGH

For Lucy.

FINDING NOWHERE

'It has been said that 'time heals all wounds'. I do not agree. The wounds remain. In time, the mind, protecting its sanity, covers them with scar tissue and the pain lessens, but it is never gone.' (Rose Kennedy)

"No problem is so big or so complicated that it can't be run away from." (Miki Dora)

PART 1

2000

GULLY

I remember so clearly the day that my childhood ended. It was a day that left a permanent scar, not only on me, but on the whole town that I lived in and the people that I loved.

I was ten years old the first time I saw the Atlantic Ocean. Moving from a small council house in the midlands to Cornwall felt like we had gone from a place about as far from the ocean as you could get to what felt like the edge of the world. Mum had bohemian ideas of living some sort of idyllic 'good life', eating cream teas and wandering the moors, but reality is never quite as perfect as we hope and dream of.

We had next to no money, but we managed to rent a little terraced house on the outskirts of Rocky Bay, a small surf town nestled in a wide crescent bay in Cornwall. In those first few years there was an old man who lived next door to us who used to come round with all sorts of things, from pasties, to sewing machines. My Mum said he was just lonely. He didn't know what to do with himself after his wife had died. One day he appeared on the doorstep with a battered, old T&C surfboard. It was a strange sight-seeing this frail old man standing there in his shorts, socks and sandals, holding a surfboard. He said he found it in his shed - he thought it might have been his sons. My Mum always tried to say we didn't need any of this stuff, but she wasn't so good at standing up for herself - maybe that's why it took her so long to leave my Dad. But I was glad the old man from next door turned up that day; the strange sight of this crazy old man with a surfboard - it was like some sort of angel sent to bring a small, lonely boy a little ray of happiness.

That surfboard changed my life - it led me to the ocean. From that point on, my entire life, all the decisions I ever made, centred around the water. It gave me focus, it gave me purpose and it introduced me to my best friends.

You can never replicate the friendships you make when you're young. The friends you make when you are a kid are the deepest and most integral in your life. This is because you are so vulnerable and exposed when you are a child, making mistakes, making a fool out of yourself and, in doing so, you are showing the worst side of you - if people can see that and still want to be your friend, you are likely to be friends forever. When you are an adult, you become more measured, more guarded, more able to hide your mistakes, and the friends we make only see a carefully edited version of ourselves; it is rare that we will ever make ourselves as vulnerable as we do when we are children, so we end up with friends and acquaintances that are skin deep rather than bonds that connect all the way to the heart and the soul.

That first summer with the surfboard, I nearly drowned. Like most ten-year-old boys, I had more energy than a labrador on speed and my Mum didn't know what to do with me. The day our neighbour turned up with that old surfboard, you could hear my Mum breathe a sigh of relief. From that day on, every chance I got I spent thrashing around in the white water of the Atlantic Ocean, desperately trying to stand up on that surfboard. I'd seen the local kids doing it, I'd seen the older boys and older men ripping it up, and I wanted some of that. It was on one of these days, late that first summer, when I had been paddling around for two or three hours and my shoulders were ready to drop out of their sockets, that the tide turned and the usually friendly shallows of Rocky Bay main break turned into a lethal shore dump; I got pitched on my surfboard, went over the falls of the wave and got the full washing machine treatment. My lungs began to burn, and I was struggling to know which way was up. Getting rolled and bounced on the bottom of the ocean, panic setting in, I thought I was going to die. Ten-year-old boys don't tend to have a sense of their own mortality, they have never considered death - they live life with no fear. But in that moment, the realisation that life is fragile hit me square in the face as I searched for air, my lungs screaming; I could feel the light of the world beginning to fade. Suddenly a small but surprisingly strong arm wrapped around my chest and pulled me into fresh air. I gulped greedily, spluttering and gasping. Jimmy was standing next to me, this wiry kid with scraggly bleach blond hair and a lopsided grin.

"You ok?"

I coughed and wretched, and half the ocean dribbled out my nose as I tried to nod my head. He just laughed and hauled me out onto the sand. That was the first time I met Jimmy.

We spent most of the next seven years on that beach. He was the best friend I'd ever had. He introduced me to Charlie and Mark - they were into skating and the same sort of stuff as us, so it wasn't long before the breaking waves of Rocky Bay became our hang out. Jimmy unofficially became our coach. He was only ten, but he could already surf with a grace and style of a seasoned waterman. After the school bell rang, we'd all scramble out as fast as we could, roll down Trevellyan Road on our skateboards, all scraggy, sun-bleached hair and sunbaked skin the colour of Cornish fudge. Coming down the hill at full tilt, we'd turn left onto Headland Road, imagining that we were sliding into a booming barrel and hooting until our lungs hurt. We'd scramble along the road desperate for a first glimpse of the sea, hoping that the sea Gods had sent some waves. And then we'd spend the next few hours paddling, popping, falling and laughing, until we all scampered home before our mum's got worried and came looking for us.

As a little crew of 'grommet' surfers we understood that, like any surf break around the world, there was a pecking order in the line up at Rocky Bay, and we were at the bottom of it. Mouthy groms who'd have to wait their turn and earn some respect if they wanted to catch any of the set waves that rolled in. We bided our time, took the banter and respected the older surfers. We had our heroes in the line-up and listened to their stories of far-off waves and exotic travels. We took whatever crappy waves came at us, but as the years rolled by the older crew gradually cut us some slack and threw us a couple of rides on the set waves. Most of them knew Jimmy's dad - he was a local mechanic and worked out of a crumbling shack just outside of town. You got a sense that they didn't want to mess with old Mac's kid - he was a hard man with hard fists that had an uncanny knack of colliding with anything that got on the wrong side of him, including his son. Too many times Jimmy turned up at the beach with a black eye or some busted ribs because his old man had had a few too many and got pissed off when Jimmy answered back. It made Jimmy tough - the toughest kid in school, although you wouldn't know it. He tended to keep his thoughts to himself - probably a lesson learned living in such a volatile household. But you could see that toughness in the water; there was a look in his eye, something a little unhinged and a little scary. He was always the one who charged the hardest, who took the heaviest waves and the heaviest beatings. He didn't care. It was like he wanted to be punished. He was the best young surfer the town had produced for many years and there were whispers in the carparks of the local surfbreaks; hopes that this kid might put Rocky Bay on the surfing map. Surfing had given him hope, it had given him a belief that he could do anything that he put his mind to, and he had discovered that he was brave. Being faced with heavy waves and pushing himself over the edge, over the lip and into the unknown, even though he had been scared, had filled him with adrenaline, euphoria, belief and a determination to take control of his own life. Surfing had changed him as a person - he had realised he could do anything with his life. He could leave Rocky Bay and never come back.

Mark and Charlie were laid back twin brothers, but despite sharing the same womb they couldn't have been more different. Mark was rangy, athletic and developing the chiselled jawline of a Hollywood heartthrob, with a gift of the gab and a charisma that was both beguiling and bewitching. He was the sort of guy that made other guys jealous. Charlie was quiet and introverted. He was shorter and stockier than Mark but still had the same refined features. Where Mark was free spirited and uninterested in school, Charlie was bookish, and career driven. They came from a good family who wanted the best for their sons, and you got a sense that their parents didn't always approve of them hanging out with two boys from broken homes and an appetite for truancy. But they had their heads screwed on and knew that there was a world beyond Rocky Bay that held a myriad of treasures and adventures for them if they wanted.

And then there was me....I didn't know what I wanted apart from to surf. I was drifting through adolescence, floating on the tides and waiting to see where it took me.

Every hour we could, we spent it in the water, surfing till our arms were ready to drop off and our shoulders screamed for mercy. Whether it was catching the heavier winter waves, unable to feel our fingers in the bitter cold, or floating around in the lazy summer waves; if we weren't in the water we were watching it from the beach like any surf obsessed kid would. The winter was good for waves, but the summer was good for girls. When the sun was shining and the waves were flat, we would sit on the rocks at the north end of the beach and gaze across the crescent of golden sand, spying on the seasonal tourists and spotting the prettiest girls. They would lie lazily on their beach towels, flaunting their newly acquired curves and teasing the teenage boys whose hormones were kicking into overdrive. And that is generally how life played out in those early teenage years - surfing and girls - there wasn't much room for anything else.

Girls. Girls are the only thing that can come between boys.

It was the summer of 2000. We were all leaving school and had plans for one final surf adventure before we took on the next chapter of our lives. Jimmy had passed his driving test and had spent the whole summer fixing up a rusted ice cream van at his old man's garage. It was the most unique surf van I had ever seen. The summer season was coming to an end; in a few weeks, Mark and Charlie were heading off to university and Jimmy was leaving too, moving up to Devon to train to be a marine. And me? I had secured a sponsor - nothing major, but it was a start. I was holding on to the dream of becoming a professional surfer, travelling the world and scoring uncrowded tropical waves.

But we were going to have one last blow out - a road trip in search of uncrowded waves. We had it all planned and were leaving after the summer beach party. The Rocky Bay summer beach parties had a reputation, and we didn't want to miss out. They were big, unruly and a lot of fun. They had gotten out of hand in recent years - the grockels getting into fights with the locals and leaving the beach littered with rubbish and broken glass. The local council had come down heavy, threatening to ban gatherings on the beach after dark, but some of the locals persuaded them to give it one more try. They needed the money. Everyone knew this could be the last one and we weren't going to miss it. We didn't know anyone who wasn't going, and the town was buzzing in anticipation.

I got out of the surf just before eleven. The good weather and high-pressure front meant the waves were below average, but if there was enough to push me, I was always going in. The other guys had bailed; Jimmy was doing some work on the van in the garage, Charlie was seeing his girlfriend, Lottie, and Mark just didn't fancy it. I was meeting him at lunch time to start a shift in the local One Stop. I stood on the sand and looked out at the rich green waters of Rocky Bay, wondering about how life was about to change and what the hell I was going to do. I suddenly felt lonely. The realisation that my friends were all leaving and I had no real plan - I felt like I was thrashing around in the whitewater again. The prospect of going to the party loomed like a lead weight - as I retreated into my head, the idea of saying goodbye to all my childhood friends filled me with dread. Some of the tourists were packing up and herding their children before heading back to their holiday lets or tents for some lunchtime pasties and ice cream, as I walked across the sand and up onto the esplanade, my brain fizzing in desperate need of a life plan. Even Mark had a plan and he was the most lackadaisical guy I knew.

We only lived a short walk from the beach, but long enough for me to sink myself into a momentary pit of depression. I was running late for work, but I didn't care. I showered, letting the hot water scald my aching back and berated myself for my failure to prepare for the next chapter of my life. I was going to be left behind. I got changed and rummaged through the back of my wardrobe for the secret stash of pot I kept for emergencies. I needed something to take the edge off. A box of loose rizzla papers and a few flakes of stale tobacco was all I could find. I heard the front door and quickly closed the wardrobe and scampered down the stairs. The moment I saw my Mum I could tell something wasn't right - she could barely look me in the eye, and I could tell from the red patches around her eyes that she had been crying.

"Mum?"

"Hey Gul."

"What's wrong?"

"Oh, nothing, it's nothing."

"Mum?" I didn't move; my stillness caught her attention. "I'm not a kid anymore."

She looked at me for a moment, and then hung up her coat.

"No. No you're not. You're off to work?"

"Yeah. I'm late."

"Well, don't let me stop you. You better get going."

"Mum?"

Mum heaved a sigh and walked through to the kitchen and turned the kettle on. "I got fired today. From the lettings agent."

I was speechless. Mum had worked for that company cleaning all the holiday homes of the rich grockles for the last seven years. She never took a sick day, worked hard and was well liked by the whole community.

"What happened?"

"Nothing."

"Mum?"

Mum sighed and poured herself a coffee before pulling out an old bottle of whiskey and adding a splash. "Some guy in the property I was cleaning this morning came on to me." She looked up at me. "I rejected his *advances,* and he didn't like that."

"The fucking…..what house was it?"

"Gully, leave it. It's not worth the bother. I'll let the dust settle and I am sure Graham will take me back in a couple of weeks once the tourists have gone."

I looked at her, she suddenly looked ten years older and exhausted. She had given me everything I had ever needed and more. This couldn't be worse timing with me about to head off on a holiday for two weeks, leaving her broke, upset and unemployed.

"You should go."

I hesitated in the doorway.

"I'll be fine. We've dealt with worse." She gave me a wan smile and I gave her a hug, before walking out the door with a teenager's rage bubbling inside me.

I walked back down the hill into town, ready to explode.

"So, he finally turns up." Bob's voice was layered thick with sarcasm. He was the store manager. There were many words to describe Bob, but very few of them were positive.

"Sorry. Lost track of time." I walked into the back room, kicking the door labelled 'staff only' and threw my bag down.

"I don't give a shit. You turn up on time or not at all. You got it?"

I looked around the empty shop and then at Mark who was busy counting the float in the cash register. Years of friendship meant a look was all that was needed to know we were both thinking the same thing - Bob must have lost on the horses. Whenever he lost money, his mood was ten times worse. There wasn't a customer around and yet he was busting my balls.

"Sure, Bob. Crystal clear."

Bob picked up his paper and put a set of keys on the counter.

"I'll be back in a couple of hours. Any problems, call me."

"Where's Levi?"

"Sick. It's just you two. There's stock in the back that needs putting out. And you can clean the fridges." He threw a cloth and a bottle of cleaning fluid at me.

"Yes sir." I mumbled as he disappeared out the back. We heard the back door bang shut as Bob disappeared to the bookies to try and win his money back.

"What's up? You look shit." Mark looked up from the pile of coins he was counting out.

"Nothing."

"Clearly not nothing."

"It's nothing."

Mark finished pouring coins back into the till. "We'll be out of here soon."

"Yeah."

"Maybe we should take this money and put it on the horses." Mark looked at the pile of notes he was counting and gave me a mischievous grin.

"Or take it and run."

"That would be stealing."

"Yup." I took a bottle of coke out of the fridge, unscrewed it and threw the lid at Mark.

A half-committed laughter trickled out of both of us.

I sat down on the stool behind the counter and the silence was filled with the hum of the refrigeration unit and the glug of liquid as I gulped the coke. With the mood I was in, a devil on my shoulder was whispering in my ear and weighing up what we had just said; it had been a joke, but when you're stuck in a hole, you tend to at least give a little consideration to all options. It would be so easy, and for a moment I wavered on the edge of the strong moral compass I had grown up with.

But ultimately, Bob was a local - an arsehole, but a local we'd known practically our whole lives, and I wasn't about to fuck someone over who I knew. I had too many roots in the town. You don't shit in your own backyard.

I was just about to tell Mark the root of my anger when the bell on the door jangled to signify the rare arrival of customers. I looked up to see a couple of rich-kid tourists confidently stroll into the shop. They browsed for a minute or so before approaching the counter and casually throwing down a box of oreos and a six pack of beer on the counter. They were what the American films would describe as 'preppy' - a look that had become all too familiar in Rocky Bay - second home owning families dripping in Ralph Lauren and Hugo Boss. These two were late teens or maybe early twenties, but with the confidence of someone much older - I guess that's what a childhood of privilege brought you. I took a deep breath and tried not to take my sudden brimming hatred of the tourists out on these two.

"Hey" said the guy who threw the beer on the counter, brushing his recently conditioned hair out of his eyes.

"Hi." I said and began scanning the goods. "You want a bag?"

"What?" His forehead creased into a snarl of a frown as if I had just said something offensive.

"Would you like a bag?"

"A bag? Sure."

They looked edgy, looking around the store as if searching for something or someone.

"Anything else?" I put the biscuits in the bag.

"No. Nah. That's good." Floppy hair guy began fishing in his too-tight jeans for some money, his friend still looking around as if on some drug induced paranoia trip. "Hey, is Levi working?" It was so casual it screamed dodgy.

I caught Mark's eye for the briefest of moments. How did these guys know Levi? Levi was scum, and that was being generous. You wouldn't put these two in the same room as Levi in a million years.

"No. He's sick."

"Oh". Floppy hair guy turned to his friend and exchanged a look. Mark stopped stacking the jars of Bisto and looked over. These two were giving off a weird vibe and the atmosphere in the shop had shifted. The other guy, pleated coat and penny loafers, gave the slightest nod of his head to Floppy hair. Floppy hair turned back to the counter and pulled out a small wad of notes - he peeled off a crisp twenty and passed it over. "It's just... he told us to meet him here today."

"He's not in. He's sick." I handed him his change.

"So, you said." He took the bag and the two of them moved towards the exit. They stopped and whispered something to each other before hesitantly turning back.

"Look, we're going to this party tonight on the beach. You know about it?"

"Sure."

"You don't happen to know where we might find something a little stronger than beer do you? Levi was meant to hook us up."

Mark stopped stacking and looked up. I caught his eye. Levi was always flushed with cash even though he was barely on minimum wage.

"What was he getting?"

"Doves. Pills."

"Yeah. I get it."

"So, can you help us? Our guy in London let us down and we're having a sort of pre-party party. It's a friend's birthday."

"How much was he asking?"

"15."

"I can maybe help you for 20".

Floppy hair visibly relaxed.

The door to the shop clanged open and Mad Mabel, one of the local eccentrics, stumbled in. We stood in awkward silence as Mark served her the usual bottle of Stones and she shuffled out. It gave me a moment to weigh things up and do some maths. Jimmy's cousin was a local dealer and I reckoned I could get mates' rates.

"He said 15."

"And I'm doing you a favour. Your choice."

Floppy hair looks me dead in the eye before cracking a grin. "Fine. 10 at 20."

"I tell you what, give me your number. I'll see what I can do."

Their faces lit up and they scribbled a phone number on a lottery stub by the till.

"You drive a hard bargain. What's your name?"

"Ian."

"Ok. Thanks Ian. Otto." They headed for the door grinning and animated like Christmas had come early.

"I'm not promising anything." I shouted as the door closed. Mark was on my shoulder.

"Ian?!"

"What? I'm not giving my real name, am I?"

Mark looked at me with hard eyes. "I don't even know why you are even considering helping them anyway."

"I need money."

"Where the fuck are you going to get…………..?"

"Tamar."

"Tamar! You've fucking lost it."

"Relax. It's just a one-time thing. I know Tamar."

Mark was jittery as hell. I had persuaded him to give me a lift but I could see he was tense and feeling out of his depth. For all of our teenage bravado, beyond a little weed, none of us have ever dabbled in drugs, so going to the house of a known drug dealer to score some Class A's was well outside our comfort zone.

We'd parked in a narrow street on the wrong side of town. There were streetlights set at regular intervals down the road, but only some of them were working. Darkness was winning here, and you could almost taste the threat of the place on the salty air. I'd only ever been here a couple of times, and only ever in daylight. Tamar, Jimmy's cousin, was unpredictable and scared the shit out of me.

Mark's thumb was drumming a nervous rhythm on the steering wheel.

"Look, I'll be five minutes. Ten tops. If I'm not out in 10 minutes, call Jimmy." I undid the seatbelt and reached for the door handle.

"Gully, you're sure this is a good idea?" Mark's eyes were shifting from one thing to the next - usually so cocksure, I'd never seen him like this.

"No. But I need the money."

"Not that badly."

"We're going surfing in the Outer Hebrides. That's a lot of petrol. It's alright for you lot - you're out of here soon." I looked Mark square in the eye. We had been friends a long time and I knew he was only looking out for me.

"What does that mean? Look, I just don't think it's necessary. Why are you doing these guys a favour?" Confusion was creasing Mark's forehead.

I let the seat belt slide off my shoulder and turned to Mark. "My Mum got fired today. Some guy tried to touch her up, so she kicked him in the nuts. His word against hers. He's the client in a three-million-pound house - who's gonna believe her? That's why I was late for work. And here I am about to piss off for two weeks and leave her in the shit. She has rent to pay. You know?"

Mark looked out at the shadows. "Shit."

"Yeah."

A momentary silence hung in the stale air of the car. "Is she ok? Your mum?"

"Yeah. I think so." Mark's drumming of the steering wheel stopped. There was an enormous crack of sound from up the road and we both jumped a little and turned to look out the rear-view window. Some kids were running down the street and looking up at a firework they had just set off. Glittering sparks filled the sky like fireflies.

"I'll be ten minutes tops." I opened the door and stepped out into the shadows before I could change my mind.

Tamar lived in a static home on an estate just outside of town. Dogs barked as I closed the car door and I could hear the muffled blare of televisions as I passed each home, the cardboard thin walls were about as soundproof as a tarpaulin. I knocked on the door of number 9. One of the screws on the number had come off and had swung around to look like a six and someone had scribbled another two sixes onto the door next to it. Messing with the devil was a dangerous game. I could hear drum and bass music from inside, the heavy bass making the door vibrate. I knocked again, this time a little louder. The music quietened and I knocked again. Suddenly the door opened a crack, the chain on and a one bloodshot eye stared out at me. A sudden waft of pungent air escaped - a heady mixture of sweat, sex and weed.

"Yeah?" His tone was brusque and aggressive, but I held my nerve and tried to come across as confident and relaxed.

"Tamar, it's Gully. Jimmys friend."

"What d'you want?"

"I just wondered if you could…sort me out with something?"

The one bloodshot eye stared at me, looking me up and down and then boring into me. He unhooked the chain and opened the door. He was dressed in just a pair of tracksuit bottoms, his muscular torso covered in cursive ink, a cigarette dangled from one corner of his mouth, like some reincarnation of Tyler Durden. Tamar's face was reptilian looking, with eyes set too far apart and tanned, leathery skin pockmarked from an acne plagued adolescence, giving it the illusion of scales. He looked up and down the deserted street outside. "Get in".

I moved out of the darkness and into the static, the door shutting behind me and Tamar securing it with two chains and a bolt - low level security that screamed paranoia and criminality. He brushed past me, leaving a trail of stale body odour which, when mixed with the pungent tang of strong skunk emanating from somewhere further inside the home, made the simple act of breathing unpleasant. "Come." I followed him through the narrow galley kitchen covered in a threadbare carpet that was heavily stained and looked like it had once been cream, but was now a mosaic of dark stains that, if I had to guess, looked like a mixture of blood, vomit and urine.

I followed him into a dark living area. A hollow-eyed woman lay on a mattress in the corner of the room, her matted hair hung like curtains around her pale face. She was braless, and her breasts were clearly visible through the sweat stained vest she was wearing. I tried not to look, half embarrassed and half repulsed. Her hollow eyes were glazed and unfocused and I couldn't tell if she was looking at me or through me.

"What do you want?"

"Um." Suddenly the confidence I had felt moments ago abandoned me and I am acutely aware that Tamar is highly volatile and highly dangerous. If I say the wrong thing I could be in real trouble.

"It's not Jimmy, is it?" He took a swig from a can of lager.

"No. Jimmy's fine. I just …I just wanted to ask if ….well Jimmy said you might be able to help me out." I shifted nervously from one foot to the other.

"He did, did he?"

"I was hoping you might be able to do me a favour." I looked at the girl on the mattress as if she might offer some guidance or support, but her eyes were now closed, and she had drifted into unconsciousness.

"A favour?!" Tamar snickered and slurped his beer. "Mate, it's Gully, isn't it? I am as likely to do a favour as to take it up the arse. You're just a kid and I barely know you, so the likelihood of me doing *you* a favour is pretty slim." He looked at me with his crocodile black eyes, before leaning over and turning the drum and bass up on the stereo so that the walls began to vibrate. He leaned in and I could feel his rancid breath pass across my ear. "Why don't you just get to the point and tell me what it is you want."

"10 pills"

Suddenly he came alive, his body full of tension. He grabbed my arm and started spitting instructions in an urgent whisper into my ear. His paranoia was overwhelming. I followed his instructions and removed my jacket and lifted my shirt. He frisked my legs, before retreating, seemingly satisfied that I wasn't wired and entrapping him somehow. He never took his eyes off me as he moved to the corner of the room. He slid the mattress a few feet across the floor and the woman collapsed onto her side, a small dribble of saliva began to run down her cheek. He lifted a corner of the carpet and began to rummage around, still maniacally looking up at me every few seconds. I slid my jacket back on and stuffed my hands into the deep pockets to hide my anxiety.

The volume of the music in the confined space was making my whole body vibrate. I could feel my heart beating at a million miles an hour, outrunning the drum and bass like it's on speed. Then Tamar was back up on his feet and turning the music down - He had his back to me, but I could see him pouring out the little white pills from what looked like a medicine bottle, into a clear zip lock baggie.

"These are no-joke shit. Grade-A strong, so take it easy right." He handed me the baggie and I looked at the small white pills. There was some sort of pattern imprinted on them but in the dingy light I couldn't make it out.

"10 at 15, that's £150". He was standing completely still, inches from me. I tried not to wretch at the smell of his rancid breath. Gone was the fidgety paranoia of moments before, replaced with the cold black stare of his crocodile eyes.

Fifteen was top whack - I was never going to make anything on that. "Listen, Tamar…..fifteen is a little steep isn't it? I was hoping it might be more like ten."

He snorted like a horse and leaned on the broken kitchenette counter, lighting a cigarette. "Like I said, I don't do favours. They're the real deal. You don't want them? Put them down on that table and get the fuck out of my house. I don't give a shit if you are one of Jimmy's little friends, you come around here again, and I'll gut you like a fish. You get me?"

I felt beads of sweat on my back. "I know. I get it. But this is a one-time thing Tamar. We're leaving town in like, two weeks. We're going away. With Jimmy too. We just wanted one last party, you know? But we've only got 120. Can we do 12 a pill?"

He stared at me for what seemed like an eternity, sucking the smoke in from his cigarette like a hoover and letting it cascade out of his nose like some sort of angry dragon. Finally, he said, "Ok. One time."

I held the packet in my hand, opened it and pulled out two of the tiny white pills; examining them to pretend I knew what I was doing before pocketing the bag of pills. I tried to smile. "Thanks Tamar." I made a move to the door.

"Hey Gully." I stopped in my tracks, eager to get out of the oppressive air of the static. Tamar was looking at me with a lopsided grin. "The money."

I paused. I knew I would have to word this right. "So…..that's the favour really."

"Uh-huh." Tamar grinds out the tip of the cigarette in a dirty bowl in the sink that is overflowing with detritus.

"I wasn't sure if you had any, and I haven't got the money on me…."

"Are you fucking kidding…"

I held up my hands in what I hoped appeared a gesture of sincerity and honesty. "I just need to nip into town and the guys'll give me the cash and I can come right back up here and give it to you. I promise."

Tamar began to laugh, and his hand slipped to the drawer next to the sink. "You've got some fucking balls Gully. I'll give you that."

"I promise Tamar. 45 minutes, tops. You know I'm good for it. Where am I going to go? You know me. Jimmy'll vouch for me."

Tamar very slowly and deliberately opened the drawer, reached inside and pulled out a gun. It's black and mean looking. It has the desired effect and brings the whole ridiculous situation into focus for me. I questioned what the fuck I am doing, but it was too late by that point. "You've got 45 minutes. You got me?"

"Yeah." I was looking at the gun. In my peripheral vision I could see the crocodile grin - he had made his point.

"But Gully, one more thing."

"Yeah?"

"You or your mate in the car outside stay here until the payment is made. You understand? I don't give a fuck if you are Jimmy's mate or not."

The twitchy paranoia was back in his body and the crocodile grin had morphed into a snarl. I was momentarily lost for words, partly because the thought of staying in this rancid shithole for 45 minutes filled me with dread, and partly because I had underestimated Tamar - how did he know Mark was in the car outside?

"Ok." Is all I manage.

"45 minutes. That's all it is, Mark. Please?" I am edgy. This isn't going to plan. Mark was reluctant to act as my guarantee, which I completely understood, and I felt like an arsehole even asking him. But equally, I didn't want to stay there either.

"This was your fucking idea, Gully. No fucking way. I am not staying here."

I momentarily racked my brain to see if there are any other options. There aren't. "Fine. Here." I threw the baggie onto the passenger seat. I looked over the roof of the little car and could see the silhouette of Tamar standing in the open doorway of his fetid home. I lowered my voice and put my head through the passenger window. "Meet Otto at the back of Reefo's. Charge him 20 a pill. That's 200 in total. Ok? But we're paying 120 to Tamar ok? Ok?"

Mark just looked at me and slightly shook his head.

"Ok?". I could feel the panic rising in me and realised I was out of my depth here.

"Fine." Mark picked up the pills, stuffed them under the driver's seat and started the engine.

"And mate. Don't hang around, eh?!" We exchanged an uncomfortable grin and the car pulled away. The car disappeared around the corner, and I had a sudden feeling of sickness as I realised that one of his tail lights was broken. I hoped to God that he didn't get pulled over by the police. Shit.

I spent the next forty minutes sitting on an old fold up chair outside Tamars. I was glad to be in the open air - I couldn't stand the claustrophobia and the stench inside the static. He gave me a lukewarm beer and we sat in silence smoking a joint and sipping our drinks. In the silence you could hear the muted music that was drifting up the valley from the party on the beach. I'd occasionally catch Tamar looking at me with those black eyes, like a predator sizing up their prey.

The throaty sound of an approaching engine felt like the stay of my own execution; both of our heads snapped towards the road, and we could make out headlights winding their way up through the labyrinth of roads that crisscrossed the estate of statics. It didn't sound like Mark's car. Tamar was up on his feet and back in the house, dripping in paranoia - the guy clearly didn't like visitors and he was presumably checking access to the handgun. His silhouette reappeared in the doorway just as the headlights swung around the corner and lit up the terrace. I tried to shield my eyes. It wasn't a car. There was only one light - it was a motorbike. Jimmy.

After an animated conversation with Tamar on the steps of the static home I saw Jimmy give him a roll of cash before he marched back towards me and threw me the spare helmet; his face was set with a mixture of anger and disgust. He didn't say anything, but I knew that once out of earshot my friend had some fierce words for me. The little 125 squealed beneath us and accelerated away from the crocodile's lair. Despite knowing how pissed off my friend was, I was glad he had come to get me, and I was glad to be out of there.

It was just after ten when we pulled up in the car park across the road from the beach. You could see a number of bonfires burning on the beach and the dry weather meant that the beach was overflowing with revellers - old hippies, tourists, teens and locals, all smiling and filling the air with laughter. Jimmy cut the engine and took off his helmet. He was off the bike and pacing like a caged animal before I had even put my feet on the ground.

"What the fuck Gully?"

I took the helmet off. "Look, Jimmy, I'm sorry."

"Jesus. Tamar? What were you thinking?" A fire was burning in his eyes, and he was physically shaking.

"I was....I don't know....I was just trying to make a little extra money."

"By dealing? What's happened to you?"

"My mum got fired today."

Jimmy stopped pacing and looked at me. "What?"

"Some fucker tried to touch her up. She.... retaliated. I just wanted to ...I don't know...I didn't want to run off and leave her with no money or anything."

Jimmy knew my Mum, he was basically a surrogate son. "Is she ok?"

"Yeah. Just...you know."

He understood - me leaving her for two weeks to disappear and go surfing when she had just lost her job and was feeling vulnerable was less than ideal.

We stood staring at each other for what felt like minutes. "Did you get the money?"

"Jesus Gully!" He reached in his pocket and threw a wad of notes at me. "Don't fucking do it again, ok? You don't know Tamar - you don't want to know Tamar. You get me?"

"Sure. I'm sorry." I counted out the notes in my hand. Eighty quid. Not bad for forty-five minute's work. But Jimmy was right. I didn't want to go through that again.

We found the others on the beach by one of the fires. Charlie was nursing a bottle of rum and Mark was draped around some girl who looked a bit like a teenage Cindy Crawford.

"Gully! Gully! Gully!" Mark cackled and threw me a beer. He was clearly already drunk, even though the party can only have been a few hours in. "Took your time! Glad you're still alive mate." I took the can and cracked it. "Jimmy give you an earful?" I nodded and took a swig of the beer. "There was no way I was coming back up there man, that guy freaks me out."

"What's up with Charlie?" Across the fire Charlie was drinking rum straight from the bottle, brooding and staring out at the growing swell.

"Charlotte Westley. She finally dumped him." Mark cackled in the warmth of his drunkenness, revelling in his brother's misery.

"No!" Charlie had been going out with Charlotte Westley since year ten. They were childhood sweethearts. Cookies and cream. "Charlie and Charlie, finally over." I began to walk over to him, but Jimmy grabbed me by the arm.

"Leave it Gully." Jimmy glared at me.

"What?" There was something in his tone.

Mark cackled some more as the girl he was draped over got up and scampered over the sand to catch up with some friends. He righted himself on his elbow. "She's in love with someone else."

"Oh. Shit." I looked across at Charlie, but his focus remained on the ocean. "Sorry mate."

"She's in love with you." Charlie took a swig of the rum and stood up, staring at me as if he wanted to rip me apart. "Has been for a long time Gully". He turns and begins to wander off down the beach, his head hung like a weight on his shoulders.

I couldn't formulate any words. I was as shocked at this news as he was angry. Charlotte Westley, or Lottie to her friends, was a beautiful girl - a little nerdy, but sweet and sexy in a bookish kind of way. We'd always got on and we had kissed at the beginning of year 10, just before Charlie started going out with her. My head was spinning. She was in love with me? No girls ever really showed an interest in me - that's what comes when you have Mark Watson as one of your best friends.

The crackle of the dry logs on the fire filled the silence. Mark lit a joint and passed it to me. Suddenly I was filled with indignation, "Well it's not my fault." I falter, looking for some support from two of my best friends. "I'll go and talk to him."

"Leave it. He'll calm down." Jimmy threw a log on the fire. "What a fucking mess."

"Is he still going to come? To Scotland?" I look from Jimmy to Mark. Mark stuck his bottom lip out and shook his head, at a loss for an answer.

"Jesus." I drew on the joint and felt the harsh smoke fill my lungs.

"Look, forget about it. He'll be fine. She was a prick tease anyway." Mark stumbled to his feet just as a sound system begins to pump out Daft Punk's 'one more time' further up the beach. "Let's get smashed."

That night we talked, and danced, and drank, and laughed like we would never do those things again. And we never would.

By twelve thirty I was drunk. Not paralytic, but walking in a straight line took a lot of concentration. Floppy hair Otto came up to me and gave me a massive hug, filling my nostrils with an overpowering waft of expensive aftershave, which made me feel a little queasy. Even in the flickering light of the campfires I could see that his pupils were so dilated he looked like he had contacts in. After thanking me a million times and kissing me on the forehead he danced off to find his other posh mates, high as a kite and having the time of his life. I looked around to try and find my own friends, but they were nowhere to be seen. I caught the eye of a girl standing on the other side of the fire. She seemed to know me, and I tried to focus my gaze to work out who it was, but the drink was playing tricks with my eyes. She began to move around the perimeter and, as she came closer, I realised that it was Lottie.

"Hey."

"Hi."

"Drunk?"

"Hammered. You?"

"Not really. Can't really get into the mood."

"I heard."

"About…"

"Yeah."

I was desperately trying to stand straight and not seem too drunk, but I overcorrected and stumbled right into her. She laughed and caught me before I fell.

"You want to take some time out?"

I looked at her, confused by this suggestion, but she was just smirking at me in her beautiful nerdy way, laughing at me through her big green eyes.

"Just take a walk, clear your head." I could feel her hand guiding me towards the sand dunes at the north end of the beach and I let her lead me; I knew if Charlie or any of the boys saw me walking off with Lottie the shit would hit the fan - it would definitely be perceived as against the bro code. I looked around but all I could see were blurred shapes. She took my hand, but it was ok because she was just a friend. That's what I told myself.

"Better?"

We were sitting in a dip within the dune system, out of the breeze and away from prying eyes.

"Yeah. A bit."

"You never could handle your drink." She threw her head back and laughed at her joke. I felt slightly annoyed that this was the image people had of me - it somehow dented my adolescent pride. "Here." She passed me a bottle of water.

"Thanks."

I took a glug. Water had never tasted so good. I lay back on the sand and looked up at the stars. I could hear the surf beyond the dunes, and the rhythmical pounding of the waves on the beach calmed my racing heart and began to clear my mind. Lottie lay down on the sand next to me and I could feel her left arm pressed up against me. The close proximity felt wrong but exciting, and the drink was blurring the lines.

"So, you broke up with Charlie."

"Yeah."

There was a shout further along the beach followed by an eruption of laughter.

"That's shit."

"Yeah."

I could feel her head nestle into my shoulder.

"You know why I broke up with him?"

I didn't want to spoil the party so I gave the answer I would have guessed at, had I not already known. "I guess, because he's going off to university and it's….well, it's sort of the end of an era isn't it?"

"I guess."

She sat up and grabbed the bottle of water and took a slug, then leaned on her elbow and looked down on me, her face only inches away from mine, her shoulder length blonde hair falling across her face. "But it was mainly because I'm in love with someone else."

I couldn't look at her. I could feel her eyes scanning my face, desperately looking for eye contact. "No shit."

"Yeah. I have been for a long time. I love Charlie. He's a great guy. But I'm not in love with him."

I couldn't help it. I looked at her. "And you are in love with this other person?"

"Yeah."

A gong of guilt clanged in my heart and I broke eye contact before I succumbed. "You want a smoke?". It was a lame change of topic, I knew she didn't really smoke weed, but I couldn't hold her gaze and needed a distraction. I didn't even want a smoke, but I needed something to focus on other than her. I patted down my jacket pockets and found what I was looking for. I pulled out a bent and mangled single skin joint from one pocket and a lighter from another.

"You think that's a good idea?"

"No." I lit the joint and took a pull.

She looked away and shivered. I took off my jacket. "Here." I gave her the coat.

"Thanks." She put it on and sat up next to me. "Are you ever scared?"

"Of what?" I handed her the joint, the buzz was too much for me - she was right, it was a bad idea. To my surprise she took it. My head was spinning, and I sat back down heavily on the sand.

"Of what comes next. You know after school. Uni, jobs, being an adult. All that stuff."

"I guess."

"In a few weeks everything will be different. We'll all be doing other stuff, spread out all over the country."

"Yeah."

She stuffed her hands in the pocket of the coat, looking for a lighter. "What are these?" She held out her hand with two small white pills. I'd forgotten I had taken two out of the packet at Tamars. Otto obviously hadn't noticed.

"Um. Doves. E. "

"Oh. I didn't know you were into that sort of stuff."

"I'm not. Not really. Why….you want to try one?"

She looked at the little pills, mulling it over and then looked up at me and I could see a recklessness in her eye I had never seen before. "Yeah. Why not?" Before I could say anything, she put one pill in her mouth and took a slug of water to wash it down. She grimaced and laughed. "That's gross."

Lottie suddenly straddled me, pinning me back on the sand and removed the jacket and her cropped t-shirt, revealing a black lacy bra. Her slim porcelain body glowed in the moonlight, and I could feel the blood rushing to my groin. She leaned in and kissed me before I could react; soft lips wet and hungry, forcing my mouth open and her tongue gently probing. I fumbled with her bra strap before she suddenly pulled away and looked at me. My hormones were raging around my body and making a beeline for my crotch. "You know it's you I'm in love with."

"I heard."

She looked at me and grinned, holding up the second pill in front of my face. "Let's get high together."

"Is that a good idea?!"

I took the pill in my hand and raised myself up onto one elbow, reaching for the water, when suddenly there is a blood curdling scream echoing off the cliffs of the bay. The music abruptly stopped and there was an eerie silence except for the gentle pounding of the surf. Something was clearly wrong back at the beach party, but I remember having the irrational thought that maybe the waves would be picking up tomorrow. Then someone yelled out for help, and all hell broke loose. Lottie climbed off me, pulling on her t-shirt and jumping to her feet. I scrambled up, doing up my trousers and wondering what the hell was going on.

"Maybe it's a fight again." I looked up the beach to where the fires were still burning.

"I don't think so." She looked at me for a moment before we both set off down the beach.

He was foaming at the mouth and his body was convulsing, spraying up sand as I broke into the circle of onlookers. Johnno, one of the local lifeguards, was kneeling on the sand next to him, trying to restrain him.

"Someone call a fucking ambulance!"

It was only then that I realised who it was. I looked across the circle of people and saw Mark and Jimmy staring at me - they weren't looking at the guy fitting on the sand - they were looking at me, fear and anger bristling and burning in their eyes. The guy fitting was floppy hair from the One Stop, Otto. The guy I had sourced the pills for. The guy that Mark had given the pills to, and the guy Jimmy had taken the money from. Charlie burst into the circle of people, phone in hand.

"An ambulance is on its way. They said eight minutes."

"Fuck." Johnno rolled Otto onto his side. Spittle and vomit were erupting from his mouth, and pooling on his quilted jacket. Even by the light of the fire you could see the colour was draining from his face and his lips were turning purple. Johnno rolled him back onto his back and began CPR. I had only ever seen someone given CPR once before, when Nicky Davis had saved a tourist who had got caught in a rip and almost drowned. They had saved the tourist that day and Nicky had been hailed a hero. But the tourist had only swallowed seawater, not some super strong ecstasy.

I ran around the outside of the crowd and grabbed Mark. "You told him they were really strong right? That he shouldn't double drop yeah?"

"What the fuck does that matter Gully?"

"But you told him, right?"

"I...I don't know."

"Shit!"

Eight minutes is a long time to watch helplessly as someone gives CPR to a person.

He was breathing when the paramedics packed him into the ambulance, but the fun of the beach party left with the taillights of the ambulance as it pulled away up Northcliff road. Where there had been laughter and music only moments before, there was now just the pounding of the waves and a few hysterical girls crying. The adrenaline of the moment had had a sobering effect on the crowd and people were beginning to drift away from the carpark and back to their beds. The party was over.

I stayed by the fire as the crowds slowly began to disperse. A few locals hung around and some people were picking up empty bottles and beer cans and putting them into bin liners. Jimmy sat down on the sand next to me. "I told you."

"I know."

"Where were you?"

"What does it matter?"

"We saw you walking into the dunes with Lottie." My world began to come crashing down, the pounding headache of a hangover beginning to kick in just to top off the worst day of my life.

"Does Charlie know?"

"Yeah."

As soon as the words escaped my mouth, I heard Lottie screaming in rage further along the beach. I could make out her silhouette against the pale light of the moon. She was arguing with Charlie. Snippets of their argument drifted to us on the light onshore breeze. "I don't love you….. Leave me alone…..It's over…." it looked like she slapped him in the face before storming off up the beach towards town. Charlie came marching back towards us.

Jimmy turned to me. "Watch out."

I got to my feet and tried to adopt a neutral and passive stance. As soon as he was close enough Charlie swung; his fist connecting flush with my nose and my mouth, and I went sprawling on the sand. He stood over me shaking with rage and a million other emotions.

"You prick. I thought we were friends."

"Charlie." Jimmy grabbed his arm and pulled him away before he could do any more damage. I put my hand to my face and could feel the wetness of blood on my chin. My top lip was swelling up and I thought that maybe one of my teeth was broken. The adrenaline rush briefly subsided, and Charlie shook out his hand as the pain of the impact began to take hold. "Fuck."

"I'm sorry Charlie." I pulled myself to my feet. "I was drunk. She took me to the dunes, but we didn't do anything. I mean, she kissed me, but that was it and then we heard the screams and came running here."

"Fuck off Gully. You're a snake. Don't come near me. You hear?"

Charlie turned on his heel and marched back up the beach, cursing and mumbling to himself before kicking over a camping chair that someone had left. I had never seen him this animated before. We watched him go, before Jimmy turned to me and held my face to check the damage. "You ok?"

"Not really."

"Well, to be fair, you deserved it. Never knew Charlie could punch like that!" He handed me the can of beer in his hand. "Have a swig of that". I greedily gulped the beer, washing down the metallic taste of blood from my mouth.

"Where's Mark?"

"Gone off with Maisie Rogers."

"No shit?!"

"Yeah."

"Fuck Jimmy."

"Yeah." Jimmy put his hand on my shoulder. "Come on. Let's go.

It'll all settle down tomorrow. The guy seemed ok and is on the way to hospital. He's in the best place."

We walked up the beach in silence.

"You want a lift home?" Jimmy was putting on his helmet.

"Nah. I'm going to walk. Clear my head."

"Ok. See you tomorrow? Think the swell is building."

"Yeah. Maybe."

With that, Jimmy straddled his bike and started the engine. He offered his fist and I bumped him before he screeched off into the night.

The next day I knocked on Charlie and Mark's door, but Charlie wouldn't talk to me. I wanted to clear the air, to apologise, to explain that I was caught in the middle, but I understood his frustration.

A rare summer ground swell had rolled in overnight and I tried to distract my guilt by physically punishing myself and surfing until I couldn't surf anymore. Jimmy came down and got in for a few hours, but we didn't talk much in the water. He tried to act like things were normal, but both of us knew that they weren't. Eventually, lying on the sand, exhausted and feeling as vulnerable as I could remember, I told him about what had happened in the dune with Lottie - the kiss… the pills.

"Fuck. That's not like her, eh?" Jimmy just stared out at the ocean.

"Nah. It took me by surprise. But I was hammered. I just….I don't know." I lay back and closed my eyes, the remnants of a hangover hovering front and centre.

"Give him some time mate. He'll calm down and it'll all work out."

"Yeah. Maybe."

The following morning a pounding on the door woke me. I tried to ignore it, hoping whoever it was would go away. My body ached from the surf the day before and my mind ached with the guilt I felt for my friend. The pounding on the door continued with increased vigour, and I threw back the covers, huffed, and made my way down the stairs. Charlie, Mark and Jimmy were standing on the doorstep. Charlie looked pissed and I wasn't sure I wanted to deal with it right at that moment.

"Get up. Get dressed." Charlie's tone was blunt and matter of fact. He looked stressed and pumped with adrenaline. He was shifting from foot to foot and unable to make eye contact.

"What?" I was defensive and being childish.

"Lottie didn't get home after the party."

My stomach momentarily dropped away. "So?"

"It's not like her."

"Maybe she hooked up with someone." I offered.

"Gully. That's not helpful." Mark was looking at me with disappointment in his eyes.

"Well, have you tried phoning her?" The harsh sunlight made me squint and sent needles into my brain.

"Obviously. She's not answering." Charlie snapped. "Jimmy told me you gave her a pill."

I looked at Jimmy and momentarily felt betrayed, but I knew I had no leg to stand on. He was right, in a way; I hadn't given her the pill, but I hadn't stopped her either. Jimmy was looking at the floor. "I didn't give it to her. She found it in my jacket, and she took it."

"What the fuck Gully?" Charlie's face was going red with rage.

"What? I'm not her keeper. Maybe that's what she wanted… a little excitement." As soon as I said it, I regretted the tone. Charlie swivelled and snarled at me.

"What, so now it's my fault she's taken some class A drugs? What, because I'm so boring?"

"That's not what I'm saying?" My stomach was twisting in knots. Things were aligning in my brain and the realisation of the situation was hitting home; Lottie was missing - last seen high as a kite from drugs I had supplied her and heading into town. A silence hung in the air. I could feel Charlie's despair.

"Her parents are freaking out."

"Have they called the police?"

"Of course they've called the police."

"Do they know? Do they know she'd taken a pill?"

"It's a bit late for worrying about saving your arse, Gully." Charlie was almost shaking, his bitterness spilling out.

"Ok, ok."

"We're going to look for her. Half the town is out looking for her." Charlie took two steps away from the door as if expecting me to follow. "You coming?"

"Ok, ok. Give me a second." I ran upstairs and threw on some clothes before coming back down. They were still on the doorstep, not having moved. "Right, let's go."

We checked all the usual hangouts, and places we would go when trying to escape the prying eyes of the community, but it was a small town, so it didn't take long. None of her friends had heard from her and news came back that no one had found anything. Lottie lived in a house on the headland to the north; it was remote and beautiful. If she had left the beach and headed straight home, she would have gone up the coastal path and along the cliffs. We walked in silence, looking out for any clues as to where she might be. Tendrils of concern began to spread to the pit of my stomach as I began to replay the image of her taking the pill, the image of her storming away from the party. Flashes of floppy haired Otto convulsing on the beach pierced my mind. "Does anyone know how the guy on the beach is?"

"Conscious and ok apparently. Pumped his stomach." Mark and Charlie's Mum worked as a nurse in the hospital. We walked a bit further in silence, a million questions weighing on my mind.

"Do you reckon he'll say anything?"

"I don't reckon. Ten pills? He'd get done for intent to deal." Mark reasoned.

"Gully, what the fuck were you doing with pills anyway?" Charlie shook his head. It felt like his tone was softening somehow. I guess Jimmy hadn't told him about my Mum.

"I was just trying to make a bit of extra money."

"Dealing?" Charlie turned and faced me. A couple of ramblers came around the corner carrying rucksacks and walking sticks, out enjoying the coastal path and oblivious to the tension between us all. We fell silent as they strolled past, nodding a 'Hello'. As they disappeared down the hill the tension bubbled again, mirroring the swirling and boiling waves below as they crashed against the bottom of the cliffs with an unapologetic violence.

"It was a one off. I had my reasons." I glared at him, unwilling to justify my actions.

"Oh Shit. Here!" Mark was at the edge of the cliff holding a flip flop. It was Lottie's. A sinking feeling filled my entire body, and I had a sudden urge to be sick. We peered over the edge of the cliff at the small cove below known as Dead Man's cove. It had been a smugglers cove in the olden days, with an intricate system of caves that wound under the headland. With difficult access, not many people went down there apart from the odd naturist when it was low tide. We knew there was a path down to the cove that you could access further along the cliffs, so we ran there and scrambled down. It was a sketchy path, rarely trod, but despite the danger it posed we descended quickly, Charlie leading the way.

She lay white and pale on the sand - the unforgiving embrace of the sea leaving an indelible mark on her once living, breathing body. I wretched, but my gaze was quickly drawn back to the prone figure. The girl I had kissed only a few hours before. Had I caused this? I couldn't quite grasp the reality of it all. It was her, even though it barely resembled her once angelic features, I knew it - it rumbled in my soul. The others stood back, tense and timid, unfamiliar with this proximity to death. Charlie rushed forward and knelt by her body. The rest of us stood back, unsure of what to say or do. Salt and brine clung to her pallid flesh, the plundering waves and greedy sea creatures having already begun to strip away any remnants of dignity or grace. Her clothes were torn and shredded, revealing swathes of bloated, swollen and bloodied flesh. I recognised the pale ochre coloured remains of her top, the one she had so casually discarded in the dunes. Tendrils of seaweed wove an intricate tapestry over her body, as if the emerald strands were attempting to shroud and protect the remains of what was once a beautiful girl. The face was brutishly distorted, mangled by the rocks and the fall, yet we all knew this girl. It was Lottie - Charlotte Westley, top of the class and the perfect pupil. Charlie turned away and vomited onto the pale sand.

From the depths of her sunken eyes, hauntingly still and lifeless, crawled a small crab. A symphony of seagulls cried out, disturbed from their feeding frenzy; their mournful cries echoing and bouncing off the steep cliffs of the cove. The sun was high in the sky now and lit the scene with a high-definition clarity. I could feel the tears begin to swell and overflow. I tried to fight it but the flood of emotion was becoming too strong to hold back. I could hear Jimmy behind me.

"Charlie. I'm sorry." It was barely audible. Mark, who was normally so good with words, was unsure of what to say. He moved to crouch next to his brother and put his arm around him. My mind continued replaying the snippets of that night in vivid technicolour. Fractured and frenetic images flashed through my mind. I knew my actions had contributed to this tragedy, but there was very little I could say or do that would make it any better.

"We need to get back." I brushed the free-flowing tears away from my face as Charlie placed a hand gently on his ex-girlfriend's cold, lifeless face. Suddenly everything Charlie was feeling, the anger, the frustration, the resentment and bitterness erupted like a wave exploding on the shore. He was on his feet and marching towards me.

"This is your fault, Gully! You fucking...." His eyes burned with a need to hurt me.

Jimmy stepped between us and Mark grabbed his brother from behind. "Charlie, I'm sorry. She took the pill. I didn't know...I didn't mean...."

"Fuck you, Gully." Charlie collapsed to his knees and wept an ocean of salty tears. The seagulls squawked overhead.

"We should take her with us." Charlie's voice was cracked and choked with emotion. Tears were cascading down his face, and he was barely able to speak. Mark clasped his brother, turning him away from her body.

"We can't." Jimmy was always the voice of reason, the pragmatist. "We need to get back and let the police deal with it. They'll come and get her and take care of her. Come on." Jimmy gently placed a hand on my shoulder and the small gesture immediately opened the floodgates and I wept uncontrollably, my body shaking and convulsing with the emotion of the tragedy. Jimmy was right. Jimmy was always right. We needed to go and get help.

The police never did find out who gave Otto or Lottie the ecstasy and the boys never let on what exactly had happened. But it didn't matter - we all knew. And the guilt I carried for the rest of my time was enough of a punishment. I was left in Rocky Bay, with demons of torment playing havoc with me every time I stepped onto that beach, or walked the cliffs, or saw Lottie's parents in town. I never saw Mark, Jimmy or Charlie again after the day we found her body. We never went to Scotland on our surf trip. We never even spoke again. I tried, but they didn't want to know. I understood. I was to blame. I did get a couple of postcards from Jimmy when he was posted in Germany and then Afghanistan, but that was it.

More than ever, the ocean became my focus. Every time I jumped in the sea, I hoped it would wash away my sins - perhaps it diluted them a little but I could never forget completely. I surfed to numb my pain; and I did pretty well - I got a major sponsor and travelled the world. I never really made the big time, never cracked the WCT, but I got more success than I deserved.

Time slipped away and I could do nothing about that. We had all gone our separate ways, wracked with guilt or afraid to reunite- it would only have resurfaced uncomfortable memories. I always wondered if fate would one day bring us all back together. A childhood brotherhood is difficult to escape. What I didn't know was the unfortunate circumstances that would bring us all together again. When people say that time heals everything, it's a lie.

PART 2

2010

A DROP IN THE OCEAN

The deck beneath their feet suddenly fell away and sea spray exploded off the prow of the small fishing boat, peppering the windscreen of the wheelhouse with cold water bullets. Kieran flicked the cap of his thermos coffee mug and took a sip of the rich, pungent liquid. The green of the boat's paintwork rose out of the water and the white name of the boat, 'Shamrock', glimmered in the gathering darkness, before plunging back into the dark green of the north Atlantic.

"Let's be quick about this. Drop this stuff over the side and let's be off. Weather's rolling in and I don't want to get caught out in it." He cut the engine as Simon and Sean exited the wheelhouse and headed to the prow of the boat. Sean opened up the hatch to the hold, the metal hinges groaning with reluctance, before he reached down and pulled up one of the heavy blue plastic barrels. Simon watched his brother and wondered how he had grown up so much - the skinny runt of the family and now...now he was twice the size of Simon. He was glad they were on the same side.

"Port side!" Kieran's voice bellowed from the wheelhouse. Simon looked over the side of the boat and saw the red buoy approaching. He reached down and grabbed the top of the buoy with the rubber handle. The engine growled as Kieran reversed the throttle to keep her steady. Sean passed his brother the first barrel. Simon deftly attached a chain around the barrel's handle and linked the chain with a carabiner, which he then latched onto the rope of the buoy. With one swift motion, he lifted the barrel over the side of the boat and watched it disappear into the depths of the ocean, taking the chain with it as it abseiled down the rope attached to the buoy.

"One down, three to go! Let's get moving boys. There's a long journey home." The three fishermen laughed and looked to the skies as the first few drops of rain began to fall.

LOST IN THE RAIN

Jimmy sat and stared at the thick black coffee in the vintage china teacup; the delicate porcelain and intricate handle feeling fragile and awkward in his rough hands. This part of town was all a little bit trendy and pretentious for him - he would be more comfortable with a mug of PG tips in a laminate covered greasy spoon. He mindlessly stirred the liquid with a teaspoon. It had been 6 months since he had entered civilian life, and he was barely clinging on. An honourable discharge had seen the end of him as a marine, and now here he was, sat in the busy cafe in Soho, in a city of nearly 9 million, with people buzzing around him - he felt alone, lost in his own thoughts. Big cities had always felt a little alien to him. He was a country boy at heart with salt and sea running through his veins.

"You done?"

"Yeah. Thanks."

The waitress swept up the empty cup of coffee like a petulant teenager who had been asked to tidy their room and glided off into the babble of the coffee shop bubble. It was busy, perfect for people watching; and his mind wandered again as he followed the ebb and flow of the human interaction in the confined space - people coming, people going, people talking, people busy…..people, just busy - busy going about their lives at four hundred miles an hour. It was humanity on speed. And Jimmy could feel its intensity pressing into his brain, and the thin tendrils of panic and depression beginning to close around him. He needed out. Out of this coffee shop. Out of this city. He needed space. He needed air. For the first time in a long time, he yearned for the sea.

His phone rattled as it vibrated on the wooden table, the display showing an unknown number.

"Hello"

"Mr MacIntosh? It's Alicia calling from Phillip Palmer's office."

Jimmy's heart lurched; his brain shifted into gear; everything suddenly being forced into focus. He adjusted his position on the hard wooden chair - suddenly alert, upright, as if he was in the interview again.

He breathed in.

"I'm sorry, but we have gone with someone else for the position."

He breathed out.

"Oh."

"We just feel like you need to gain a little experience in the industry before you would be ready for a position like this."

"Sure."

"We'll keep your details on file...."

Jimmy didn't hear the rest of the sentence. He zoned out. Another 'gentle' let down.

We respect you, but....

We like you, however...

Life had been easier in the army. It was black and white. It was straight talking with none of the bullshit. He put the phone down. Sixteen job interviews and not one offer. Jimmy's army career was over, and he felt like he was sliding down a hole. His phone buzzed again - a message notification.

"Gully's dead. Funeral is Saturday." Five words. Succinct and to the point. Despite the misery of the message, this was the language Jimmy understood. Jimmy hadn't spoken to Gully in over ten years, but he had heard how his childhood friend had been sick - a brain tumour someone had said. He had meant to visit - to patch things up. He'd sent a couple of postcards but never anything more than that. But for whatever reason he had put it off and now it was too late. Death was all too familiar to Jimmy. He viewed death as just something that was inevitable. We would all die at some point but Gully had been like a brother; despite the hiatus of their relationship, this news stung a little more than he was used to. Jimmy had lain awake contemplating death many times - it was something he could not run away from when he was fighting on the frontline. He had accepted his own death was inevitable even before it had stretched out its scrawny claws for him - it was just a question of working out how he would eventually pass onto the other side. Would it be calm? Peaceful? Dying in his sleep or blown to smithereens? A gentle drifting into old age until the component parts eventually fall apart, withered from a full life of wear. Drowning? Apparently, that was peaceful - although he wondered how anyone knew that it was peaceful if they were already dead. More likely it would be a violent end for Jimmy; a reckless car crash, being crushed by falling debris in an earthquake, maybe he would end up jumping off a building, or being shot. Shot. He'd seen a lot of death. It was what he was trained for. He was a marine. He was. He wondered if Gully had suffered. He hoped not. More death falling into his lap. Gully was dead? Gully.

A song broke his daze. Jimmy turned and looked at the bearded barista behind the counter and asked him to turn it up. He loved this song; it was one of Gully's favourites.

He stood up and walked out into the street, falling into step with the people of the city. The rain was getting heavier, and umbrellas were beginning to explode into life everywhere. Jimmy moved with the determined fluidity of those around him, those who were going somewhere, even though he felt like he was just drifting.

Warm, summer rain streamed down his face; his leather shoes began to saturate. Jimmy stepped out of the crowd and ducked into a small convenience store to buy some cigarettes. He needed to quit, but everyone needs a vice when the chips are down. He stood under the awning of the store watching the rain hammer down in angry torrents and smoked a cigarette. The noise was thunderous, nature showing off and blasting the sounds of the city away.

The screech of a siren penetrated the bass rumble of the rain; an ambulance ploughed down the road, followed by a second. The piercing wail of the siren momentarily taking him back to the events that had led him to be standing there at that moment. Jimmy dropped his cigarette in a pool of rainwater and ran for the underground station.

****

It was still raining as Jimmy exited the tube station at Elephant and Castle. Deep puddles lay dotted across the pavements like the craters of a minefield, but the smart brown, leather brogues he wore were already sodden and his mind was focused on something else other than the dampness of his footwear. He felt reckless, like he used to when hanging in the lip of a monstrous wave. He wanted punishment. It was almost five o'clock on a Thursday, and the streets were filling up rapidly as people piled out of their workplaces; a desperate dash in the hope of an early escape, a long weekend perhaps, a few more precious minutes with friends or family. People weaved and meandered along the narrow pavements, bumping and bouncing off one another like the heavy, angry waters of a flood. Within five minutes Jimmy had reached the Kings Head - the old and familiar Edwardian building emitting a sense of fading grandeur, with peeling green paintwork and rotten sash windows. The low wattage lights inside projected a warm yellow glow onto the street outside, and the heaving mass of sweaty bodies that filled the interior of the pub lined the frosted windows with a slick of unhealthy condensation. Jimmy pushed open the heavy wooden door and was hit by a wall of sound - the chatter and laughter of grown men, and the clinking and clanking of glass on glass. The pub was filled with working men; Hi-Viz vests, plaster covered work trousers and steel toe-capped boots were everywhere. The only female in the whole of the pub was standing behind the bar, surveying her kingdom. Shelley hadn't changed in the four years since Jimmy had last seen her - fake eyelashes thick with mascara, rich red lipstick and the carefully coiffured, peroxide blonde curls of a 1980's hairstyle. She still commanded the bar though and kept every man in that pub on their toes and in their place. She was old school - there weren't many like her around anymore.

The atmosphere within the pub had an animalistic intensity to it - hard men hell bent on having a good time and releasing some of the pent-up tension of the working week - a fine line between having fun and having a fight. As the door closed behind Jimmy, he could feel all eyes on him - he knew this pub well, but he hadn't been here for nearly half a decade and was for all intents and purposes a stranger in their bar. And this was not a pub you wanted to be a stranger in on a Thursday or Friday afternoon. In his peripheral vision Jimmy clocked the large, shaven headed thug standing at the corner of the L-shaped mahogany bar, guarding the cardboard tray laden with rolls of cash - things clearly hadn't changed. The Kings Head had long ago established itself, among those in the know, as a pub where you could get anything you wanted, from drugs, to guns, to knocked off electrical goods, but from four o'clock on a Thursday afternoon it filled with labourers and tradesmen who would exchange their weekly wage cheques for cash. A lot of cash sat in that cardboard tray, and Jimmy knew first hand that there was a shotgun lying within easy reach behind the bar. He didn't look directly at the men looking at him, he knew that direct eye contact would be seen as confrontation by any one of them, and although Jimmy would fancy his chances if it came to it, he wasn't here for a fight.

He looked to the bar and locked eyes with Shelley. There was a brief moment of silence in the bar, it must have only lasted a second or two, but it felt to Jimmy as if it lasted minutes. Shelley's eyes lit up with recognition and her cold, hard stare broke into a broad grin.

"Jimmy Mac. Well, isn't this a surprise!"

Like a switch being flicked, the tension in the pub immediately dissipated and the men went back to their rowdy banter and their drinking. Jimmy approached the bar.

"Alright Shelley".

"It's been a while, Jimmy. Home from fighting someone else's war?"

"Something like that."

"What do we owe for the pleasure?"

"Was just in the area. Wondered if there might be a game?"

Shelley looked at him, the eyes boring into his soul. Shelley was a gatekeeper, and her job was to smell out a rat as soon as it stepped through her door, and she had a gift for it. After a few seconds, she gave a brief nod of her head, it seemed Jimmy had passed her assessment.

"There is as it happens. Andy's gonna wet himself when he sees you walk in. Come on through. Darren? Watch the bar."

Jimmy followed Shelley through the wooden door at the side of the bar, the shaven headed Darren eyeing him suspiciously as he passed. Despite being close to sixty, Shelley was still an attractive woman and Jimmy couldn't help admiring the way she sashayed up the staircase in front of him, the black leather trousers clinging to her petite frame. Jimmy knew she enjoyed having men's eyes on her, knowing that they were fantasising about her, but there had only ever been one man for Shelley, and even though Frank had died ten years earlier, she would never be with another. They reached the top of the bare wooden staircase, and stepped onto a small landing with heavily patterned, threadbare carpet. Three doors led off the landing and two burly men stood outside the door to the right. They were caricatures of gangster bodyguards, pantomime 'baddies' whose facial expression and gesture were so loud and placed it was almost comical. They were both dressed in jeans, black leather jackets, and black turtlenecks. Shelley spoke to the man on the right of the door, a large Nigerian who had a thick gold link chain around his neck.

"Dokes. This is Jimmy. He's an old acquaintance. He's come to play. Some of the boys will know him. You can let him in."

With that she turned around and headed back down the stairs, her platform sandals clip-clopping down the bare wooden staircase.

Jimmy stepped towards the door and both of the bodyguards took one step towards each other, blocking the way. Jimmy looked at the man named Dokes and was met with an impassive stare. The other man, a white eastern European type with short cropped dark hair, held up a wooden tray.

"Guns, knives, weapons, phone."

Jimmy took out his mobile phone and placed it on the tray. The bodyguards looked at him but didn't move.

"I don't have any sort of weapon."

"Please raise your arms".

Jimmy followed the request and the muscular Dokes expertly patted him down, checking all pockets, armpits, ankles, waistline and the small of Jimmy's back. Satisfied, the two men stepped to the side of the door in perfect synchronization, as if performing a choreographed routine.

"You have phone when you leave."

The Eastern European opened the door and Jimmy stepped through.

The room was dimly lit, shadows everywhere creeping in from the outer reaches - the darkness winning the war against the light. An old fashioned standard lamp stood in the far corner of the rectangular room, feebly throwing out a pale straw light onto the surrounding wooden floorboards, unable to penetrate the thick, tasselled lampshade; a single white bulb, topped by a reflective stainless steel, industrial lampshade dangled over a large circular table in the centre of the room; small, picture lights lined the dark, wood-panelled walls, softly downlighting the grained wood in the absence of any pictures. Jimmy looked to the corner behind the door he had just entered and met the cold black eyes of a small Asian man in a white shirt and black bow tie. He was small in stature, but Jimmy was in no doubt that he was someone who could take care of himself should he need to; if he worked this closely to Deaf Andy, the likelihood was that he was dangerous. The man stood behind a low black bar, behind him a sideboard loaded with every kind of spirit you could possibly want, along with crystal cut glasses and buckets of ice and bottled beer.

"Can I get you a drink?"
"Single malt?"
"Of course. Ice?"

"No. Thanks."

Jimmy turned back to the table. Deaf Andy sat on the other side, a little more wrinkled and a little greyer in the temples, but still the same measured manner. Gone was the old prominent NHS hearing aid in his left ear, replaced by a more subtle modern version. He was looking at Jimmy, elbows on the table and the harsh light of the bulb casting shadows across his face.

"Well look what the cat dragged in."
"Hello Andy."
"Sit down. Make yourself comfortable. You're just in time."

The game was Texas hold'em and there already seemed to be a considerable pot on the table. There were five people at the table; Jimmy recognised Alfie 'the rat' Green, the petty criminal from Camden who Jimmy had last seen in this very room almost five years ago. He hadn't changed all that much, his unwelcoming sneer still fixed to his ratty, pockmarked face. Opposite Deaf Andy was Neil Aldridge, the Mancunian who ran the Northwest branch of Andy's firm; Jimmy had only met him once, but he never forgot a face. Next to Aldridge was a younger, fashionably dressed guy, all high line haircut and neatly pressed shirt. He looked familiar but Jimmy couldn't put his finger on where he had seen the guy before. Jimmy took a seat between Alfie and the fifth member of the group, who he didn't recognise, but he met the man's gaze with strong eye contact and a neutral expression, unwilling to give away any 'tells' to the unknown challenger.

Andy leaned back in his chair as Jimmy sat down, never taking his eyes off his old acquaintance. The pile of chips in front of Andy was already substantial - green, red and black chips neatly stacked and looking like an impressive outline of a city skyline - the empire he was building.

"I think you know a few of the boys. You remember Alfie and Neil?"

Jimmy gave Andy a curt nod and acknowledged both men.

"And this is Danny, Neil's brother. Coming up through the ranks. Making a bit of a name for himself." Jimmy noticed a flicker of a smile on Danny's face at the praise from the boss.

"And this….."

A silence lingered in the room. Jimmy looked up from the table and realised that he was meant to finish off the statement. Jimmy looked at the man, with his immaculately presented appearance, the manicured hands absent-mindedly flicking a chip between his fingers, but he couldn't place his face. He was young and athletic looking, but somehow didn't seem to fit in with this crowd of mobsters and petty criminals. Jimmy pursed his lips and shook his head.

"Kevin Armstrong. Rising star of Millwall. This time next year, my money's on him being starting nine at Chelsea."

Kevin Armstrong bowed his head, embarrassed by the praise, but a slight twitch at the corners of his mouth belied the modesty. Jimmy made the connection, seeming to recall seeing the man's face on the back pages of the newspapers a few times - he was a bright young star who was typically being overhyped by the English media as the next world beater.

Jimmy pursed his lips and shook his head again.

"Sorry. Not really a football fan."

Deaf Andy snorted a disappointed laugh.

"You haven't changed a bit."

Jimmy wasn't going to give Deaf Andy the satisfaction of seeing him impressed with the company Andy was keeping.

He wasn't impressed. Jimmy was fairly certain that Andy had only extended an invitation to the footballer to show off to his entourage, and because the sporting celebrity was likely to be an easy target around the poker table - a rich, naive kid willing to throw some cash around to buy him friends with influence. Jimmy looked at Kevin and noticed he was looking at the table, perhaps a little crestfallen, perhaps just a realisation that he was a little out of his depth.

"You know the rules. Things haven't changed since you've been away. Fifty quid minimum bet."

He felt the presence of someone behind him.

"Two grand buy-in"

Jimmy sighed as he looked up. A small smirk spread across his face as he held Deaf Andy's gaze.

"I'm here to play." The Asian barman unloaded a pile of chips onto the table in front of him.

LIFE SAVER

Charlie lay crushed into the sofa; his stocky frame bent and contorted in a brave attempt to find comfort. Thank-God he had an eye mask. The counselling room was the only room he could find tonight to try and get twenty minutes of sleep. This was his eighth night shift in a row, and he needed every second of sleep he could find. Only he couldn't sleep tonight. Partly because the sofa was possibly the worst sofa he had ever had the unfortunate pleasure of trying to sleep on, partly because every time he moved the motion sensors in the room turned the glaring lights on, but mostly because in 3 hours' time his shift ended and for the first time in God knows how long he was taking some time off.

He moved. The lights came on.

"Fuck"

Charlie sat up, pulling his legs towards him with his arm, trying to dig out his limbs from the decrepit and inhospitable sofa. He pulled off his eye mask and blinked at the intensity of the sterile strip lighting in the hospital. He looked up at the TV hanging limply on the stand on the wall, clinging on for dear life. It was one of those compact, all-in -one TVs you used to get in the 90's , with the inbuilt VHS player . It was old and looked like it was thinking of just rolling off that stand and ending it. His phone began to violently vibrate. He picked it up and looked at the screen. Multiple messages were flooding in with details of a major incident in London. Charlie grabbed the TV controller and flicked it on. The sombre expressions of the news reporter said it all - he found the controller and turned on the sound.

"We are just receiving reports of an explosive device being detonated at Stockwell tube station. It is currently unknown how many casualties there might be but there are large numbers of people emerging with what appear to be significant injuries."

Charlie stood up. He was watching the clean cut, sharply dressed reporter standing in front of a scene full of carnage. In the background, smoke and dust were pouring out of the tube station entrance, paramedics rushing from casualty to casualty.

"Shit."

He turned off the television and walked purposefully out of the room.

The Accident and Emergency department was eerily quiet as Charlie strode towards the central nurse's station - the calm before the storm, he thought. Chloe was on the incoming. She put the red receiver down and opened her mouth to say something.

"I've just seen. How long?"

"Three minutes out."

"Call plastics. Get Mahafferty down here and clear as many of the beds as we can. We're going to need them."

Charlie looked up at the clock. Three hours until the end of his shift, but that was now looking unlikely. This was just typical. His phone pinged in his scrubs. A text message. It was Dibs, his old school mate in Rocky Bay. What the hell was he texting for?

"Gully's Dead. Funeral is Saturday."

Oh Christ.

As he marched through the double doors into the secure accident and emergency area his mind was doing mental acrobatics as he tried to organise his thoughts. Gully dead? He could feel his heart almost jumping out of his chest and overriding the innate tiredness he felt. A tingling ran down his arms and up his legs. He stopped momentarily in front of a set of double doors and took a deep breath. His body was struggling to process this thunderbolt of news. He was amazed that a simple text message could have such a physical impact on someone. He moved through to the ambulance bay, he could hear the sirens of the city echoing through the narrow streets, getting rapidly closer. He couldn't process this now, he needed his mind focused, ready to deal with the casualties who were about to be landed in his lap and who needed his help. But Gully's face kept filling his thoughts, and then the image of Charlie lying on the sand replaced it. He pressed his palms into his eyes and took another deep breath. He looked around him at the crew of nurses and doctors awaiting the delivery of injured people - people were restless, moving from foot to foot, furiously chewing gum or continuously looking up and down the road to spot the first 'blue-lights'. It struck him that the answer he was looking for at the end of the ridiculously long days, when he questioned why he had gone through so many years of training and exams, questioned why he worked so hard for comparatively little money, why his job had cost him his marriage, was right here in front of him at this very moment: in a dark, macabre kind of way, this was it - it was the excitement, the adrenalin, the toying with life and death in dangerous and challenging situations. That's why he and so many of his colleagues did it. He put thoughts of Gully and Charlie to the back of his mind. Shut them temporarily in a room inside his mind palace. He would deal with that later. Right now, there were people that needed him; the buzz and the thrill of an emergency began to get the blood pumping. *He couldn't believe Gully was dead.*

A convoy of three blue lighted ambulances came tearing down the street. Charlie looked at the message again.

"Gully's dead. Funeral is Saturday." Charlie's mood dipped. He had heard Gully was sick but didn't realise that it was life threatening. A wave of emotion washed over him and he felt clammy and sick. He would have to think about it later.

Nicola Andrews, one of the A&E consultants, put her phone into her pocket. "Here we go everyone."

FLOATER

Jimmy's feet actually left the floor, and he came down hard on the crumbling tarmac in the alley behind the pub, the puddles from the rain the night before not deep enough to soften the blow. The metallic taste of blood dominated his senses as his nose gushed claret. He rolled to the side and spat the blood into the puddle he was lying in. His head was still ringing from the gentle reminder that Dokes had given him about paying his debt to Deaf Andy, and as he tried to focus on the two intimidating figures which loomed over him in the alleyway, he suspected that he might have a mild concussion, or it might be the whiskey…he couldn't tell.

"Two days. Then we come find you."

Nico, the Eastern European, tossed Jimmy's phone onto the floor beside him and then the two goons turned their backs and walked casually back into the pub. Jimmy lay his head back down on the tarmac, oblivious to the wet, the dirt and the grime of the London alley. The first rays of the new day were breaking through and filling the dark recesses of the city with light and hope. Jimmy looked up at the sliver of baby blue sky framed by the dark and malevolent outlines of the buildings which lined the narrow alley. He loved the early morning, before the world had properly woken up, when the unnatural sounds of human existence were muted, and the sounds of nature filled the air with a sense of unashamed freedom. A rustle to his left made him turn his head, and he could see a large black rat cautiously moving through the pile of bin-liners outside the back door of the pub. It momentarily looked up and locked its beady black eyes on Jimmy, before dismissing his presence as one of little threat, and going back to scavenging for its breakfast. He hated rats, he always had.

"Fuck."

A memory of his squadron leader telling him that rats were just rats came flooding back to him. Rats weren't good or evil, they were just rats. They just did what they had to do to survive, just like any soldier.

He sat up and watched the rodent root through the detritus that littered the alley floor and a smile spread across his bloodied face. Maybe he shouldn't fear the rat. Maybe he and the rat had more in common than he thought. He had hit rock bottom. He was bleeding, sitting in a pile of rubbish in an alley in a questionable part of town. He had slid down the scale. He was vermin. He picked up his phone. The screen was cracked.

Jimmy had never classified himself as a gambler, but more as someone who liked risk. High risk, high reward. Unfortunately, he had always focused on the high reward part, but it seemed that recent events were doing a damn good job at reminding him that the flip side of that, the risk side, was dangerous and at times, life threatening. His stupidity, bravado and obstinate machismo had just landed him in a very big hole. A hole the size of twenty grand. As he lay there his brain suddenly kicked into overdrive, the adrenaline of panic flooding his body. A quick calculation of what money he had in the world. Not much. His savings were dwindling rapidly since leaving the army. His brain was fuzzy, pulsing and throbbing, not letting him think clearly. He gave up. He would need at least fifteen grand, maybe more. He had two days.

Like an old man, he staggered to his feet. Blood still dripped from his chin. He felt his nose. The blood flow was stemming as it began to clot. The bridge of the nose was swollen. It was probably broken but it didn't feel too bad; he'd had worse, and right now he had other more pressing problems.

SLEEP NO MORE

Although Mark hadn't yet opened his eyes, he could sense the new day had dawned. He didn't move; something was off, and he needed a moment to work out what it might be. The throb of a hangover lay slumbering at the base of his brain, ready to unleash its full power the moment he moved. He used to laugh in the face of people who whined that hangovers get worse with age, but at this particular moment, he was asking for their forgiveness. However, it was a silent plea, because his mouth was stuck together and felt like he'd been chewing on a Pritt-stick.

He opened his eyes, the lids feeling heavy and crusted, and he stared at the smooth soft skin of a naked female back. Long dark hair spilled out across the pillows, and he could see the bold black lines of a tattoo snaking down from the woman's neck. He closed his eyes again and immediately a montage of images flashed through his mind, recollections from the night before - music, dancing, drinking and good times. From what he could recollect it had been an enjoyable night out. He rolled over to reach for the water bottle and saw the bright red LED display of the alarm clock on his bedside table.

"Shit!"

Mark exploded off the bed and his head filled with a searing pain behind his eyes.

"What? What's going on?"

The woman in his bed rolled over, half sitting up and staring at him through one open eye. Mark silently congratulated himself on the fact that she was attractive, perhaps not the sort of girl he would have taken home to meet his mother, but still.

"I've got to go. I've got to go to work."

"Oh. Right."

She didn't move.

"I'm, like, really late."

"Oh. Right. Ok." The woman slipped out from under the sheets and stood self-consciously next to the bed, covering her breasts and trying to locate her clothing. An awkward silence hung in the air and Mark, racking his brain to try at the very least to remember the woman's name left the room to give her some privacy and hurriedly get his stuff together for work.

As he pulled on his shirt and slurped the boiling cup of coffee he glanced at his phone and saw he had a message.

"Gully's dead. Funeral is on Saturday."

Gully was dead?

MILLENNIALS

Mark stood at the front of the lecture hall, 200 faces looking at him and he knew he had to pull his thoughts together to do his job, but the text message about Gully this morning, together with a raging hangover and the news of a terrorist attack was making it difficult for him to concentrate. The students seemed sombre and fidgety after the news of the attack on the tube, and he sensed he needed to pull something out of the bag to distract them. Mark was a popular lecturer and had a reputation for delivering engaging and interesting talks. He just wasn't feeling it today.

He continued with his train of thought.

"A sobering thought. Are we set on self-destruction through our own selfish desires? Who here has more than one brother or sister?"

Mark looked around the theatre and an array of hands were heavily lifted into the air. Mark laconically put his own hand up.

"Who wants kids when we grow up?"

He fixed the room with a searching look. Again, the majority of the room raised their arms to the ceiling, grins spreading across their faces as they began to identify Mark's line of questioning. A ripple of amused chatter echoing around the small lecture theatre. He was winning them back. The sea of hands began to ebb.

"More than one?"

"More than two? Getting greedy? Selfish?"

Mark laughed as he looked at the grinning faces. The human race just couldn't help themselves. They were weak...including himself.

"Ok hands down. Think about this. The current world population is approximately 7 billion. If fertility remains at current levels, the population will reach the absurd figure of 296 billion in just 150 years. 296 billion. Worrying, yes? Why can't we just slow it down? Come on millennials....what are you going to do about it?"

Mark paused for effect. Despite his banging hangover, the lingering threat of terrorism and the tragic news of his childhood friend, he was beginning to get into his stride; it was at times like this that he loved his job; he could feel the tension in the room, they were listening, engaged and feeling challenged....or maybe it was just the performer in him that vainly enjoyed having a crowd hanging on his every word? Mark deduced that it was probably a bit of both.

"Apart from the fact that 1/3 of the current population growth in the world is the result of incidental or unwanted pregnancies, what about the fact that one billion teenagers are just entering their reproductive years."

There were 'whoops' and cheers from groups around the theatre.

"Yeah, yeah."

Mark smiled and leaned casually on the table next to the lectern.

"The largest 'youthquake' ever. The world is growing by more than 76 million people a year."

Mark pointed over his shoulder at the projection screen as the slide changed to a worrying looking bar graph.

"At the current rate of growth, even accounting for a continual decrease in the growth rate, the world population is headed for double digits within 50 years. Where are we all going to live? How are we going to feed everyone? Every 20 minutes, the world adds another 3,500 human lives but loses one or more entire species of animal or plant life - at least 27,000 species per year."

Mark propelled himself away from the table and nonchalantly clicked the projection screen onto the next slide of his presentation.

"Your assignment is a 1000-word proposal for how you, the millennial generation, are going to combat the population crisis. Due after the holidays, the first Monday back please everyone."

Groans reverberated around the room.

"Have a good break!"

There was a flurry of activity as students stood up and began to pack away their laptops and folders, desperate to get out of the cramped lecture theatre. Mark turned and began to gather his lecture notes together.

"Mark?"

Mark turned around to find Tilly, a second-year geography student coyly eyeing him.

"Tilly"

"I wondered if I might come and see you about my last essay. I think I could do with a little *hands-on* guidance "

It struck Mark that subtlety was the thing that this generation needed a little more guidance on. He looked at her. She was attractive. Mark could feel danger signs flashing all around him.

"Er....yes. Yeah, sure. Well...um drop me an email and we can arrange a time after the break."

"Great"

And as if she was in some hair commercial, she flashed her million-dollar smile, batted her eyelids and turned on her heel, her immaculate hair flicking out into a perfect arc. She sashayed away up the stairs to the exit at the back of the theatre, clearly aware of where Mark's eyes were lingering.

"A little bit young Mark."

Mark spun around, feeling like he had been caught with his hand in the sweet jar. Jacquie was standing in the doorway at the back of the stage, leaning against the door frame with an amused look on her face.

"They're the same age. I just keep getting older."

Jacquie smiled. Mark's boyish grin spread across his face. Mark was a rogue, a charming rogue - there was a playful charisma about him which many women seemed to find irresistible. In fact, she wasn't sure she had met many women who hadn't wanted to sleep with Mark Watson.

"Did you hear about the explosion on the tube?

"Yeah." Mark wasn't in the mood for small talk. "What do I owe the pleasure?"

"I thought we should maybe talk. About...well, Tuesday."

Mark paused as he continued to pack papers on the table.

"Listen, I'm going away for a few days. Can we talk when I get back?"

"Sure." Jacquie leaned on the table next to him. "Anywhere nice?"

"What?"

"Where are you going?"

Mark continued packing his bag. He didn't want to get into this now. "Home. To Cornwall. An old friend of mine just passed away. It's his funeral tomorrow."

"Oh. I'm sorry." Jacquie put her hand on his. Without looking at her he withdrew his hand and continued stacking papers.

"Yeah. Me too."

Jacquie stood up from the table and began to retreat towards the exit, sensing this wasn't the time to address their complicated romance. "Sure. Let's talk when you get back."

Mark hurriedly closed his work bag and slung it over his shoulder. He moved towards her. She held her ground, uncertainly blocking his exit.

"I've got to go."

Jacquie held his gaze for a moment.

"Yeah. Me too."

"We can talk when I get back."

And with that, Jacquie stepped to the side and Mark slid past.

"And Mark?"

Mark stopped and turned.

"I'm sorry about your friend."

Mark forced a polite smile before turning and disappearing through the door. For a moment she didn't move. She knew she was making a mistake chasing Mark Watson, but she couldn't help herself.

LAST ONE IN

It was almost ten thirty by the time Charlie lumbered through the door of his ground floor flat. Over two hours after he was meant to finish his shift...still, what was he to do? Those people needed him. Why did people do these things? He had made a difference this morning and no matter how tired he felt, that was what he always reminded himself of. The basement flat felt dank and cold as he shrugged off his rucksack and dropped it next to the front door. He picked up the small pile of lurid flyers that had been posted through his door, and made his way through to the kitchen. He discarded the junk mail into the recycling bin and turned on the kettle. He could never go straight to sleep when he came off a shift - the adrenalin was still coursing through his body, and his mind was still struggling to wind down after so much stimulation. He would wash away the grime of the hospital in a shower, have a cup of tea and curl up on the sofa and let sleep take him whenever his body and mind felt the urge to succumb to it. He couldn't think of a better way to start his week's holiday. An escape into the ecstasy of slumber. Today was a good day for doing nothing, and then he would get on with the task of sorting out his life. He looked around the bare kitchen, the brown boxes neatly stacked against the wall. Red writing for her. Blue for him. The stamped and addressed brown manila envelope that was sitting forlornly on the kitchen surface. The divorce papers. He had finally got around to signing them. It had been six months and Sarah's patience was beginning to run thin. The flat was sold - the last remaining connection severed. He had no choice but to sign them - the dying embers of his hope had finally been extinguished. Now all that was left to do was to post them; but posting them felt like the final act he wasn't sure he was ready for.

He poured himself a cup of tea and watched the steam rise from the chipped mug. He had been with Sarah since they were at university and he had been so certain that they would last, that they would be together until death do them part. But it turned out that she had ambitions for a life beyond a dingy, cramped two-bedroom flat in Brixton and a husband who was never at home. Being married to an A & E doctor hadn't turned out quite how she had expected, and she had ultimately become resentful of his job, feeling neglected and second best. Charlie was sure it probably hadn't taken much for her smarmy boss to tempt her away from the stale and stagnant marriage she found herself caught in. Charlie had only ever wanted to make her happy, and if she wasn't happy with him then he wasn't going to force it. A pang of emotion surged through him and he pulled out his phone. He looked at the phone message. *'Gully's dead'.* Memories triggered of Charlie Westley. Of her sixteenth birthday when they had had sex for the first time at Gully's house; of the sting of her slap that night on the beach. Even though it had been over a decade since he had seen Gully, he could feel the tears beginning to pool in his tired eyes. He was tired and feeling emotional. He needed to get a grip. Gully had stolen his girlfriend and then caused her death. Hadn't he? Did he deserve forgiveness? What had his own role been in her death? If he hadn't had a fight with her that night on the beach, if he hadn't been so angry…..

The clink of a key in the lock interrupted the battle raging in Charlie's mind. He felt a gust of the fume filled morning air waft through the flat and then the door slammed. Jimmy slunked into the kitchen and threw his keys on the countertop.

"What the fuck happened to you?" Charlie looked at his friend's swollen nose, a nasty cut sitting proudly on its bridge, his chin encrusted in dried blood.

"It's nothing." Jimmy went to the sink and began to fill a glass of water.

"Let me have a look."

Jimmy took a long gulp of the cold water before Charlie carefully and expertly assessed the damage.

"Did you see the news?" Charlie asked as he gently pressed around the swollen nose.

"Saw some headlines." Jimmy winced as Charlie pressed a little harder.

"Fucking terrorists."

"You don't have to tell me about it." Jimmy winced under his friend's touch.

"No. I guess not." Charlie let go and opened the freezer, throwing Jimmy an old packet of frozen peas. "Don't think it'll need re-setting, but pretty nasty. What happened?"

"It's nothing." Jimmy turned away.

Charlie looked at him with concern. His friend had struggled since leaving the army and Charlie had tried all he could to help and support him. He was glad Jimmy had returned from the wars he had been fighting physically unscathed, and it had been nice to have him staying with him since Sarah had left. It had been good to have some company, good for both of them. But there was a shadow that followed his friend these days, a dark, intense and stormy shadow and he could see that mentally Jimmy was scarred and damaged. He could see his friend was steadily imploding. He wondered if He had got the text about Gully too?

"What happened yesterday?

"With the job?"

"Yeah."

"What do you think?"

Jimmy took another gulp of water. His throat was dry and cracked after all the booze he had consumed.

"You stink."

"Thanks"

Charlie looked him up and down; he'd always been complex, angry and in many ways introverted, but he knew him well enough that things were on the cusp of going very wrong indeed.

"So, it didn't go well?"

"No. It went well. I just didn't get it."

The bitterness of the response lingered in the kitchen.

"You want a brew?"

Jimmy silently nodded his head, his jaw clenching and unclenching as he wrestled with whether to tell Charlie about the hole he had dug himself with Deaf Andy. He couldn't ask him for money. He couldn't ask him for more help. He already felt bad sponging off him by crashing at his house. And what about Gully? Should he tell him about Gully?

"Have you heard?". Jimmy looked at Charlie, searching for some sort of reaction.

"About?"

"Gully."

Charlie momentarily paused as he removed another mug from the cupboard, caught off guard. "Yeah." An audible sigh emphasised that Charlie still hadn't really processed the news and it was weighing on his mind.

"You going to go? To the funeral?"

"It's tomorrow."

"Yeah."

"I don't know. Unlikely. I haven't…..I haven't really…."

"I'm going." Jimmy paused. "We should all go."

"I don't know Jimmy. I've got stuff to sort out - with the house, the divorce."

"You've got a week off, haven't you? The flat is packed, the divorce papers just need putting in the post. Don't run away from this. We should go."

The deep throated rattle of the ancient doorbell reverberated around the kitchen and cut through the tension. Jimmy involuntarily stiffened.

"I'll go." Jimmy went to the hallway. Once out of ear shot, he moved lightly over the creaking floorboards until he reached the front door. He peered through the spy hole expecting to see some of Deaf Andy's thugs, but a sense of relief flooded through him as he saw who it was, and he opened the door.

"Fucking hell Jimmy. Who've you upset?

Jimmy gave Mark a lopsided grin and stepped aside to let his friend in.

"Thanks." Mark pushed past him into the house. "What the fucks happened?" Mark looked closely at Jimmy's mangled face as the front door banged shut.

"Just a bit of a disagreement."

"Ever just tried talking it out?!"

"Words were never my strong suit."

Mark smirked. It was so true. Jimmy had never been good with words. "No! Hey, have you guys seen the news?" Mark burst though into the kitchen to find his brother stirring a steaming cup of tea.

"Yeah, I was mopping up most of it."

"Long night then? Fuckers. Hey. You heard about Gully?"

This was big news for his brother, given the history. His brother had gone through a lot recently, what with the divorce, the sale of the flat and the stress of his job; he wasn't sure how Charlie would have taken this news - it had been over a decade since it had all happened, but despite everything, Gully had been one of their best friends, almost family.

"Yeah. Got the text from Dibs."

"How're you feeling?"

"Not sure. Haven't really processed it."

Jimmy took a sip of his tea. "Mark? You going to the funeral?" Mark shared a look with Jimmy. Jimmy could see he was conflicted. "Erm, Yeah. I think so. Or I was thinking of going." He looked at his brother who hadn't really moved in the last few minutes, just standing there lost in his own thoughts and sipping his tea.

"I think we should go. It's Gully guys! He was practically family." Jimmy had always been the one closest to Gully but the four of them had been inseparable for so many years. They both looked at Charlie.

Charlie was anxiously twiddling with the toggle of his hooded sweatshirt. He was torn between a love for his boyhood friend, and the anger that was still raw and was now resurfacing. But he owed it to Gully, didn't he? Forgiveness was strength.

Charlie filled his lungs and audibly exhaled. "Yeah. I guess. We should go."

Mark's face lit up, relieved that his brother was on board. "Road trip!" Jimmy's heart suddenly began to pound. Maybe this wasn't such a good idea, considering he needed to front up twenty grand for Deaf Andy in the next two days. What was he doing? He couldn't just run away from his debt. Or could he? Would they come looking for him? Could he just keep on running? Would they chase him over a sleazy, drunken back room bet? Spasms rippled through his body at the potential danger the decision he had just made might put him in. But then, it might just be perfect….a bit of time and space to get his shit together. Doubt's icy fingers began to crawl across his heart. Maybe he should stay. He might find the money. Somehow. And if he didn't….face the consequences like a man. No. He needed time. Time to make a plan. Right now, he needed to get out. Evade, escape, hunker down and take cover. Disappear. And apart from anything else, he needed to say goodbye to his friend.

DISAPPEARING BELOW THE SURFACE

Jimmy hated church. It made him feel false.

God is kind and loving and will welcome Gulliver into the light of Heaven.

Jimmy bit his lip. He could feel a trickle of blood seep into his mouth. He had witnessed first-hand the compelling evidence that God is not kind and loving, but cruel and unjust; inflicting pain and suffering upon innocents on a scale that would have Amazon chomping at the bit to make a blockbuster documentary on God, for 'Psychopath Season'.

A warped image bolted from the recesses of his mind; a girl of about eight or nine years old, her right leg torn apart and dark arterial blood pooling in a perfect mirror-glass crimson lake on the floor beneath her. Screams and shouts echoing and reverberating around the concrete carcass of the building. The piercing scream of her mother.

He closed his eyes and tried to breathe, tried to block it out, but the air was old, ancient and musty and did little to wash away the memory.

But we cannot understand Gods' will. He has his own plan for each of us and it is a mystery to humankind.

The chaplain's voice washed over him. With his eyes closed Jimmy searched in the darkness for something positive but began to spiral. Memories swirled - Jayden, a young private on his first tour, talking late one night around a small campfire in the desert.

"So here me out yeah....like, I think it's....yeah, like nine million children die each year before the age of five. Nine, bruv. Kids, yeah? Put that into perspective right - think about that Tsunami in 2004 right. That killed two hundred and fifty thousand people, yeah. So nine million - that's the equivalent of one of those tsunami's happening every ten days and only taking out children under five."

Bobby Fairweather chips in, "Justin, you are wasted bro - you should be on countdown or somethin'!"

Justin just smiled. White teeth gleaming in the darkness. "That's twenty four thousand kids a day....that's a thousand an hour...or seventeen a minute."

"I'm gonna call you Carol Vordaman. But she's better looking!". Bobby rolled onto his back, laughing at the stars.

Justin smirked, the embers of the fire casting shadows across the embarrassment on his face.

The three of us are silent for what felt like a long time, but was probably only about a minute; then Bobby threw a dry piece of brush on the fire and sparks lifted into the blackness like fireflies on the breeze. "What's more mad y'know, is that all them kids, their parents, yeah, a lot of them probably love God, yeah. Like whatever religion, wherever they come from, they are probably praying and shit. For their kids."

Justin prodded the fire. "Exactly my point man. It doesn't matter what God you're praying to - he ain't listening or he just simply doesn't give a shit."

The Chaplains voice broke the memory. *"Let us pray."*

Jimmy snapped open his eyes and cast them around

the cavernous stone church. Heads bowed, eyes closed - subservient to a mythical power. Karen, Gully's mum was two pews in front of Jimmy, her bowed figure heaving as the tears began to flow again. Her boyfriend, Gavin, put his arm around her and handed her a crisp white handkerchief. Gully would have hated this. He was always so full of life when they were kids, so effervescent. He couldn't stand people being miserable and negative, which is why everyone wanted to be his friend. What had happened to their friendship? One mistake. And they had been so young and naive. And so full of hate and blame. And then they had all just drifted, full of resentment, anger and secrets. Gully - this little blond surfer kid with the big smile and the dirty laugh, always telling jokes and always wanting to please. He would talk to everyone, from the homeless guy on the street corner, to the supermarket cashier, to the cute girl at the party, to the kid standing on their own, to your Mum or Dad….it didn't matter…within five minutes they would love him. As people prayed to their mythical God, Jimmy thought about what it was that had made Gully so loved; it was the fact that whoever he talked to, he gave them a hundred percent - he made you feel like you were the only person in the world. That was why Charlie Westley had loved him. And it wasn't his fault. He wasn't one of those people who looked around the room as they talked to you, looking for a better option - even if he didn't like the person and never wanted to speak to the person again, Gully still gave them his full attention until the exchange was over. It was just his way. He gave everything one hundred percent. He filled a room with positivity and people loved him. Gully *was* love. And God is love. So why the fuck has God taken him so young. Maybe God was jealous. God moving in mysterious ways - the anger began to rise in Jimmy's throat again. But what about forgiveness, isn't that something that God encouraged? Was that why Jimmy, Charlie and Mark had come back? To forgive? Did he need forgiveness? Was he to blame? Was it all just a little bit too late? None of these people knew what truly happened that night of the beach party, but surely Gully deserved forgiveness, they all did - it had been an accident, a reckless decision fuelled by anger, desire and a teenage naivety.

Suddenly there was movement, and everyone was standing. Mark on one side of him and Charlie on the other. Charlie was leaning over and saying something, but Jimmy couldn't make it out, his right ear had never been the same after the second tour - clearing out a cave system somewhere near Kandahar and in the darkness and confusion Jimmy had found himself too close to a stun grenade. Mark nodded at whatever it was that Charlie had said, and then they both turned back to face the front as the organ erupted and the coffin slid slowly beyond the curtain.

The church was full - a testament to the impact Gully had on people, the respect he had within his small community. Because of the volume of people, you could hear the hum of murmured voices under the boom of the organ. People began to file out, sombre faces and bowed heads, a few tears. Jimmy wondered how many of these people actually knew him - really knew him. Maybe they knew him better than he did these days. But still, he was glad his friend had had a good send off. He wondered how many would turn out for him - nothing like this.

A light drizzle was falling outside, the parched earth lapping it up after weeks of an unexpected summer heatwave. Umbrellas popped into life and people milled around on the gravel path, making polite small talk and murmuring condolences. Jimmy wanted to get out of there, his mind was imploding, and he felt like he was about to scream. He wasn't sure how much more he could take. He pulled out his phone and saw a single notification flash up. It was a text from an unknown number. Three words, one sentence.

ONE MORE DAY.

Jimmy swiped the message away and tucked his phone back into his jacket. Back in the day, it would have been Gully he would have talked to about his problems, it would have been Gully. No judgement, he would have listened and helped him work out the problem. But Gully was gone now, and Jimmy felt regret that it had taken the death of his friend for him to return home. He couldn't talk to Charlie without him getting all high and mighty with him. There was no point in talking to Mark about anything more serious than the latest drama in his love life. He had to work it out himself, but he didn't know where to start. Since leaving the army, how had his life become so complicated? He wasn't cut out for the real world.

The wake was at Gully's mum's house, She had moved from the town house in the bay to a Gavin's detached house just a ten minute drive from the church in a small cornish village on the coast. Sandwiches and crisps dotted the trestle table in the kitchen/diner, taking shade under the long petals of a million lilies. The pungent smell of the flowers filling the room with the scent of death. It was overwhelming. Jimmy stood in the corner nursing a cold beer, listening to Mark sharing amusing anecdotes about Gully when they were a kid. The time he stole some wax from the local surf shop only to return it the next day because he couldn't stand the guilt; the time he complained how Annabel Simpson hadn't even kissed him after he had played her a song on his guitar. Charlie was notably quiet - this was probably most awkward for him, and to be honest, Jimmy was surprised he had even come.

Suddenly there was a gentle tap on his arm and Jimmy turned to see Karen standing next to him, a broken woman who had to say goodbye to her only son that day.

"He loved you boys."

Jimmy felt words forming in his mouth, but no sound came

out. Mark broke the awkward silence.

"We're really sorry, Karen. You don't need us to tell you that he was one of a kind. We'll all miss him."

"He was so looking forward to you coming back home, Jimmy."

Jimmy could feel the tears pooling in his eyes and the guilt ripping through his insides.

"He wanted me to give you this." She held out an envelope with Jimmy's name written in Gully's spidery cursive, and a small navy-blue cardboard tube. Jimmy took the envelope and tube. It was heavy.

"Look after him won't you." Tears glistened in her eyes. "It's lovely to see you boys. You were like the brothers he never had. Stay in touch. Our door is always open."

With that she turned and disappeared through the melee of people.

THE PADDLE OUT

Mark and Charlie had a static caravan on the south side of the bay. After they moved away, both of their parents had died; their Mum succumbing to an aggressive cancer, and their Dad not lasting much longer. They sold the family home but had kept the static caravan the family had owned on the headland ever since any of them could remember. 'The box' as it had come to be known, became their little headquarters when the four of them had been growing up surfing every day; stashing their boards there, drinking before parties, taking girls there - Mark even lost his virginity in the old tin box. It came with picturesque views looking out over the breaking surf and memories a mile long. But neither of them had been back to the van for almost ten years, choosing to become one of the people they grew up hating, and letting it out to tourists in the holiday seasons.

Mark's primary love had always been photography, but he was smart enough to understand that this wasn't a profession that would allow him enough funds to live the life he wanted to lead. Mark was clever, he always had been. He hadn't worked hard at school, not like his brother - he didn't need to - he was just naturally intelligent. He was one of those guys that was sickeningly good at most things - athletic and sporty, clever, musical, charming and ruggedly good looking. So when it came down to planning what he wanted to do with his life, with so many avenues open to him, he had approached it with a logical and mature mindset. When the careers advisor had spoken to him at school and said to him, "Mark, I really think you should push the Oxbridge angle. Perhaps pure maths or environmental sciences. You can do anything. What do you want to do?".

Mark had simply replied, "I just want to be happy."

He didn't need the advice and guidance of the career advisor, Mrs Soames. She was a nice lady, but there was nothing she could do for Mark Watson. He already knew what he was going to do. He had a plan - he needed money, sure, not too much money - he wasn't greedy, but enough to pay the bills and allow him to travel and pursue his passion of taking photographs, of studying people and the natural world around him. Teaching seemed the obvious choice. It was never going to make him rich, but it paid enough and gave him lots of time off to pursue his passions.

So that's what he'd done. He'd gone to university to study Geography and Oceanography, graduating with first class honours. After a masters and a doctorate, he had taken a position as a professor at UCL in London, living in student digs and lecturing on physical and human geography. London had been alien to him, and he missed Cornwall, but being in the capital allowed him quick and easy access to the rest of the world when he wanted to escape. Mark had secretly yearned to come home and live a few weeks of the year in 'the box', to escape and reconfigure but had stayed away for Charlie - his wounds had never really healed, and Mark kept his distance out of respect for his brother.

Mark wondered how damp and musty the tin box would be. He stood with Charlie for a moment on the little decked terrace outside the front door. It was an idyllic spot. The late afternoon sun slowly making its way down to dip into the ocean and cast the Cornish coastline into an array of purples and pinks and pastel hues. It was a stunning view directly across Rocky Bay, and precisely why the family had held onto the place, even when the property prices began to skyrocket, as Cornwall became 'trendy' and people began buying up their own little piece of paradise. Even the price of a little static caravan was eye wateringly high as all the second homeowners pushed the locals out of their homes, offering money that was difficult to turn down for the residents of one of the poorest counties in the country. But as Mark stood there, he realised how much he had missed this place - he was so relieved they hadn't severed all ties with Rocky Bay. They had this view. They had direct access to one of the best beach breaks in the county and a roof over his head. He didn't need much else. Maybe now they would be able to reclaim the box as their own.

Charlie and Mark were suiting up to be part of the paddle out in the bay in memory of Gully. The Rocky Bay boardriders club had organised it and he suspected that most of the local surfing community would be there, and probably a few from further afield too. As a professional surfer, Gully knew a lot of people, making friends at most of the breaks in the southwest peninsula and beyond; he was a well-established face in the carparks of most decent breaks in the British Isles and many of those in Europe too. Wherever he turned up, he would inevitably know someone in the water - he was just one of those guys.

"I can't believe Jimmys not gonna paddle out." Mark didn't take his eyes off the surf in the bay. As always, the summer was generally disappointing for waves; the tourists arrived and the waves died, but there was a small swell running now, small feathering lumps marching towards shore. It wasn't much, but even so, the peak was packed with people, boards flying everywhere and people dropping in on each other left right and centre. It looked like carnage, but once the tourists all went back to their over-priced holiday cottages in an hour or so, the tide would be on the push, and it might be worth a little paddle. Gully would have been in. If there were waves, Gully was always in, regardless.

"Yeah. I think he's struggling. You know how he is."

"Intense."

"Yeah. He needs time to process."

"He's probably seen more death than most of us will in a lifetime."

A cloud passed over the sun and the afternoon light took on a moody feel.

"Let's get suited."

The air in the caravan felt stale and musty but not as damp as Mark had expected - the recent low pressure, bringing with it sunshine and blue skies, would have helped. Still, he opened the windows to air the place whilst they changed. He wasn't sure how long he was going to stay down for, but he needed to make it feel like home again. Gully's death had caught him off guard and had thrown his plans into disarray; he was warming to the idea of being down for a couple of weeks whilst he worked out his next adventure.

In ten minutes, they had their summer wetsuits on, the evening water and light offshores would bring a chill. Carrying their boards down the rough gravel path to the beach, they stepped carefully so as not to snag a toe or cut their feet. Mark had brought his camara and water housing to take a few shots of the paddle out. He was caught between feeling the emotion of losing one of his oldest friends and having a unique opportunity to capture such an event on camera. He kept telling himself that Gully would have been the first to encourage him - he was all about capturing the moment and following your dreams.

As they walked in silence, Mark cast his mind back to those early teenage years when Gully decided that he was going to try and make it as a pro surfer. They had all grown-up surfing together, dawn sessions egging each other on, pushing each other to be better. But it was Gully and Jimmy who had been the standout surfers from an early age, winning local grom competitions and attracting the attention of local sponsors. But whilst Jimmy had been desperate to escape the confines of Rocky Bay as soon as possible, finding sanctuary in the armed forces, it had been Gully who had fully committed. Getting onto the World Championship tour (the WCT) was his ultimate dream, and despite Gully winning the English national surfing championship twice, he hadn't quite had the results internationally to push himself up the world rankings and into the world elite. At sixteen years old Mark had bought his first water housing and remembered swimming out at north point to try and get some shots of Gully, Jimmy and Charlie. It had been onshore and messy, and Mark had got caught in the lip of a head high wave, trying to get a shot of Gully's bottom turn from above. The wave had pitched him and pounded him into the rocky shelf below, before turning him over in the 'spin cycle'. He had desperately clung on to his camera and in doing so had lost a flipper. The two hundred metre swim back to shore had been brutal with only one flipper and one hand to swim with. But he had made it, and when looking back over his shots, realised that his commitment had brought him gold; he had nailed the shot, and that photograph of Gully leaning back in towards the wave, an intensity in his eyes as he focused on where he was going to snap his board around at the top of the wave had earned Mark and Gully their first cover shot on Wavelength magazine. As two sixteen-year-olds, it had catapulted them into the limelight. That shot had changed both their lives overnight - suddenly it felt like everybody in the surfing world knew who they were and wanted a piece of them. It had opened up a whole new chapter for both of them and Mark would never forget that.

They had reached the rocks at the bottom of the path. They could see that there were already a number of people on the beach with boards scattered on the sand of all shapes and sizes, Hawaiian leis around their necks. The tourists were beginning to drift off the beach, looking at the group of locals with an air of curiosity. The sun was low in the sky, the ocean like liquid gold. Within five minutes of stepping onto the sand they were paddling out, hoots and laughter echoing across the water as they celebrated the friend they had lost. They saw old faces they hadn't seen in a decade and were greeted like long lost brothers by the local crew. The atmosphere was one of celebration and positivity. Just beyond the peak, a circle of nearly a hundred people formed, all sitting on their various watercrafts (from kayaks, and SUPs, to thrusters, bodyboards and longboards) and holding hands, as small A-frame waves peeled into the bay. It was picture perfect and Mark couldn't have wished for a more beautiful evening to send his friend off - the priest was right, God was clearly opening the pearly gates and letting Heaven's warmth flood down. He rattled off a few shots, capturing smiling faces obscured by the flare of the sun. For about twenty minutes the group sat there exchanging stories about Gully, mostly about his surfing exploits as well as a few other poignant anecdotes about how he had touched people's lives. Mark listened and tried to stem the images of Charlotte Westley lying prone on the beach of Dead Man's Cove. As the pulse of the ocean floated beneath them, the president of the boardriders club said a prayer for Gully, asking for God to provide him with good waves and a pint of decent cider, then everyone splashed the water and hooted as loudly as they could. As everyone began to paddle back in, a perfect set rose up on the horizon and people began to scramble to get into position to catch a wave. Mark pulled up his board in the channel and began to reel off multiple shots as people shared party waves into the beach, hooting and cheering as they went. Maybe this was Gully telling them he was ok - maybe he had sent these waves as a final farewell.

INSTRUCTIONS

Jimmy sat on the bed of his childhood bedroom. He looked around the room, untouched since he had left over ten years ago. The posters on the wall curled and faded, images of his childhood heroes, Occy, Irons and Slater tearing up another tropical, turquoise wave. The camouflage duvet cover and shelves lined with miniature toy soldiers creating a philosophical conflict of interest. War and peace coexisting to create a confused and angry young man. He was filled with self-loathing, at the bottom of the pit of despair. Somehow, he felt he had let his friend down even though there was nothing he could have done to change anything….it was fate or God's will….

He could hear his old man coughing downstairs, slumped in his recliner chair, creased and crippled from a life of hard labour and hard drinking. He never liked coming back here. He had done everything he could to leave. But he owed it to Gully to come back. He wouldn't have to endure the presence of his old man for too long - he was no threat anymore.

The blue tube and the envelope that Karen had given him lay unopened on his bed. He was too scared to open it, too scared to know the truth, which is what he knew Gully would have written - he always told the truth, and Jimmy wasn't sure he was ready to hear it. His phone pinged with a text message. It was Mark.

2-3 FT AND OFFSHORE. CLEAN AS JENNIFER ANISTONS LOVE HOLE.

You could always rely on Mark to make any comparison to the female form. His imagination hadn't progressed since they were fourteen. After the wake, Charlie and Mark had headed down to the bay for a paddle out with the local crew in honour of Gully. He had been an integral part of the local surfing community and too many people connected to the ocean wanted to pay their respects. But Jimmy couldn't face it. He couldn't look into the eyes of all of those people, it would be too painful, too many memories.

He turned back to the envelope and tore it open. Inside were two neatly folded sheets of A4 paper. Doodles of waves and surfboards adorned the margins, just like the notes they had passed in the lessons at school. Jimmy couldn't help but smile.

Dear Jimmy,

If you are reading this, I am dead. It's a fact. I imagine you're angry and frustrated at the world right now. But that's life. I had a good one. And I want to thank you for being a major part of it. You were always there for me, always looking out for me - remember that time when Chris Jackson tried to kick the shit out of me at Rocky's because Ali gave me her phone number?! You sat him on the sand and told him to grow up. I'll never forget that! The look on his face! No one would mess with you and having you as a best friend let me be who I wanted to be. I probably would have had my face smashed in a million times if it wasn't for you. I only wish that we had stayed in touch. But I understand - and I take full responsibility.

A tear rolled down Jimmys face and spattered onto the page, smudging some of the writing.

But I am dead. I am gone and it's time to move on. Not too quick. You can cry a bit more if you want!

Jimmy let out a brief chuckle and wiped his eyes. Typical Gully. Always making a joke - making the world lighter.

I have missed you. I have missed all the boys. I only hope that you are all still in contact. I hope that life has healed your wounds, and that the army has given you what you were looking for. I suspect that you have been through a lot, that you have some incredible and haunting stories to tell, your head is probably even more messed up than it used to be! But I hope that my death can bring some closure to past events and that some good can come of it. So I want you to think of this..... Remember when we were kids? When we were angry teenagers? Whenever you were pissed off with me or Charlie or Mark, or your old man, what did we do? We dived into the ocean to wash away the pain and clear our minds.

So.....

I have something for you.

Jimmy's heart skipped a beat, and he wondered if somehow Gully was going to give him money - something he desperately needed with Andy breathing down his neck. But Gully never had any money. Did he?

I have a request....a dying wish if you like. A lot has happened in my life in the last ten years, and I have some things I want to share with you. Before my mistake, before I ruined everything, we were all taking that trip to the Hebrides - remember? For obvious reasons, we never took that trip. But I did. I went many times. And I found a place - the most beautiful place in the world, with perfect waves and no one out.

Inside the envelope you will have found a key.

Jimmy looked at the discarded envelope on the bed and picked it up. Inside was a small, flat silver key. It looked shiny and new.

This key opens a lock up (number 11) just off Trevellyan drive - you know, the garages where we used to go and smoke Mark's shit weed when we were kids. Round the back of the Budgens? Go and open it. There you will find your next instructions! Oh....and bring Mark and Charlie with you. They're involved in this too!

I am with you always, brother. See you in the juice.

Gully.

Jimmy looked at the key in his hand. He noticed his hand was shaking a little. Tears were streaming down his sun kissed cheeks. He didn't even realise he was crying. He smiled. This was so typically Gully.

99 WITH A FLAKE

The next day the seagulls were cawing loudly as the three friends stood outside lock up number 11 in the warmth of the summer sunshine. The dusty ground was littered with the overflow of the bins behind the Budgens, and the seagulls had clearly marked this as a reliable feeding ground, circling and swooping. It had been some time since the three of them had been here and memories of their childhood cascaded through their minds. They were unsure of what was inside the lock up; sitting on the deck of the static caravan, they had thrown out some ideas when Jimmy caught up with them after the paddle out, but the mystery left them both excited and nervous. Knowing Gully, it could be anything.

Jimmy pulled out the shiny key and turned it in the lock. It was an old up and over garage and the door was heavy and stiff. It creaked loudly as they lifted the door, as if it was reluctant to reveal its treasures, wailing in pain at the realisation that this meant its owner was now dead.

Dust motes danced in the early morning sunshine. It smelt damp and musty, with a lingering undertone of petrol. It took them a few moments for their eyes to adjust to the darkness, but then they saw what Gully had left them; it looked exactly the same as they remembered, but maybe a little more polished, a little more 'finished', but there was no mistaking it - it was the van Jimmy had been working on all that summer before it all fell apart. The ice cream van. Jimmy's heart fluttered, he could feel Mark and Charlie' eyes on him. How the hell had Gully got hold of this?

Mark picked up a big brown envelope that was pegged under one of the wipers on the windshield. 'BOYZ' was scrawled in black marker on the front. He opened the envelope and took out three sheets of folded paper and a large key attached to a wooden key ring in the shape of a two-dimensional whiskey barrel. Mark unfolded the paper and began to read aloud as Jimmy began to inspect his old van, reunited with an old friend. Charlie remained in the threshold of the lock up, still troubled by the ghosts of their childhood.

Dear Jimmy, Mark and Charlie,

I hope you're all here. I would understand if you weren't, but I hope you are. I only wish I was with you.

Look at her! Jimmy, I can't believe you just left her to rot in your old man's garage. I persuaded him to sell her to me a few years back - I think he took me for a ride in what he charged me, but I don't mind - call it penance for all my wrongs. He gave her a good once over and she runs like a beauty - your old man was always the best mechanic in town.

So, if you are here, then I am hoping that you are willing to carry out a dead man's final wishes? I am not expecting forgiveness for what I did and the mistakes I made, but I want to give you guys something. These are your instructions:

I want you to take this van (I called her Bonnie by the way) and follow the directions on the sheet in the envelope. The directions will take you to a very special place - the place we should have gone to together before I messed everything up. I want you to take that trip like we should have done. There is a house you can stay in. It's a house I bought after you all left. For a long time, I was very lost and alone. I bought this place to escape, to give me time to think and to surf.....and boy is there surf. I hope you enjoy it because it is yours - I have left the house to the three of you. There is nothing I can do to change the past; there is nothing I can do to make up for the pain I caused; but I hope that you can forgive me enough to accept this gift.

I am hoping my Mum has given you some of my ashes. Please take me with you, so I can be a part of this trip in some way. Scatter me on the break in front of the house.

So long. I hope you score big.

G

A loud silence hung in the garage. "Gully has a house in the Hebrides?" Mark broke the silence and opened up the map.

"The guy never ceases to surprise you. Even from the grave." Charlie moved towards the van and began to inspect it. "But I'm not coming."

"What?" The other two whirled on him and looked at him in surprise. "Why not?"

"I'm not traipsing up to Scotland on the wishes of Gully Jones. I've got stuff to do. It was one thing to come down here for his funeral. A whole other thing to go off galivanting around chasing waves."

Mark began to follow him around the van. "You're on holiday."

Charlie turned on him. "A holiday I booked to sort out my life."

Mark stood his ground. "You're so fucking boring. Maybe this is exactly what you need to sort out your life…a little excitement. A bit of adventure. Instead, you're going to take yourself back to London and sit staring at four bare walls beating yourself up about how shit your life is. Fucking hell. Loosen up." Even in the gloom of the garage, Mark could see the heat begin to rise in his brother's face. He had poked the bear. He knew him better than anyone and he could sense the heady mixture of anger and stubbornness seeping out of every pore of his brother. "It's been ten years Charlie. Ten years. This is a chance to put it to bed. We've never talked about it. Any of us. Maybe Gully is right - maybe this is a good idea. A form of closure."

Jimmy emerged from behind the van. "I'm pretty keen to see this place of his. And to see how the van goes - I never did get to give it a good run."

Charlie looked at them, his expression one of grim determination. But deep down he knew he wasn't going to win this battle, and Mark's words held some sort of truth to them. Jimmy and Mark exchanged a look. Mark's face broke into a mischievous grin, "You know we've always been stronger than you. Kidnapping you is not off the cards. It's time for a road trip."

ROAD TRIPPING

Perhaps it was because the van had been left in a lock up for God knows how long, but the description of the van 'running like a beauty' was some way off the mark considering the way it spluttered and rumbled up the M40, sounding like an old man with emphysema; black exhaust fumes propelling it along the slow lane of the motorway, occasionally belting out enough power to overtake one of the many articulated lorries trundling along. Their only reassurance was the fact that Jimmy was a mechanic's son and knew more about engines than most. If it ground to a halt, they were confident that Jimmy would be able to fix it and get them on the road again - he had been the one to originally restore it after all. Mark had managed to negotiate the traffic laden A30 as the 'exodus' of tourists on any given Sunday of the summer made their way home, clogging the few arteries into the southwest. Then he had pointed the van north on the M5 and the van purred and coughed its way up the motorway. Now they were approaching Birmingham, Mark sat hunched over the large steering wheel, staring intensely ahead at the red taillights of the cars ahead. The earlier downpour of summer rain had passed, but the spray from the surface water and the creeping darkness was making driving conditions a challenge. The deep furrowed lines running across his forehead conveyed the intense concentration needed to combat the creeping fatigue he was feeling. He was just starting to wish they had delayed their exit from Cornwall until the following morning, when Charlie's voice broke the silence.

"I could do with a piss. Let's pull over at those services." Charlie pointed at the 'Welcome Break' sign, indicating that the next service station was just one mile away.

They left Jimmy asleep in the back of the van; a bespoke set up that was comfortable and surprisingly spacious, whilst they relieved themselves and then loaded up with snacks and overpriced, weak coffee. On the way back to the car Mark threw Charlie the keys and told him that he needed a break.

The heavy metal door creaked on tired hinges as the driver's door swung open and Charlie climbed in.

"Fucking hell Jimmy!"

The inside of the car was engulfed in a cloud of pungent smoke. Jimmy was sat with his feet up across the back seat, staring intently at his phone. A conical joint dangled limply from his lips. Mark swung up into the passenger seat and shut the door, letting out an excited "whoohoo!"

"Now this is more like it!" Mark turned and grinned at Jimmy.

"Mate, couldn't you have sparked up outside?"

Jimmy looked up momentarily from his phone, a maniacal glint in his eye. As he spoke the joint comically waggled up and down with the minimal movement of his lips, "Thought there might be cops about, fuelling up with coffee and donuts."

"And if those policemen decide to pull us over....."

"I thought we were on an adventure. Crack a window. Relax. I remembered I built a secret stash compartment back here in the side panel and had stashed some weed ready for the journey."

"So, you are smoking a ten year old joint?" Mark chuckled.

"I can't say it matures with age! A little stale and harsh but seems to be doing the trick!"

Charlie passed a coffee cup to Jimmy and a cold pasty. "Thanks."

"We're going to drive in shifts. Hopefully get there for sunrise. I'm taking this shift. You're up next - so don't smoke too much of that shit, will ya?" Charlie was always the sensible one. The realisation of their mission and the excitement of the road trip was just beginning to settle as Charlie started up the engine with a throaty roar, flicking on the headlights as he pulled out of the car park and onto the slipway to rejoin the motorway. They were giggling and laughing like they hadn't done in years - this could be just what they all needed. Jimmy slid open the service window and after a moment's hesitation threw his mobile phone into the bed of an open pick-up truck they accelerated past, a sense of reckless abandon and freedom washing over him. He followed the trajectory of the phone and took a long hard tug of the joint. He exhaled the smoke in a slow trickle, watching as the wind took it out of the open window, his mind running over the troubles he was running away from. Well, if they tracked his phone, that should lead them on a merry chase. He leaned forward and gave the half smoked joint to Mark as Charlie pulled onto the motorway and into the river of cars flowing north.

"So, you sent off those divorce papers yet?" Mark asked the question in hushed tones. Jimmy was asleep in the back, enveloped by the darkness seeping in. Air's 'Moon Safari' was gently playing in the background, fighting with the rumble of the engine. Mark felt a tiredness creeping over him but didn't want to fall asleep - he had a duty to keep Charlie company whilst he drove.

"Yeah."

"You want to talk about it?"

"No."

Mark pushed his bottom lip out and nodded his head. "Good

chat."

Charlie gripped the steering wheel a little harder, the thought of Sarah decimating any sense of relaxation he had begun to feel. He focused on the taillights in front of him and pressed the accelerator a little harder. He pulled out into the middle lane to try and overtake the car in front of him, willing the van to go a little faster. It whined and strained, sliding past the white ford fiesta inch by inch. When the van's rear end was clear he indicated and pulled back into the inside lane. He felt a bead of sweat trickle down his spine.

"I don't want to talk about it."

"I can see that."

"It's just….it's just that….I don't know."

"Charlie. I get it."

"Do you? I mean, really? You've never been married, Mark. I'm not sure if you *can* get it. I mean, you couldn't be further from ever getting married if you tried. You have no idea what it means to stand in front of all your friends and family, in front of God and tell them that you are going to fully commit to someone and spend the rest of your life with them, only for it then to fall apart because….well, because…"

"Mate, it's not your fault." Mark looked at his brother and shook his head. In the dim light of the cab, he could make out a solitary tear rolling down his brother's face. He had always been the sensitive one and Mark had always been so blasé about emotions - especially when it came to women.

"Isn't it? If I was at home more, if I had a normal job, if I had shown her more attention, more love, made her more of a priority, then…." His voice was rising, and Mark could hear the hurt. They were twins, but they were so very different.

"No. It's not. You love someone for who they are don't you? For the good and for the bad. And she did the bad, Charlie. She went and fucked her boss. So fuck that. It's not your fault. You were off saving people's lives and helping people in need whilst she was dropping her panties and spreading her legs."

"Nice." Mark had a point. He never put things eloquently but that was part of his charm. Charlie tried to stop a glimmer of a grin creeping across his face.

"So, stop mourning her. Stop moping. You're better off without her. This is a new chapter of your life man."

Mark was right. People only ever saw the roguish charm of his brother, more often than not, viewing him as charming but childish, with the emotional intelligence of a five-year-old. Charlie knew that was a misconception. If anyone knew his brother, really knew his brother, then they knew that he was perceptive and intelligent, and when things got serious, he was as wise and mature as anyone. But only a few people ever saw that side of Mark. It was normally when no one else was looking.

"I never liked her anyway." Mark grinned and turned to look at Charlie.

"Really? I thought you really liked her."

"Nah. I found that stupid laugh of hers so fucking irritating."

Charlie laughed. "Yeah. I guess."

A moment passed and they listened to the windscreen wipers scrape across the windshield. "She didn't like you either."

"What?!" Mark pretended to be offended. "Her loss."

The traffic was slowing, and the red taillights ahead were clustering suggesting there might be an accident further ahead. Counting Crows 'Omaha' came on the radio.

"What about you?" The slow traffic relieved the intensity of the drive for Charlie momentarily and he looked across at the sharp features of his brother.

"What about me?" Mark began flicking the lid of the zippo lighter Jimmy had given him earlier. He didn't like being questioned about serious stuff, and he could sense his brother wanted to have a serious conversation. It was one thing for Charlie to be offloading, but that had never been Mark's style.

"Well, any girls that are more than just a one-night fling?"

"Not really."

"Not really?"

"I don't want to talk about it!" Mark grinned at Charlie. "There is a woman at work. But….it's complicated."

"Ok. I'll take that."

"It's not fucking serious or anything ok? It's just…I don't know, maybe she, maybe she's got under my skin a little." Mark looked out of the window and thought about Jacquie. What was it about Jacquie? It wasn't love or anything, but he had certainly been thinking about her, and that was something he'd never found himself doing before.

After nearly thirteen and a half hours of driving the van pulled into the ferry port at Ullapool. It was pitch black and there seemed to be very little life about. Mark pulled the van up and switched off the engine to wait for the first morning ferry. Charlie was asleep in the back seat and even though Jimmy had tried valiantly to stay awake for his friend's second shift at the wheel he had eventually succumbed to tiredness and drifted off, his face pressed against the cold glass of the passenger window. Mark looked at his watch - it was five thirty in the morning, meaning that they had an hour and a half before the first sailing. The rich amber light of a solitary streetlamp illuminated the deserted ferry port. Mark closed his eyes and before he knew it, he was asleep.

An explosion of sound jolted all three of them awake.

Looking around, it took them a moment to get their bearings and remember where they were. Another blast from the approaching ferry, seared through their sleepy brains. They looked out of the steamed-up windows and saw that they were now surrounded by other cars, lorries and Winnebagos. Jimmy, his hood pulled up and with dried saliva encrusting his chin, looked out of the passenger window at the car beside them. An old man was sat eating sandwiches from some Tupperware and sipping coffee from a steaming thermos. A woman sat next to him and looked across, smiling at Jimmy. For some reason, Jimmy felt the urge to raise a hand in a childish wave. He turned to the others.

"What's the time?"

"Twenty to seven."

Jimmy opened the passenger door and stepped out into the amber lit car park. The first thing he noticed was that the temperature was significantly lower than the stifling and oppressive heat of London. A cool coastal breeze was coming in off The Minch (the stretch of water between the islands and the mainland), and Jimmy zipped up his jacket and pulled his hood further over his head. He pulled out the pouch of tobacco in his pocket that he had bought during one of the few pitstops they had made and rolled a cigarette. As he smoked, he moved around the van, admiring the restoration work he had done on the van. He looked out across the water and the dark shapes that sat ominously on the horizon. The water was calm, almost glass-like and you could see the reflection of the early morning sky on the mirrored surface. A man in a Hi-Viz jacket was moving between the cars.

"We're going to start loading now. So, if you wouldn't mind getting back into your vehicle, please sir."

Jimmy took one last drag of the cigarette. As he stood there looking out across the waters off north-west Scotland, the fears and worries that he was fleeing felt more distant now, more diluted- he wondered whether running away had been the right decision; he was in one of the remotest parts of Europe - maybe things would work out. But despite the dissipating fear, there was still a nagging feeling in the back of his head - Andy's fingers had a long reach. It almost felt like something was watching him. Maybe it was just paranoia from the weed. A pang of regret surged through him and filled his heart as he longed that Gully could be there with them. As he clambered back into the van, he lifted the blue tube of Gully's ashes and placed them on the dashboard. "Here you go buddy" he whispered as Mark turned over the engine.

Two ferries later and they were disembarking on one of the remotest islands in the Hebridean archipelago. It felt like they had been transported into another time, or that they were entering the film set for Jurassic world. Steep cliffs rose out of the ocean, and the sky was speckled with a million seabirds. A wide east facing bay opened its arms and the small ferry puttered towards the stone jetty. Charlie was constantly checking the now, well-thumbed pages of directions that Gully had left them, uncertain that this could be right. But there was no mistaking the clear directions of which ferry to get and which island they were headed for; it was just hard to imagine Gully in a place like this.

Looking over the side of the ferry, the teal water was calm and the shimmered with life. The horn of the ferry gave a loud blast and the crackle of the tannoy announced that they would be disembarking in ten minutes.

DAY 1

(MONDAY)

FINDING NOWHERE

The steam from the tea swirled up into the cold morning air before dissipating as Gordon blew into the chipped Rangers FC mug. His hand reached out and grabbed the brown envelope. He could feel the brick of money inside and it felt good to have it in his hands. His wife was wanting a foreign holiday this year and Gordon wanted to surprise her - Greece maybe, or Croatia. He'd always fancied the idea of Croatia, but she would decide in the end - that was just marriage, wasn't it?

"Thanks."

Geoff smiled at his old friend. "No worries. Duncan says there's going to be another one in a couple of days."

"That's quick."

"Aye. Business is booming it seems. And the next one's a big one."

Geoff leaned back against the flimsy brown wooden walls of the shed and surveyed Gordon. His long black beard now had streaks of white running through it, giving the impression of badger. Gordon was an integral cog in the island's operation; they all had their roles to play, and all it would take would be for someone to open their mouths and give the game away. They'd known each other for a long time, but you never knew did you? Everyone had their price and if the authorities ever got to Gordon, it would bring down the whole, entire operation. Gordon was the gatekeeper, and that was why Duncan paid him well.

Gordon sat up in his chair and peered out of the salt encrusted

Perspex window, the green iris' standing out against the unusually pure white sclera of his eyes.

"Oh aye, here we go!" He stood up and shuffled to the door and opened it, just as what looked like an old ice cream van pulled up off the ferry and stopped outside the shed.

The sun was low in the sky behind the van, reflecting off the mirror-flat blue expanse of water. Gordon stepped out of the shed as the driver poked his head out of the window.

Jimmy handed over the orange ferry ticket to the shuffling man with the salt and pepper beard. Another man stood in the doorway of the ticket hut watching with a mug of tea in his hand. He lit a hand rolled cigarette without taking his eyes off Jimmy. His gaze was a little fixed and certainly didn't go very far in making Jimmy feel welcomed to the island. The man with the beard snapped Jimmy back into focus.

"You boys visiting?"

"That's right."

"Well, mind yourselves. These islands can be a dangerous place." He gave a throaty chuckle.

"Ok. Thanks"

"If you need anything, you'll find me here, down at the harbour. The name's Gordon." The man gave all three of them one last look and then disappeared to the back of the vehicle and slapped the tailgate to signal them to move off, as he walked back towards the next car behind them.

The myriad of different seabirds squawked and circled the small harbour as the van pulled off the slipway and onto the quayside.

"These islands can be a dangerous place - what's that about? Weird thing to say. The guy gave me the creeps." Jimmy changed gear and began the ascent up the road that led away from the small harbour.

Mark looked back out of the rear window at Gordon, who was now waving through the car behind them; Jimmy was right, there was suddenly a strange vibe in the air.

Jimmy joined the main road out of the town. The road was wide and empty with lazy grasses lining the hedgerows and walls, speckled with the purple hue of the thistle. Charlie sat in the passenger seat, staring at the vague directions on the paper Gully had left them.

"Just says, go straight to the end of the road. It's the last turning on the left. What sort of directions are those?"

Mark leaned forward from the back seat.

"Seems pretty clear to me. How hard can it be?"

The van continued its journey into the central part of the island. Either side of the road were lush green fields, a healthy scattering of white sheep eyed the vehicle suspiciously as it sped past. The wet, black asphalt of the road lay like a dark and moody trail across the stark but beautiful landscape. The road was lined with dry stone walls, the odd white crofter's cottage nestled into the contours of the landscape, hunkering down against the unpredictable weather. The road climbed over an outcrop of the metamorphic rock and revealed a mirror black loch to the right of the road, sinister and beautiful in every way. The three men took in the landscape and the sense of its remote isolation, a landscape which stood its ground against the fiercest of weather and the full-frontal wrath of the north Atlantic ocean. They tried to picture the happy go lucky Gully in a place like this, but for whatever reason it didn't seem to fit. A sense of moody power emanated from the land. It was bleak, desolate, remote and extreme. The car slowed and gently came to a stop. Ahead a crofter was ushering a flock of sheep through a gate on the side of the road, driving them from a field on one side of the road and into the field on the other side. He wore the marks of a man who had spent his life outside, who had seen hardship; his face wrinkled and lined, wind beaten and tanned. The steely blue gaze of his eyes stood out against the stark white of his full beard. He held a staff in one hand like the image of an angry Neptune and set an uncompromising gaze on the three strangers in the unusual vehicle. There was no smile or welcome for these foreigners. Charlie, Jimmy and Mark attempted to smile at the crofter, but got little back in response. The toughness of the island emanated from the old farmer - to survive in this outpost of the British Isles, these people clearly didn't piss about.

The last of the sheep crossed the road. The crofter stood to the side, and the van moved past him. The old man's eyes never left the van, watching it drive off along the road towards the north of the island until it disappeared out of sight.

"I feel welcomed." Charlie looked at the other two and the tension within the car suddenly dissipated and the three of them burst out laughing.

"Here, this must be it. Nowhere."

A simple white picket sign stood next to the main road, with 'Nowhere' painted in black letters and an arrow pointing down to the left, where a narrow, single-track lane meandered down towards the ocean.

Jimmy turned into the road,

"Do you reckon Gully named it? Sounds like Gully. I like the sense of humour." said Mark as he leant forward, eager to get a better view of their home for the next week.

"That is one thing Gully definitely had." Jimmy offered.

The crofter's cottage came into view half-way down the track. Like all the others they had seen on their journey across the island, it was whitewashed and squat in the landscape as if clinging on to the land, desperate not to get blown away.

Whereas many of the cottages they had seen had replaced the traditional thatch roofs with more hardy slate, this still retained the original thatch style roof.

Mark grinned. "Sweet."

Suddenly, Charlie tensed up and stamped his foot into the floor of the passenger's footwell.

"Whooah!"

Jimmy reacted, slamming on the brakes and bringing the van to a screeching halt, the abrupt stop propelling everyone forward; Mark, who was casually reclining in the back, came crashing into the front seats, cursing on impact; Charlie and Jimmy were propelled back into their seats as the car jolted to a standstill. Jimmy cranked the handbrake and looked at his two friends. Fragments of memory briefly enveloped him - a dusty road in a war-torn country and the heat of an explosion in front of him; soldiers shouting and screaming. Jimmy's heart raced and he focused on controlling his breathing. "Everyone alright?"

"Massive fucking pothole." said Charlie as he got out of the car to take a look. Jimmy followed. In front of the car, a large crater the size of a half-submerged Swiss ball had been gauged out of the tarmac and the ground beneath, and was now half full of rain water.

"That would have been the tyre," said Charlie.

"Or the Axel. Good spot, Too fucking busy looking at the view!" Charlie and Jimmy exchanged a grin, and took in the majestic panorama in front of them - the track they were on wound down a little further with nothing but lush green fields as far as the eye could see, before ending at a small white cottage. Beyond that was the sea, glinting in the morning light, a mosaic of different shades of blue. They both sucked in a lungful of salty air and a calm settled on them that neither of them had felt in a long time. It was quiet too. Eerily quiet except for the soft sounds of nature. This was raw and isolated; no wonder Gully had sought solace here, there wasn't another soul around, let alone another surfer. They climbed back into the van, skirted the pothole and slowly made their way down to the cottage.

"Well, it's not the Ritz."

Mark stood in the centre of the living room and surveyed the out-dated decor. Net curtains covered the narrow, recessed windows; a small uncomfortable looking two-seater sofa in a densely floral pattern sat opposite a large inglenook fireplace, a moth eaten velvet wingback chair with 'doilies' on the armrests next to it. Bric-a-brac aplenty adorned almost every available surface in the room. The rough stone walls had been whitewashed and displayed moody, stormy paintings of life at sea, in dark wooden frames.

"I like it," said Charlie as he moved through the room, picking up a China dog off the sideboard. "It's got character."

Mark moved through the space -his lanky frame slightly hunched to avoid the black oak beams stretching across the ceilings. "Would be helpful if the ceilings were just a little higher."

Jimmy dropped his bag on the flagstone floor. "Doesn't feel very 'Gully'." He moved through to the small kitchen. The units were hand built of lightly stained wood, with a small free standing four ringed stove wedged into the corner, which immediately reminded him of his grandfather. He opened the back door off the kitchen and a gust of fresh salty air hit his face.

Jimmy walked out into the back garden, closely followed by Charlie and Mark. The unmistakable smell of the air hit them like a wall - a pelagic scent mixed with undertones of earthy peat filling their nostrils and seeping into their lungs. The garden gently sloped for twenty metres or so, away down towards the beach below - a dry stone wall with a small rickety wooden gate leading to a sandy path which took you a further fifty metres onto the beach. Charlie, Jimmy and Mark stood in awe at the breath-taking view in front of them- the green velvet of the grass scattered with the white pearls of moisture left from the morning dew, glinting in the bright morning sun. Their eyes were drawn down to the ocean. Corduroy lines of swell were stacked to the horizon, with three-to-four-foot waves peeling and breaking onto a golden white sand beach. Gully hadn't been lying. Empty, glassy, turquoise walls of water invited them to suit up and jump into this watery playground. It was like they had stepped through the gates of Heaven. Suddenly Mark let out a deafening 'hoot', a war cry for action.

Like three over excited groms of their youth, the three men turned on their heels and shot back through the cottage to unload and suit up.

The fine, white sand crunched and squeaked under feet as they sprinted across the beach towards the pushing tide. The ocean lapped their bare feet as they stood in the shallows and assessed the rips and currents of the unknown beach break. The temperature of the water was surprisingly tolerable for somewhere this far north, the gulf stream waters providing that extra little bit of warmth. A cloud of seabirds squawked and swooped overhead as the three men strapped on their leashes and began to paddle for the central peak in the bay, where perfect A-frames were breaking about fifty meters out.

Jimmy paddled hard, the adrenaline and excitement fuelling his tired limbs, and the cool, clean ocean washing away the grime of the long journey, invigorating him. It had been a long time since he had been in the 'juice' and the familiarity of the board beneath him felt good. A set exploded twenty metres in front of him. He pushed his board down under the first line of white water, feeling a surprising amount of power considering the size of the waves. The water was crystal clear, and Jimmy could make out the small boulders of rock scattered on the sandy floor of the ocean, and the fizzing foam of the breaking wave reeling away across the bay. Jimmy duck dived the second wave, and by the third, he wished he had selected his shorter board rather than the higher volumed fun board he thought might be more suitable to the conditions. Maybe he was just a little out of shape. The waves were better than they looked from the beach and the period of the swell was clearly building as each wave packed an impressive amount of power. Charlie was already sitting on the peak in prime position as Jimmy emerged from under the last wave of the three-wave set, a huge grin spread across his face.

"I can't believe it's just us. Look at it." Jimmy smirked and said a silent prayer of thanks to ocean Gods.

"It's been a while, eh?" It was the first uninhibited smile he had seen on Charlie's face for a long time.

Mark joined the other two, looking a little tired. "Got fucking pummelled by that second one!" They were still laughing as the next set arrived on the horizon. Blue humps filled the horizon and the laughter petered out and was replaced with focused eyes full of steely determination. Unsure of where the exact take-off spot was, they jostled and paddled in the hope of being the first to ride this new break, each of them feeling a little nervous; none of them could recall the last time they all surfed together, and each of them was desperate to lay down a good first wave, their childhood competitive streak kicking in. The first wave arrived, jacking up to shoulder height, feathering in the light offshores. Charlie was sat slightly further out and turned, paddling hard. Despite his effort, the wave slipped under him. Jimmy and Mark were too busy watching Charlie and urging him into the wave to react in time to turn and paddle, instead opting to reposition themselves in readiness for the second wave of the set. Mark was slightly further inside as the three surfers dropped into the trough behind the hump of the first wave; he began to paddle hard to his right, angling across the bay. Charlie was also paddling hard just outside Mark, in case he missed it. Jimmy watched from the shoulder as the ocean stood up like a spitting cobra ready to strike; a similar height to the first wave, it picked Mark up, carrying him in the feathering lip. Mark exploded up to his feet in an athletic pop, muscle memory taking over his body; he crouched, knees bent and arms pointing down the line of the wave. Jimmy watched as Mark pressed his left foot down on the front of the board, tipping him into the now vertiginous face of the wave. He accelerated, dropping down into the chasm of the wave, and then he was gone as Jimmy felt the rise and fall of the wave passing beneath him. He turned to watch the wave press on towards the shore, catching glimpses of Mark's cherished fish throwing spray off the back of the wave, creating rainbows of colour as the morning sun refracted through the water droplets. Jimmy was still watching over his shoulder, watching Mark make his way on a long ride towards the shore, when he heard Charlie hoot - he turned to see Charlie taking off on the best wave of the set. It was easily head high and Charlie had taken off just behind the peak, the light offshores standing the wave up and making it barrel. Jimmy caught sight of Charlie backdooring the wave and slipping into a small but perfectly formed barrel. A barrel on his first wave for who knows how long? Gully must have sent that one. And then he was gone, and Jimmy found himself alone out the back. He looked to the horizon in the hope of another wave, but Huey (the God of waves) was making him wait. He paddled further over towards what seemed to be the peak and pushed himself up to sit astride his board. He checked the headland to the right and left and then looked to the shore searching for markers that could help him find this spot again if it transpired that he was sitting on the peak. He could feel the pulse of the ocean as he sat and stared at the horizon, he could hear the mix of seabirds squawking and the laughter of his two oldest friends as they paddled back out. Jimmy took a deep breath of the north Atlantic air, a flood of emotion washing over him as all of the negativity of the past few months diluting in the lap of the ocean and being replaced with a calm clarity he hadn't felt for months. He could feel his heart beat slow and he closed his eyes momentarily, trying to register this moment, trying to store it in his memory. He turned and could see his two friends paddling towards him over the rhythmic pulse of the ocean. He had priority, the next wave was his. A building sense of pressure began to grow as he positioned himself for the next set. It had been a long time since he had last caught a wave and despite having been one of the best in the country whilst growing up, he was nervous. The wait was short, and a new set began to march towards him. He turned and began to paddle for the first of the set waves, stroking deeply to maximise his power and to bring his speed up through the water quickly. He could feel the power of the ocean as the mountain of water picked up the tail of his board, tilting him down the face of the wave. A sheer drop opened up beneath him and before he knew it, Jimmy was on his feet and accelerating down the face of what felt like a roaring monster of a wave, its jaws gaping, ready to swallow him whole. Jimmy flew across the face of the wave, keeping a high line. He transferred his weight to his heels, digging in the rail of the board and making a smooth arc down the face of the wave before adjusting his weight once more, onto his toes and pulling into the pocket of the wave - his speed slowing. He stepped down on his front foot and accelerated again along the face of the wave. He could see the section closing down and so he pointed the board towards the summit of the wave, rising rapidly and exploding off the top of the wave with a hoot of joy. He plunged into the ocean and let the cool water wash over his elated body, trying to contain the grin which was spreading across his face. A short ride, but an immense high. He suddenly felt alive again. Just like riding a bike, you never forget.

The session lasted another hour or so until the tide became too full, and the waves became too fat. The clouds had moved in, and the wind swung around and was blowing onshore now, forcing the waves to crumble into the bay. Jimmy's arms were tired and his body aching after the long drive north. He had caught his fair share of perfect peeling walls. He had gone over the falls a couple of times, but the three friends had revelled in the isolation and sheer joy of having empty waves to themselves. Jimmy turned and paddled late under the lip of a breaking wave. He allowed the wave to break behind him, before climbing to his feet and casually riding the white water towards shore, dropping down onto his belly as the wave began to lose power. He rode the wave to the shallows and slid off the board. Mark and Charlie were already on the beach, huge grins were plastered across their faces, and they were talking animatedly about the best waves of the session as Jimmy emerged from the ocean.

"I need breakfast."

The three of them laughed and headed back towards the cottage, satisfied, exhausted and hungry.

THE SALTY DOG

The sun was low in the sky as they walked along the tarmac road towards the pub; the days were long in Scotland during the summer months. Jimmy could see some squalls rumbling on the horizon, but the direction of the breeze suggested that the adverse weather might be moving away from them.

They felt a little more rested and alive than they had a few hours before. The surf had exhausted their limbs and, together with the mental fatigue of the long drive, it had allowed them all to get a few hours sleep in the cottage. They were now awake, hungry and eager to explore a little of the island.

The road was quiet, all they could hear was the delicate sounds of nature around them, balanced and muted, the rustle of the long grass in the breeze, the sounds of the seabirds overhead, the occasional bleat of the sheep in the fields. Their footsteps on the tarmac and the crunch of the stones beneath them felt prominent and alien in nature's soundscape, like they were intruding. The earthy smells of the peat fields wafted past them and there was no mistaking that they were now in a rural setting. Suddenly they heard the sound of music drifting across the fields, the vibrant, upbeat bowing of a fiddle and the strum of a banjo, followed by the unmistakable muted, raucous cheer of inebriated customers in a pub late on a Friday evening - some things are the same wherever you go.

"Oi, snowy?!!", Mark suddenly bellowed.

Jimmy raised a lopsided grin, catching on to a childhood game and turning on his best Aussie accent, "What?"

"I can see the pub from here." Their pace quickened.

The white-washed, squat building stood at the end of a small line of stone buildings; a black wooden sign hung from a weather-beaten and rotting post outside, with a picture of a scraggy dog in a pirate's hat, silver cursive writing spelled out its name, 'The Salty Dog'. A small convenience store occupied the building next door, with a few run-down stone cottages lining the road beyond. Town.

Mark smirked, "The wild west of the United Kingdom. No fighting in this saloon Jimmy MacIntosh."

"Just whiskey and women Marky Mark." Jimmy retorted.

"Don't encourage him." Charlie delivered in a deadpan, knowing that these two things were his brother's favourite things in the world.

PUB GAMES

The 'Salty Dog' was steaming when Duncan entered. It had been over a month now since the argument with Maggie in the pub. He still couldn't understand what her problem was and why she had suddenly just ended their relationship. He had tried to reason with her, but when she slapped him in front of all those people in the pub, it was like twisting a dagger in his gut. These people respected him, relied on him, looked up to him, but most importantly, they feared him. Having a jumped up girl from the mainland making him look like a fool in front of the island community was not ideal, but it was Maggie..... So what could he do? What's more, he had chased her, waited for her and the English surfer to end their relationship and bided his time. It made him look weak. He'd kept his distance and let things settle down again in the hope that people would have forgotten about it and brushed their memories of the event under the carpet - but that was pretty unlikely in a small community like this where everyone thrived on a good yarn or juicy bit of gossip.

So, although he wouldn't show it on the hard exterior he presented, he was nervous as he entered the pub, unsure of what kind of reception he would get when he walked in. But he needed to go - he needed to pay Sam.

As it was, he needn't have been concerned, the locals didn't miss a beat as he walked in - he was part of the furniture and people were glad to see him, wondering why they hadn't seen him in so long. Albert and Malcolm were playing in the corner by the fire and the evening was obviously just getting going. Duncan greeted a few people, a slap on the back here, a ruffle of the hair there, people had clearly forgotten, or maybe they were too polite, or maybe they were just too scared to say anything to him.

The 'Salty Dog' was a small squat building, like most of the buildings on the island, and the inside was cramped and low ceilinged. The walls had once been white but were now a nicotine stained yellow from all the years of pipes, and cigarette smoke - the smoking ban had been happily met with two fingers on this island, and there was no one to enforce it anyway, with Stuart Ferguson, the chief of police on the island, a 'forty a day' kind of man. Threadbare Persian carpets scattered the cold flagstone floors, and a mishmash of chairs, settles and tables hugged the edges of the room. Duncan eased his way through the crowd, the air dense with smoke, sweat and song as the community geared up for the annual festival that was held at the end of every summer. He reached the long mahogany bar and leaned casually on it. Kelsie, Sam's daughter, was leaning over to get a bag of crisps from the bottom shelf, for Greg Brown at the other end of the bar. She was only nineteen but was blossoming into a fine-looking girl. Duncan took a moment to admire the way her tight denim jeans accentuated her toned legs and pert, petite posterior.

"U-huh"

Duncan was brought back to the moment and his lascivious facial expression was quickly removed by the appearance of Sam in front of him.

"Not lusting after my daughter, are you Duncan?"

"Turning into a beautiful young woman Sam".

"She's nineteen. You keep your hands off."

Duncan smiled at Sam. "She's not a girl anymore, Sam. As I say, a beautiful young woman." It was brave of her to warn him off, knowing that it wouldn't make a blind bit of difference to what he decided he wanted to do - he ruled around here, and she knew it.

"Here."

Duncan handed over an envelope stuffed full of used twenty pound notes. It was important to keep this channel of the island open - it wasn't as sophisticated as parts of the operation, but it was easy and it meant that the whole of the community was invested in his business.

"Thanks. You want a drink? Been a while since you've been in here."

"Been busy. Pint, thanks Sam."

Duncan turned his attention to the bunch of locals that were filling the pub, whilst Sam busied herself with pouring him a pint. He caught the eye of Flannagan in the far corner and gave him a nod. He was sat with a bunch of lads from the distillery. He had been apprehensive about taking on Flannagan to run the distillery operation at first; he had been a waste of space a few years back, always smashed off his face and barely able to hold down a job, but with a little help from Duncan, he had cleaned himself up, sobered up and was now a key man in Duncan's complex and lucrative team.

By the fire, Stuart Ferguson was laughing and joking, cigarette in one hand and single malt in the other, bouncing his foot on the flagstones to the rhythm of the jig that Malcolm and Albert were playing. Christian Fletcher was leaning on the far end of the bar, chatting to Kelsie, probably spinning her some bullshit line about his next big 'gig' on the mainland and how he was going to be a famous rockstar - anyone who really knew Christian knew that he was a pretty average guitarist and a less than average singer, but that didn't stop Kelsie from fluttering her eyelashes and Christian leaning in a little bit further.

Suddenly the door to the pub opened and the silhouette of three men stood huddled in the doorway. Slowly, the locals took notice of the strangers, and the chatter began to falter, as everyone turned to look at these new faces. They were unused to strangers in their bar. The music faded and faltered. For a brief moment there was a silence, it probably only lasted a millisecond, but to Charlie, Jimmy and Mark standing in the doorway, it felt like it lasted minutes.

Jimmy entered first; years of dealing with hostile groups of people when he was in the marines had given him a confidence which the two friends standing by his side did not feel. A smile and an open gait went a long way to appease someone who is uncertain of you or your intentions; at least some of the islanders must know who they were, even if they didn't give anything away - a small community like this meant news travelled fast - they would all know that they were the English staying at 'nowhere'. Mark and Charlie tentatively ducked their heads and followed Jimmy through the low door and into the crowded pub.

Charlie and Mark followed Jimmy's lead and beamed smiles around the room, making brief eye contact with whoever they could before looking away in a gesture of respect. As they made their way to the bar, the locals began to turn back to their conversations and their own friends, seemingly satisfied that the new arrivals were of no threat and did not seem sufficiently interesting to sustain their curiosity. To the Englishmen's relief the Celtic folk music started up again, and their unwelcome interruption to the evening's proceedings seemed to dissipate.

They squeezed and slipped their way through to the bar, apologising to everyone and anyone that they passed. A stern looking woman behind the bar walked over.

"What cannae get yous?"

Jimmy looked at the top shelf and was impressed by the array of fine whiskeys backlit behind the bar.

"Three Laphroig, 10 year please,"

The woman gazed at them with an air of suspicion before turning to get glasses and pour the drinks. She placed three tumblers on the bar, uncorked the bottle and poured three generous measures into the glasses.

"Where are you lads from?"

"England."

"Really? No way." Sam smiled at the three uncertain faces in front of her.

"And you're the lads staying over at old Elsie's place?"

"Er, the cottage down the road. Nowhere?"

"Aye. Elsie's old place. Another English lad bought it off her a few years back. Friend of yours?" Sam smiled at Jimmy and corked the bottle.

The three friends exchanged a look. Mark answered for them, "Yeah. But he died. Left the house to us."

The bar lady paused, and they could feel ears listening in to their conversation. A weathered looking man with long hair had sidled up to the bar and was staring at them. Jimmy recognised him as one of the men in the shed when they arrived. He never forgot a face. "Be with you in a second Geoff." Sam turned back to Jimmy, "Well you boys enjoy the islands. Don't get into no trouble, eh?!"

She turned and moved over to the long-haired Geoff, leaning in to speak to him conspiratorially.

The Salty Dog turned out to be everything a remote Celtic drinking hole should be - loud, raucous and full of drunken revelry. Jimmy, Mark and Charlie stumbled out the door somewhere around one o'clock in the morning, the fresh sea air hitting them like a battering ram and highlighting for them just how drunk they were. Charlie could vaguely remember singing along with the local who was playing the banjo….or was it the ukelele, Jimmy had been locked into a deep conversation with a captain Birdseye look-a-like, but he couldn't recollect the details, something about the history of the island, and Mark had spent most of the night at the bar, chatting up the young barmaid. Their recollections of the evening and laughter suddenly felt empty and out of place as they made their way along the deserted and remote coastal road back to the cottage. Halfway along the road, Mark stopped and bellowed into the night sky. A nearby cow answered his call with an elongated 'moo', which made the three friends laugh until their sides hurt.

SEND IN THE DOGS

Niko and Dokes stood in front of the large, lacquered desk in Deaf Andy's office. The late afternoon sun filtering through the Venetian blinds was casting parallel bars of light across the dark interior giving a theatrical impression of the bars Deaf Andy had seen enough of in prison.

"So?"

Niko momentarily unclasped his bear-like hands from in front of him and covered his mouth as he nervously cleared his throat.

"He staying at his friend's flat in Brixton. His friend. He doctor at hospital in Tooting."

"And?" Deaf Andy leant back in his leather chair sensing that the stuttering procrastination of the muscle in front of him was indicating he wasn't going to like the next part of the conversation.

"They not there. House is packed up. In boxes."

Dokes chipped in, "Looks like they left."

Deaf Andy swivelled in his chair ninety degrees and looked out on the street below, the street he grew up on. A silence hung in the air, the shuffle of the two big men the only sound.

"So. We've got a runner." Deaf Andy picked up an Arturo Fuente Anejo cigar from the wooden box on his desk. "I have to say, I never had him down for a gutless pussy. You know what we do with a runner don't you boys?"

"Yes Boss."

"Find him and bring him to me."

"Yes Boss."

Deaf Andy took the gold-plated cigar clipper from the top drawer of his desk and sliced off the end of the cigar.

"I don't like people who don't pay their debts." Deaf Andy looked up from the caress of his cigar. "Speak to Nigel and get him to track his phone and look into his bank cards. Gently remind him he owes me a favour. Jimmy can run, but he can't hide from me."

Niko and Dokes nodded their heads like a couple of marionette puppets.

"Well go on then. Get going."

DAY 2

(TUESDAY)

MEETING MISTER NICE

Charlie pulled up the zip of his Patagonia jacket. He marvelled at how warm something so lightweight could be - technology in clothing and adventure gear had gone crazy. His mind filled with the imagery of his old, crusted winter wetsuit he used to fight to get on in the freezing garage of his parents' house, a smirk creasing his face at the memory. A brief recollection of standing in the garage with Gully, getting suited up reared its head, but he quickly squashed it back down - unsure if he was ready to deal with that yet. Still, it was a good thing the jacket was warm - it had cost him an absolute fortune - more than he should really spend on his meagre junior doctor salary. Having said that, he never went out, never did anything, he just worked, worked, worked; he never had the opportunity to spend any of the money he worked so hard to earn. But that is what he had always wanted, wasn't it? Perhaps being away and having a break was just what he needed to get some perspective and recharge. At some point he needed to address the loss of Gully, but the moment would come. Right now he needed to get some air.

As he stepped away from the front door, he could feel a brisk onshore breeze which had built throughout the morning. He had left Jimmy and Mark, who were sleeping off the morning surf so he could get out and explore a little. A good walk and some sea air was exactly what he needed. He looked up to his left and then to his right and looked at the contours of the land.

The cottage sat in the lee of two headlands, with the lush green fields of the land sitting stark against the steel grey of the ocean. There was a light sea mist rolling in, curling in over the sea grasses, heather and gorse, giving the landscape a vintage hue. He could just make out what looked like an old stone chapel on top of the headland to his left. He took the sand path that ran down the side of the house on the other side of the dry-stone wall, thinking that he must be able to pick up a path at the end of the beach and climb the headland from there.

As he made his way down the path, the smells of the land evoked strong memories in him. The damp sand and salty air taking him back to his childhood and the endless days he spent on the beaches of Cornwall with his three best friends. Smells could be so evocative and he felt a physiological reaction in his body, the adrenaline beginning to course through his body, as vivid flashes of memories shuttered through his mind; remembering the quiet of the beaches in the early mornings, broken by the banter and bravado of teenage boys as Charlie, Jimmy, Mark and Gully would regularly make their way to their favourite spots for a dawn surf, before all of the grockels stumbled out of their beds with their holiday hangovers and filed down to the beaches to eat fish and chips and stuff their faces with the local ice cream.

Charlie came to the end of the path and stood atop the sand dunes. He had been so amped and excited to jump into perfect waves when they'd arrived, he still hadn't fully taken in the lay of the land, but now he looked out at the ocean, a frothing, bubbling cauldron of whitewater and angry shore dump, and he studied the arc of the beach paying more attention to the beauty of his surroundings. The sea mist was obscuring his view in some directions, laying thick and heavy in the air. As he turned to his left the mist was more wispy, and tendrils coiled and caught the rays of sunlight fighting to break through, giving the land a gothic and almost magical feel. He could see what looked like a break in the undergrowth at the foot of the headland and a trodden path snaking its way up towards the small stone chapel silhouetted black against the gothic sky. He pulled his old fisherman's beanie out of the pocket of his jacket, wedged it onto his head and set off towards the far end of the beach and the path that promised to lead him up to the chapel.

*****

By the time Charlie reached the summit of the headland his legs were feeling heavy, and his breathing was a little ragged - it felt good to exercise and have his heart rate up a little. After Sarah, he'd thrown his whole self into work, as a sort of subconscious distraction, and he'd stopped looking after himself- going to the gym, eating properly. But already he could feel the glow of his body reviving, waking up, and he felt alive, and for the first time in a long time he felt a little seed of hope inside him. Maybe this trip was a new start, a new beginning. He turned around to try and get his bearings from the vantage point of the headland, but the mist now lay like a thick blanket, hugging the land and it was hard to make out any distinguishing features, or even to get any sense of where the sea became land or vice versa. An old Toyota pick-up truck stood parked on the rough gravel road leading up to the chapel, its once bright red paint job and 1980's stickering, now faded, rusting and peeling. He pushed open the iron gate in the low stone wall that surrounded the chapel, delineating the boundary of the small cemetery. It felt like this was a frontier for nature's battle to reclaim this land; the moss and lichen swarming over the perimeter wall, and the headstones inside being overrun with weeds and grasses. It was overgrown and unkempt; headstones leaning at tired angles, as if they were stumbling or had had enough, perhaps beaten by the extreme weather they experienced up here on this exposed piece of land. It wasn't a 'pretty' island chapel, but more like something out of one of those low budget horror films they all used to watch when they were teens. Charlie felt a little apprehensive as he reached the heavy wooden door of the chapel, which was darkly stained and riveted with iron studs like the fortress of some ancient kingdom. He tried the ringed handle and the door swung open, creaking on unwilling hinges. He tentatively poked his nose across the threshold and looked around, hesitant to enter the house of God without an invitation. From the open doorway, Charlie could see a stark and bare place of worship; stone flagged floors and exposed stone walls punctured with small, recessed windows He took a step into the space and could smell the damp of the building. Light from two stained glass windows cast coloured patterns across the small space, constantly changing as the mood of the weather outside shifted with every second.

"Hello?"

Charlie's voice echoed through the building, bouncing off the hard walls. He stood in the aisle between the rows of old wooden pews and looked towards the neatly presented altar at the eastern end of the building. The placement of the altar gave Charlie some sense of direction and he took note for when he went out and continued to explore the island. Silence hung heavy in the building, dust motes flittered and danced in the light, shifting and swirling with every disturbance of the air.

"Hello?"

The tension in his body was high as he waited to hear a response. It was something about being in a building like that on your own. The silence felt heavy. He could hear the whistle of the wind as it forced its way through the cracks and fissures of the building. Charlie had never believed in God - he was a scientist after all, but he was not an atheist, but an agnostic; somewhere in his being he believed that there was perhaps some higher power? And he could feel that power now, that presence. In this silent chapel, the eerie silence carried some sort of energy in the air…. maybe it was God? Maybe it just gave him the creeps. Suddenly an unnatural noise broke the silence

- a heavy buzzing reverberated around the room. It had a muted quality and Charlie deduced that its source was outside, on the other side of the wall he was facing.

He retreated outside and traced his way around the perimeter of the building, a light wind whipping his face on this exposed piece of headland. He rounded the corner on the ocean facing side of the chapel and had to stop abruptly to avoid crashing into a large ladder leaning up against the building. A man was cutting lengths of wooden baton with a chainsaw, his back to Charlie, facing out to sea. Charlie looked up to the roof and saw sheets of blue tarpaulin flapping in the breeze, desperately clinging on to what appeared to be the vestry roof.

The chainsaw stopped and the end of the wooden baton dropped to the floor with a musical thud. The man with the chainsaw, sensing he was not alone, turned around brandishing the chainsaw in front of him as if he were ready for a fight. He looked Charlie in the eye, his was tense and alert - a physical reaction to being taken by surprise. The man visibly relaxed at Charlie's friendly demeanour and cut the engine of the chainsaw.

"Only thing I could find to cut the wood". He smirked at Charlie. "Can I help you?"

"Hi. Sorry. Didn't mean to sneak up on you. I was just going for a walk and popped in to have a look at the chapel. We're just staying in a cottage down in the bay."

"Old Elsie's place, eh? You friends of Gully's, are you?"

"Yeah." Charlie paused, before adding, "We were".

"Yeah. Sorry. I heard he passed. Real shame. Decent lad. Cornish, are you?"

"Yeah. Originally."

"Oh aye. Beautiful part of the world."

"You know it?"

"Been a few times. Where're you now?"

"London now."

"Ah. Maybe not quite so beautiful."

"Not in the same way."

There was a slightly awkward pause as the two men looked at each other, unsure of where this conversation was going.

"Sorry about the state of the chapel. Not been here that long and just trying to patch it all up....I'm Tom Green. I'm the priest here."

"Charlie."

Charlie extended his hand - Tom took it and shook it with the firmness of a gorilla.

"Problems with the roof?" Charlie surreptitiously massaged his hand, checking that Tom hadn't inadvertently crushed one of his metatarsals.

"Just a few. Think a storm's coming in and I'm running out of buckets! Wanted to patch it while I can."

'Do you need a hand?"

"If you've got time, that would be very generous of you."

For the next hour Charlie helped Tom to cut the baton, hold the ladder and pin down the tarpaulin over the vestry roof. It wasn't the best job in the world, but it was as watertight as they were going to get it for the time being. Within the hour the storm rolled in proper, and the rain came lashing down in thick droplets, forcing the two men to down their tools and retreat inside.

The shelter of the chapel was a welcome relief even after enduring just a few seconds of the torrential downpour, despite the dark overhead rain clouds making the chapel spookily cast in shadow.

"Come through. It's a bit warmer through here. Cup of tea?"

Charlie heard the upbeat tones of Tom's voice disappearing as he watched his retreating figure stride into the depths of the gloom of the chapel. He hastily moved after him, following the trail of wet footprints across the flagstones. A block of light suddenly flooded the building and Charlie found Tom standing at a small doorway in the far corner.

"So? Tea? Doubt you fancy heading out until this passes? Shouldn't be too long. They normally only last an hour or so, sometimes less."

"Sure. Thanks"

They were in a good-sized vestry. A kitchenette lined one wall, A camp bed lay nestled in one corner with a sleeping bag that looked like it had only just been vacated, lying discarded and crumpled. A big brown dog lay snoring on the bed. Tom saw him assessing the room. "Don't mind Keegan. He'll be out for a while. Took him for a long run first thing." A desk stood next to the bed overflowing in papers, books, photographs, a computer and empty coffee mugs. Above the doorway the tarpaulin which they had been fixing moments ago was hammering nature's drum beat as the rain played rockstar. It was loud and they had to almost comically raise their voices to be heard.

Tom looked at Charlie and raised his eyes to the improvised roof. "It's pretty loud."

"Not leaking though".

"Ha. Not yet!". Tom moved to the kitchenette and produced two mugs, throwing the tea bags in them like a practiced professional.

"Milk? Sugar?"

"Yeah. Both please. One. "

The two men stood there in mutual silence listening to the

hammering rain, accompanied by the whine and gurgle of the cheap but functional kettle. Tom stood facing the counter, hands clasping the edges, listening and lost in thought. Charlie used the moment to take in the room and get a sense of the man in front of him. There were a number of pictures hung on the walls, including what looked like some sort of religious icon, and three scrawled children's paintings on pieces of white paper blue tacked to the wall. There was also a framed black and white photograph of someone in a wetsuit and hood, surfing a solid double overhead wave. Charlie looked at Tom. The kettle clicked and he began to assemble the tea.

"Go through into the chapel. Not sure I can sit in here!"

Tom threw him a box of extra-long matches. "If you can find any candles, light them."

Tom walked back into the chapel and immediately the thumping beat of the rain mellowed and was replaced by a hollow-shell stillness. Charlie could see a couple of candles on the sills of the recessed windows. He lit those on the two windows on the far side of the chapel, furthest from the vestry and the pounding rain. Immediately a warm arc of light erupted from each recess and gave an inviting glow which reminded Charlie of Christmas. Charlie was suddenly overwhelmed with a brief moment of raw emotion as the memory of the Christmas he lost his father came flooding back. Charlie had been seventeen. It was Christmas Eve and he'd been down to the 'The Anchor' with Mark, Gully and Jimmy where they had downed some festive beers before rolling up the hill to the village church for midnight mass. He and Mark had come home after the church service to find an ambulance outside his family home and his mother crying on the doorstep. His father had had a serious heart-attack, and he was pronounced dead on the scene.

Charlie was jolted suddenly out of this visceral flashback.

"It's almost like they give out a bit of heat, isn't it?"

Tom was standing in the next pew down and just behind him. He offered Charlie the tea and noted the troubled gaze as his guest took it.

"Have a seat." Tom indicated the pews and the two men sat. "It should pass pretty quickly. They come through all the time. Weather's constantly changing up here, eh?"

"Yeah." Charlie took a sip of his tea. "Thanks."

"No problem. Sorry about the lights. The wiring is a bit dodgy and is all on different circuits…it's a nightmare. Just another job on the list! So ….anyway."

Both Men sat in silence for a moment and sipped their tea.

"So, is that a Geordie accent there?"

"Waye-aye!. Used to weather like this, eh?!"

Another silence. Another sip of tea.

"You have kids?"

The question caught Tom off-guard, and he hesitated for a moment.

"The drawings on the wall." Charlie indicated backed towards the vestry.

Tom was not a man who shared a great deal. He was a private person and more comfortable listening to the troubles of others. Charlie could see that he had touched a raw nerve.

"Aye. They live with their mother." Tom took a sip of his tea. Charlie waited but it was clear that this was a subject Tom was unwilling to expand upon.

"I noticed in the vestry a picture of a surfer on a pretty serious wave. Is that you?"

"Uh huh. Few years back now though. I saw you guys surfing the bay yesterday. Looked pretty nice."

"Yeah. Really fun. Is it often like that? Just what we needed after the drive."

"Yeah, I bet. The bay can have some great waves, especially when the tide is on the push. You caught it just right. It's nice to have some more surfers on the island."

"There aren't many surfers?"

"There's a couple, but not many. Most of them just surf a reef break on the northwest of the island, but I'm the only one that really surfs the bay or any of the reefs down here on the south of the island. That was until your friend Gully turned up. That boy could surf."

"Yeah." Charlie smiled - Gully would have loved to hear someone compliment his surfing. It's what he had lived for.

Charlie nodded his head towards the vestry and smirked as he said, "And is the photo from around here?"

Tom smiled, looked up to the heavens of the chapel. He looked at Charlie like a kid in a sweet shop, eyes wide, trying to suppress a grin. "Aye."

"Shit. Ooh, sorry. I didn't..oh..."

Tom smiled at Charlie's reaction to his own blasphemy. "A slip of the tongue. It's fine. The Lord will forgive you." Charlie looked at Tom and was reassured by the amused smile he received. "It's a wave out by the lighthouse. Only breaks every now and then. It's heavy and dangerous and not many folk like heading out there. It's a long paddle if anything goes wrong. About a mile or so offshore." This was clearly a subject he was more comfortable with.

"Listen, this swell is set to build over the next two days. Some of these spots are going to be ....well, put it this way...decent. I don't mind showing you around a bit. To be honest, I could do with the company."

The rain continued to increase in intensity and was accompanied by some rumbles of thunder for a few minutes. Tom showed him around the Chapel and the battle he was facing to keep the building watertight and functional. He showed him the crypt which he had converted into a makeshift store for all of his surfboards. The tombstones were stacked with surfboards of every shape and size, from long, narrow big wave guns to small, stubby twin fins. "Don't people get a bit funny with you piling your boards on top of their dead ancestors?!" Charlie was admiring a longboard that was lying against one of the walls; the darkness of the crypt made it hard for Charlie to really see, but he was pretty sure it was a Takayama.

"They don't mind. Not many people know about the crypt. Not many people come up here anymore, and the dead don't have much to say!" Charlie and Tom talked about surfing and drank tea for the next half an hour whilst the storm continued overhead, travelling east towards the mainland. Tom openly talked about his journey and how he ended up here on this remote outcrop of rock, his travels around Europe and his obsession with cold water waves. There was no more mention of a wife or children though and Charlie didn't press him - he knew the pain of divorce and a broken marriage. Tom suggested a few things on the island that he would recommend having a look at whilst they were here, including a small freshwater loch at the top of the hill directly east of the cottage, and the distillery. He said you could drive around the island in about 45 minutes, and there were some amazing coves and beaches, as well as some beautiful coastal roads.

As the storm began to pass and its ferocity abated, the shadows began to be beaten back by the tendrils of sunlight streaming through the narrow leaded windows. Tom gave Charlie his mobile number and said that if he was going surfing, to give him a call. Charlie gave Tom his empty mug, zipped up his over-priced coat and stepped out into the blustery sunshine which was now enveloping the headland. The rain had passed, leaving the wet grass gleaming in the now brilliant sunshine. The wind was whipping across the headland in fits and bursts but was retreating and losing its power. Charlie looked around. The storm had blasted the sea mist away and you could see all along the coast from up on the headland. Charlie could see the cottage in the bay that his two friends were presumably still asleep in. His eyeline traced its way in-land and he noticed that there were two other white cottages in the bay. Further east still and he could see the small hill with the purple gorse and bracken adorning its summit, like some miniature volcano, where Tom said that the loch was. It didn't look that far. The sun was shining. Charlie put his sunglasses on and began to walk.

TRACKING THE TECH

Nigel stirred. A noise had jolted him out of his slumber. His eyes felt dry and crusty and he could feel the river of dried saliva across his cheek. He didn't move but slowly opened his eyes and let them scan the small room from where he lay, on the broken and stained sofa. Chipped bowls and plates encrusted with the remnants of food eaten days...maybe even weeks ago...lay scattered over all the work surfaces. Empty beer cans littered the floor and the coffee table in front of him. A light breeze was attempting to break into the room, blowing through the metal bars that lined the windows and valiantly pushing at the heavy velvet curtains that were keeping the day at arms-length. He was living behind bars. Were windows of his own home barred to keep the criminals out or keep the criminal in? The corner of his mouth curled in mild amusement at this thought. The world was a fucked-up place. He could hear the whirr and the hum of his best friend and lover in the corner; flashing eyes blinking and twinkling at him. His MSI GS66 laptop with a core i9 sat stealthily in front of a bank of computer screens and hard drives, carefully and meticulously constructed with his own bare hands. This was his world. He could do anything from this little corner of Hackney - he could change the whole world if he wanted to. But small steps. Little jobs. He didn't want to live behind the bars of his majesty's prison system again.

A sudden rumble shook the whole of the bedsit, the plates rattled on the table and an empty can of beer toppled over onto the floor. The rumble was quickly followed by the clanking and screeching of iron as the sound of an approaching train from Stratford and Hackney Wick came clattering in. He closed his eyes and imagined all the hipster wankers with their oiled beards and their artisan coffees standing on the platform, pontificating about plastic pollution and saving the planet. Bunch of hypocrites. Maybe if they wanted to save the planet, they should stop working for huge corporations, spending their money flying around the world on luxury holidays, and having deliveries from amazon every other day. So very humble and 'eco' of them. He had watched as they had all moved into his neighbourhood, watched the old businesses forced to close and sell up; watched the price of housing driven up to the point where it was simply unaffordable for the locals who had lived there all their lives. Then again, his bedsit had doubled in value in the last five years, so who was he to complain - he was as selfish as the rest of them. Maybe he would sell up, move out of London and find a nice quiet cottage by the sea so that he could hear the sounds of waves lapping the shore rather than police sirens and commuter trains. He listened as the train rumbled off into the distance. But then again, he liked the sounds of the city, the energy and the buzz of a world wired on caffeine and egos. From his basement bedsit he could hear someone hocking up and spitting on the street above.

The re-enforced, communal front door banged shut and he heard footsteps coming down the stairs. Coming down to his bedsit. Not going up. Someone had come in without buzzing. Or maybe they had buzzed. Maybe that was what had woken him up. Maybe it was the police. Panic surged through his body. Adrenalin pumped through his veins, and he burst into action; he scrambled across the floor and over to the table. He scooped up the laptop and fumbled for the threads of carpet in the corner. His eyes fixedly gazed at the light coming from under the door to his bedsit. Two shadows blocked the light. He lifted the carpet and the loose floorboard beneath. There was a firm knock at the door. Nigel slipped the laptop in the recess beneath the floorboard. Another knock, firmer this time. He scanned the room for any kind of weapon and settled on a small screwdriver he used when building his computers. He slipped it into his dressing gown pocket and moved to the door.

In an affected, sleep-riddled voice he called out, "Hello".

"Nigel. Mr Andy has sent us to speak to you. You owe favour."

Nigel looked through the spyhole. 'Fuck!' Two of Deaf Andy's Goons. What did they want? He owed Andy a favour he'd said. How many favours would he have to owe? He took a deep breath and tightened his hand around the screwdriver in this pocket before cautiously opening the door.

"What do you want?"

Nigel was roughly pushed backwards into the room and the door closed behind the two gorillas who were there to collect a favour.

THE RED LOCH

It took Charlie about forty-five minutes to make his way across a number of fields, having to climb over a seemingly endless series of low walls, across the coastal road and up the hill. It was bigger than it looked when Charlie had eyed it from the chapel on the headland - perspective can be a devil. Charlie was halfway up the hill and thinking that he should never have been so ambitious, perhaps he had overdone the exercise for one day. He stopped and breathed deep lungful's of the fresh Hebridean air. It was amazing what fresh air tasted like - it felt like he hadn't breathed any for a long time. It felt light, invigorating and full of goodness. He felt a renewed vigour seeping through to his weary legs. He turned and surveyed the rolling landscape in front of him. An alternative perspective to the one he had eyed from the headland - here he was looking out to sea, whereas before he was looking along the coast and inland. With the sun shining, the luscious greens of the landscape rolled gently into the twinkling ocean, flecked and rippling with white horses as the wind cuffed the rising ocean swell. From here, Charlie could see that the swell was indeed building; he could see the tell-tale humps of solid ground swell silhouetted against the horizon. His shoulders and back ached at the thought of a second surf in the day. He was unfit and out of shape.

He turned and continued to climb the last hundred metres. Paths had been cut through the gorse, heather and bracken, by regular footfall, and he followed one of these narrow arteries through the sea of red, spilling from the summit of the hill. As he crested the hill, he was presented with the most picturesque landscape he had ever seen. The top of the hill was very reminiscent of a volcano, with a large crater seemingly scooped out of the top. The entire crater was covered in the same deep red gorse. At the pit of the crater was a mirror black lake surrounded by small out-crops of rock. In the milliseconds that Charlie took all of this in, he also noticed movement below him at the edge of the loch. A woman was standing with her back to him at the edge of the water. She was looking out across the loch and slowly removing all of her clothes. Charlie momentarily froze, unsure of what to do - he suddenly felt very exposed even though he was the one who was fully clothed. He threw himself to the ground - if the girl turned around and saw him whilst she was in the midst of stripping off for a bit of naked wild swimming, there is no question that she would freak out and he would be labelled as some complete voyeuristic pervert - he would probably end up in remote Scottish prison somewhere, where you were only ever fed gruel. He lay on his back on the path, sandwiched by the gorse bushes, and stared at the azure sky. He could feel his heartbeat thumping out of his chest. Part of him desperately wanted to look, but the gentleman in him was fighting hard against his male instincts. Perhaps, if he shuffled down the hill a little bit and then stood up and walked up over the crest of the hill as if he didn't realise anyone was there - yes that was what he would do. He began to move himself along the wet, dirt footpath, cursing as he reaslised that his new expensive jacket was going to be ruined. When he felt that he was far enough down the hill he stood up, brushed himself down as best he could and composed himself. He took another lungful of the fresh Scottish air and strode over the top of the hill, trying to act as oblivious to the naked woman in the loch as he could.

NAKED ATTRACTION

It had been a week since Maggie had been in the loch. She used to go every day of the year, but for some reason she had begun to find excuses not to go. But she needed it today. The sun was shining, and she needed some space to clear her head and think. She needed to work out what was going on in her head, what she was doing with her life and where she wanted to go with it. Then again, she wasn't sure she had many options. As she stood on the edge of the loch letting the cold water lap her feet, she could smell the richness of the earth hanging in the air which the rain always brings. There was less breeze down here by the loch, but a wisp of fresh sea aroma floating on the air brought goose bumps up on her exposed flesh. She walked into the dark, cold water, letting it envelope her pale naked flesh. The cleansing sensation of nakedness in the wild never ceased for Maggie, it was thrilling and exciting, but also physically liberating and it felt amazing. Her mind was racing with a million thoughts - a yearning and desire to drop everything and leave the island, leave her home and everything she had ever known. The death of someone close to you can have a sobering effect on your fragile mortality. It had all become too complicated. But at the same time, this was her home, and she didn't know any different.

As she submerged her body up to her neck, the coldness intensified her breathing. Her heart began to race. She fought the panic as her body froze and her lungs screamed. She mentally focused and took control of her breathing, regulating each breath as she floated out into the middle of the loch. She moved into a vertical position and stared down into the dark depths of the water, taking a deep breath and submerging her head. As she came up out of the water, her head pulsed with a brief spasm of pain from the cold. She closed her eyes, fighting against the 'ice-cream head'. When she opened her eyes, she could see a man standing half way down the slope. He had sunglasses on, so it was hard to see where exactly he was looking, but he appeared to be looking anywhere but at the loch.

"Hello!", Maggie called from the water. There was no point in trying to hide.

The man turned his head towards her.

"Oh, hi!", he called. "Didn't see you there."

Maggie could see the awkwardness radiating from the stranger and a smile crept across her face.

"Are you coming in?" Maggie shouted, the grin on her face broadening.

"Um…No. I'm…um…just…I'm just walking. Just visiting. I'm ….er…we're…er… sorry."

"It's no drama."

An awkward pause followed. Maggie stayed in the middle of the loch, treading water.

"I'm Maggie."

"Charlie."

"Well it's nice to meet you Charlie, but this water is pretty cold, and I'm not wearing anything so….. Would you mind?"

Charlie seemed to get the hint and, raising his hands in apology, turned and walked up and over the brow of the hill. Maggie gave it a couple of minutes after he disappeared from view before she swam to the edge and grabbed her towel, wrapping herself up and still smiling as she thought of the awkward Englishman. These must be Gully's friends.

WHISKEY MEET

Stuart Ferguson took hold of the metal bar that hung limply from an ancient nail in the back of the door and swung it in a clockwise direction, from left to right and let it settle in the clasp on the door frame, locking them in and barring anyone wanting entry. The 'deiseal', the Gaelic custom of moving from left to right to mimic the movement of the sun, was ingrained in every action of island life and Ferguson was reminded of this as he went to take his seat. It was a silly superstition really, but he was not a man to challenge the traditions of the ancients or the wrath of the Gods.

The small group of Islanders sat huddled in their own corners of the room, the atmosphere heavy and the group were eager to have the meeting done and to be out of the confined space. Flannagan sat on a stool with his back to the room, facing the bar and nursing a Tonic water and ice, his nicotine-stained fingers, crooked and curled, clamped onto the defeated stub of a roly cigarette. He hated these meetings, they felt claustrophobic and uncomfortable. He had never thought of himself as a criminal, a fuck up....yes, but not a criminal, but here he was and he felt dirty. Six more months and then he would disappear. He had enough to melt away and start again, start afresh.

Sam leant over the bar a little further down, serious and conspiratorial in her expression. Duncan picked up the zippo lighter that lay on the table in front of Christian MacIntosh and laconically flicked the lid open. With one smooth motion his fingers came down and sparked the flint - a theatrical statement of his misspent youth. He casually held the flame to his cigarette and inhaled. He flicked the lid on the zippo and tossed it back onto the table, where it landed with a reluctant clatter.

"I think you boys have got to stop smoking in mae Pub!" Sam grinned at Duncan and then Flannagan.

"Pub's closed." Stuart Ferguson countered.

Duncan smiled and took a step forward. "So, where are we at?"

Flannagan picked up on his cue. He took a sip of the tonic water and turned to the room. "The latest batch has just gone off. Geoff should get to Manchester tomorrow morning."

Duncan paced the flagstone floor. "Good. Good work, Pete."

Flannagan nodded and opened his tobacco tin. He needed something to do with his hands. He wanted a drink, and occupying his mind with small tasks to concentrate on satiated the craving. Even after all these years his body still yearned for the anaesthesia the drink would bring - something to dull the stress and strain of the real world.

Duncan turned to Christian. "And what about our fisherman friends?"

Christian cleared his throat. "The new shipment's landed. It's in the bothy. It's a big one."

Duncan paused his pacing and looked around the room. "Good. And that's why it's important for us to meet and talk through it. We don't want to fuck this one up, otherwise we'll all be in the shit. Things are obviously going to be a bit trickier with this one, with the festival and the size of the shipment, so we've got to think about things a little more carefully. More people around is going to make things more difficult, but we have a timetable to keep.....We're going to shift the barrels on Saturday, the day after the festival. Use the barrels from the pub as cover when you move them up to the distillery and then the usual process. No getting pished. No fucking about. Do this right and it's a big payday for everyone. We need it out on the Whiskey road by the end of the week. Okay?"

The realisation for Christian that he would have to stay sober during the Fire and Whiskey festival was suddenly very evident on his features.

"But. But…"

"Have a drink man…just… don't get smashed. Right?"

"But why are we doing it *then*, with so many people around. Eh?"

"We don't make the schedule do we. They want it done now. We do it now. Empty kegs being moved around the night after a festival on a small island shouldn't raise any eyebrows. Listen, there are lots of visiting folk then, but we need to get this shit packed and shifted. We are just a small cog in a big wheel. So in the given circumstances and the poor timing of the shipment, this is what we are going to do."

Duncan fixed Christian with a vice of a stare.

"Understand?"

"Aye."

"Don't fuck it up. Flannagan? Make sure everything is set and ready to go at the distillery. This one is important."

"Aye. We're ready. More people on the island means more people in the distillery though. But don't worry. It's all in hand."

DROPPING IN

Charlie had never sat in a more uncomfortable chair in his life - it had looked so inviting, with it's classical wing back, and the plump cushion in a faded brown corduroy, but as soon as he had sat down with his cup of tea and his book he had very quickly deduced that this was a chair he would never like to sit in again. He was so looking forward to spending some time unwinding, letting the pace of life slow in comfort, but the seemingly plump cushion had the springiness of a sea boulder, and the back of the chair was so erect and upright that Charlie felt like if he closed his eyes he felt about as relaxed as if he was at the dentist.

He moved to the sofa. Pressing and padding to check for comfort points - this was marginally better. He placed the cup of tea on the frilly doily coaster that adorned the top of the spindled side table and let his weight fall back into the loving arms of the sofa. He was knackered. The fresh air of his walk had temporarily cleared his head, but he was now entering the lethargy stage of his hangover, and the sofa suddenly felt like the comfiest thing in the world. He took a sip of his steaming cup of tea and was immediately enveloped in a hug of weariness, with thoughts of Sunday roasts and lazy afternoons in front of a fire settling on his mind. He stretched his frame out on the sofa and mused over the fact that despite not being at work for the first time in God knows how long, he was still sleeping on a sofa. This was a substantial improvement on the last one though. He caught sight of the cardboard tube that held the remains of Gully, perched on the mantlepiece. It felt like Gully was there in the room with him and was wanting to talk. "I don't know what you want me to say Gul. I don't think I'm ready to talk yet." His voice sounded empty and alien. Was he talking to himself? Was he that tired that he was delirious? As he began to close his eyes, his senses readjusted, and his heightened hearing picked up the pitter-patter of someone in the shower. One of the boys must have got up whilst he was making tea. Tea. 'I can't even be bothered' he thought to himself - he'd make another one when he woke up.

As his eyes closed, images of the calm mirror of the loch, bathed in the rich red reflection of the surrounding heather filled his mind with vivid intensity. He could hear the soft calls of the seabirds in the distance and hear the dull thump of the waves breaking not 200 meters from where he was lying.

He was under the water of the loch but he could see Gully's face through the water distorted and blurred, as he sunk deeper into the water. Muted colours and a soft focus blurred the red heather on the surrounding banks of the loch. He could feel his lungs beginning to burn and he knew he needed air. He went to push off the bottom, but his foot kicked empty water. He looked down and just saw a never-ending abyss of darkness below him, his naked body glinting white in the sunlight filtering from above, contrasting to the murky black below. He looked to the light above him and began to pull and kick his way to the surface. He could feel his body tense with the panic of running low on oxygen, even though he knew he needed to stay calm, and that panicking would eat up precious oxygen. His lungs were burning. He felt his hands break the surface and touch fresh air. He began to move in slow motion. He looked up. Light. Air: air he would not get to breathe because something had grabbed his foot and was pulling him down. It was immensely strong and powerful, whatever it was. Suddenly he felt lips on his lips and the soothing balm of air filling his lungs. He opened his eyes, but his vision was obscured by a rainbow of air bubbles. The lips were no longer on his and the bubbles dissipated, and he could just see the pale figure of a naked woman swimming away from him into the darkness below. With oxygen in his lungs, he rotated and plunged after her. She turned to look over her shoulder and Charlie pulled up. It was the woman from the loch, only she had the tail of a fish and the body of a human. She smiled.

There was a loud bang and Charlie sat bolt upright, years of being woken after a sleep lasting minutes, not hours, in the hospital, meant that he was immediately on full alert. His breathing was erratic, and, despite the mild temperature, he could feel a bead of sweat running down his forehead. The tension in his body began to dissipate as Charlie began to process where he was and what he was doing. He looked down at the floor and realised that, as he had sat upright, he must have knocked the side table and his cup of tea was now a puddle on the pale Persian rug.

"Shit. What the…"

Suddenly Mark was striding into the room in nothing but a towel. His muscled body still wet from the shower. Mark caught sight of Charlie.

"Door mate?"

And with that Mark was at the front door. He yanked it open and the dark and musty room was suddenly flooded with sunlight. Charlie could see the silhouette of someone standing in the doorway, the flare of the sunshine momentarily making him blink. And then he heard his brother purr.

"Hi."

A brief pause.

"Can I help?"

Mark momentarily shifted his weight and Charlie caught the briefest glimpse of the woman's face, and an explosion of recognition. The woman from the loch. The naked woman in the loch.

"Oh, hi."

Mark stood in a pose of unashamed casualness, leaning with his arm resting up against the top of the door, letting his bicep flex just enough to compliment his adonis like posturing. Charlie had always envied his brothers ease with women. He made it look so easy. The woman pulled back her wet hair from her face and tied it behind her head and smiled at Mark.

"I'm, er , looking for someone."

"I am someone."

The woman chuckled.

"Aye. But not the someone I'm looking for."

Charlie, feeling a little more composed and awake, took this as his cue to make his entrance, and stood up.

"Er, hi."

She was silhouetted by the sun, rays of white and gold radiated from behind her like she was some sort of ethereal being. Charlie felt his tongue go thick and his communication skills beginning to drift.

Mark looked at Charlie. Then he looked at the woman.

"You two..er..know each other?"

Without breaking eye contact with Charlie, the woman replied.

"Well...er..sort of."

Her soft laughter floated into the room.

"Er...Maggie. I'm Maggie."

Charlie passed her a cup of tea and picked up his own off the kitchen sideboard. The warmth seeping into his hands felt good. At least, having something in his hands would stop him fidgeting and looking like a complete idiot. He tried to gain some composure. Why was he feeling like this - so awkward. He couldn't remember the last time a woman had had this sort of effect on him. Maybe it was because he had already seen her naked.

"I'm sorry about before."

"Don't be ridiculous. Just unlucky on my part. You don't often see folk up there at this time. So…it's when I like to go for a swim."

"Naked"

"Naked"

"But it's… fucking freezing."

"I grew up on this island, I'm basically half seal."

There it was again. The soft lull of laughter floating. It was like a siren's call. The briefest moment of silence appeared as they let the laughter sit before Charlie frowned.

"So, how did you know I was here?"

"It's a small island." Maggie gently blew the tea, making small concentric circles spread across the surface. "I used to own this croft. Well, my gran did, that is. She's dead though. And then I sold it to Gully. You boys friends of Gully's?"

Charlie could feel his mouth wanting to move and formulate words, but he was momentarily caught, unsure of which words to choose.

"Yeah. Sort of. It's complicated. We were….we were …well sort of all grew up together."

"Oh Aye. I'm…sorry."

"What for?"

"I heard Gully died." It was hard to tear himself away from her eyes. There was movement below the surface, something she was keeping hidden.

"Yeah. It was …tragic." Charlie took a sip of his tea and regretted it - it was far too hot. "I'm sorry about your Gran."

Maggie laughed. "It was a while ago. It's fine."

"Oh." That moment of silence reappeared, awkward and adolescent. Maggie sprang into action, moving through into the living area, breaking the intimacy of the cramped galley kitchen and heading for space.

"So, is everything alright? With the house and all that? I've not been in here for a while. Doesn't look like much has changed."

Charlie followed into the living area and found himself gravitating towards the most uncomfortable chair in the world, ever.

"Yeah. It's great. A little …..well, not very Gully! But great." The formality felt all wrong. What happened to the natural chemistry of the kitchen?

"I don't think he did anything to it. He was only ever here for a few weeks at a time. So how come you're here? Staying in your friend's house?"

"He…well…he sort of left it to us. I'm not sure the ins and outs of it all - we haven't worked it all out. But he….well…he wanted us to come and take a look."

"Yeah?" Maggie looked at the boardbags stacked along one of the walls. "You're surfers?"

"Yeah. Well…sort of. We all used to surf together. But not for a while."

"Sounds complicated." She smiled.

Charlie noticed the big stain from the tea he knocked over when Maggie arrived. He quickly picked up the cushion on the chair and threw it onto the floor in, what felt like, an overelaborate charade in order to cover the crime of a stained carpet. He followed it up with an exaggerated collapse into the rock-solid chair and an audible sigh.

Maggie looked at him and smirked. Her eyes drifted over the carpet where Charlie had spilled the tea and now thrown the cushion, lingering as if deep in thought.

"So, there's three of you staying here, right?"

"That's right." Charlie took a sip of his tea and burnt his mouth, "Ow. Shit. Hot." Charlie put his tea down on the side table. " Er, there's…Mark…at the door."

"Oh. Yup. The muscles."

"Yeah. And Jimmy, who..um…I don't know if he's up yet. Not sure. I've only just got back really. He might still be asleep. We had quite a heavy night last night. At the pub."

"I heard." Maggie continued to pace the room, taking in the various ornaments and pictures scattered around. She paused at the mantlepiece and gently touched the tube of Gully's ashes. It was like she knew what was in there. But how could she? Were her and Gully just friends, or was it more than that?

She smirked.

"Oh.. Er.. OK."

"It's a small island."

It had been a long time, but if he wasn't mistaken, Charlie was convinced that this very attractive local girl was flirting with him.

"A few too many whiskeys!" Charlie felt the paralysis of self-doubt seeping through his body and tongue tying him. He had just never managed to control his nerves when he was in a one-to-one situation with an attractive woman, and he felt very out of practice. Even with Sarah he had initially been a complete buffoon - it's what she later told him made him endearing. He just couldn't believe he was so different to his twin brother - he only wished he could have had some of his brother's natural charisma. He took a breath.

He looked up at Maggie, "And then. Me."

Maggie held his gaze for what felt like a moment too long as she said, "And you."

"Charlie boy, you made some coffee?" Mark rolled into the room like a boulder of energy and joie de vivre, and smashed the delicately poised moment.

Charlie leaned back and pointed to the kitchen. "There's tea on the side."

"Tea?!"

"Trust me. I'm a doctor!" Charlie caught Maggie looking at him. "I am. I am actually a doctor." Charlie smiled and Maggie smiled back. "So, where do you….er..?"

Mark's voice boomed out from the confines of the kitchen, "Jimmy's gone in. Can you believe it. The guys a fucking machine. Looks a bit blown to shit for me." Mark reappeared from the kitchen. "So, Maggie, you're from here?"

"She owns the cottage. Or she used to own the cottage. Her Gran did. And they sold it to Gully." Charlie made circular motion with his finger.

"Oh. Right. So, you knew Gully."

"Aye." Charlie briefly caught Mark's eye. There was definitely an air of mystery to this woman.

Maggie put her tea down on the mantle-piece next to Gully, her eyes momentarily lingering on the ashes before she picked up her coat from the coat stand by the door and began to put it on. "Listen, I'm not going to stay - I was just popping in to apologise and well, introduce maeself and that, so…Anyway. Listen, will I sees you all at the festival?"

"Festival?" Mark looked confused.

"The Uisce Beatha. The Fire and Whiskey Festival. It's an annual thing here. It's on Friday."

"What day are we on now?" Mark looked like a confused adolescent.

"Tuesday! You lads really are on holiday! Loads of people come from all over. Normally pretty fun. You might find it a bit weird mind, but you should come."

"We'll definitely be there." The words slipped out of Charlie's mouth before he could stop them/rephrase them/erase them…anything…but.

Maggie let her gaze rest on Charlie. There was the merest hint of a smile, the faintest upward turn at the corners of her mouth.

"Great."

Maggie turned and headed for the door. As she pulled open the front door she threw over her shoulder, "Have fun…. don't get yourselves into any trouble!" The door shut and she was gone.

In the silence and the flutterings of dust motes Mark turned to Charlie, who was staring at the front door. "Dr. Silvertongue. I like it. Skills."

DAY 3

(WEDNESDAY)

ISLAND LIFE

Charlie, Mark and Jimmy stood on the beach of the little bay watching the rising sun glint and sparkle off the calm ocean, casting it in a shimmering silver blanket. Mark dug his hands in his pockets and let out an audible sigh.

"Flat."

Charlie looked at his friend. "I think we can see that, Mark." Charlie picked up some sand and threw it in the air to check for wind. "I thought the swell was building."

The three men stared at the ocean as if expecting something to happen, willing a pulse of swell to break the perfectly horizontal horizon. A seabird squawked overhead, and a voice sounded out from behind them.

"Beautiful morning, eh?"

The three of them turned in unison and were initially drawn to the large brown dog bounding towards them with boundless enthusiasm. It leapt up onto Jimmy who stood his ground and rubbed its ears in playful greeting.

"Got to make the most of the mornings like this when you live in these islands." Tom came striding towards them across the sand. "Keegan. Get here." The Vizzla immediately dropped off Jimmy, turned and trotted back to Tom's heels. "If he likes you, you must be alright! Gully loved this bay. I'd see him out here most mornings he was up here, surfing or stretching, or something. Wasn't a man to sit around doing nothing eh?"

Charlie squinted towards the voice, the rising sun silhouetting the figure, before Tom approached a little closer and Charlie recognized the Geordie vicar. "Oh. Hi! More obedient than my ….than my wife's….ex-wife's dog.""

"Think you're gonna be disappointed today." Tom nodded towards the glistening ocean. "But I reckon you're in for a treat if you're here for the festival. You know about the festival? You'll get a proper taste of island life." He laughed and the three friends looked at each other, sharing an unspoken agreement that the laughter insinuated some deeper meaning.

Jimmy looked back at the ocean. "Some swell coming in then?"

"Sorry. Tom, This is Jimmy, and my brother, Mark." Charlie proffered.

"Nice to meet yers. Low pressure moving in behind Ireland and could…maybe ….bring in something decent."

Jimmy stroked the dog's ears. "What about tomorrow?"

Tom looked at Jimmy - there was something about him that Tom recognised, his gait, his posture. Had they met before? This one certainly looked like he had frayed around the edges and there was the stamp of the armed forces visible on him. "A bit tomorrow but I think the winds might be a little too much. Might get something in one or two spots. You never can quite tell around these parts though. Small windows of opportunity."

"You knew Gully?" Mark searched the man for some indication as to his relationship with his dead friend.

"Aye. Not much. Surfed with him a few times. Seemed a good man. I'm sorry to hear about him passing."

Mark relaxed a little. This man seemed honest and humble. He was hard to read, but he seemed friendly.

"What are you fellas up to today?"

Charlie, looked across at Mark and Jimmy - they were going

to scatter the ashes today, but they weren't sure this was information to divulge to a complete stranger. They all subtly shook their heads and pursed their lips. "Not much", Charlie offered.

"Well how about I show you around the island a little? Show you a few spots. Give you a little tour of the island."

The black fumes spluttered out of the exhaust of Tom's old truck as it trundled north along the smooth tarmac of the road that acted as the main artery of the island, dissecting it from north to south. The sun was out, and Mark watched the grass in the surrounding fields bend and kneel in submission to the gentle coastal breeze as he stared out of the mud spattered window of the ice-cream van.

"So what's the priest's story?"

Without looking around, Charlie shrugged his shoulders. "Don't know. He's not a local, local. He's a Geordie."

Mark chuckled from the back seat. "Yeah, I think I can work that one out."

"Seems a nice guy. I went up to the church on the headland yesterday morning and gave him a hand fixing the vestry roof."

"Aren't you the little hero?"

"He surfs. Surfs most of the breaks around here pretty much on his own. Used to surf with Gully apparently. Saw a picture of him on a pretty solid looking wave. Seems pretty happy to share some local knowledge."

"Aren't the locals friendly, eh? I don't know. There's something not quite adding up with him. Do you know what I mean?"

Charlie scoffed. "Seems pretty friendly to me."

Jimmy remained silent, focused on the road ahead and following the truck in front of him. He listened to Charlie and

Mark; Mark was right, something didn't quite add up about this guy, but maybe he was just being paranoid. But he couldn't think about that right now, his mind was still distracted with what he had left behind in London and it danced between relief and fear, with spikes of panic as he considered what his next move would be. Now he had had a few days to think and escape, maybe running away had not been the right option. It had been playing on his mind since they had arrived. When the time came to leave this remote island, what were his options? He couldn't go back to London - that would be signing his death warrant. He needed a plan. He desperately wanted to share his troubles, but he didn't want to worry the brothers or dampen the mood of the trip so early on.

Charlie pointed ahead. "Here. He's turning off."

Jimmy swung the heavy wheel and followed the rusted red truck down a rutted farm track that headed towards the west coast of the island. The track opened up into a small, fenced clearing, and Tom's truck pulled up to a stop. Jimmy pulled up and they all got out. Tom unhooked the tail gate of his truck and it squealed mournfully. Keegan, the Vizla, leapt off the flatbed and bounded around Tom's feet.

"Thought we'd start with a little history." Tom smiled at the uncertain look he received from his fellow countrymen and sauntered off down a narrow footpath that led from the clearing and ambled down through the sloping field towards the ocean. After a moment's hesitation, the three friends followed.

Mark dropped his voice and spoke out of the side of his mouth, "I fucking hate history."

After a five minute walk the group of men came to what looked, at first impressions, to be just a pile of stones in a grassy field, with the blue of the ocean beyond, flecked with white as the breeze clipped the crests of the small waves that were haphazardly breaking in the wide bay below them.

Tom stopped by one of the piles of stones and it now became clear that there was some order to them and that they were looking at what appeared to be some ruins of a building or buildings. Straight lines of stones clearly delineated the outlines of some form of settlement.

"If you are up on this island for a while, I thought it might be good for you to understand a little about the island and its people. It might help give yous some context to the festival."

The three of them exchanged a look. Why was everyone painting this festival out in such a weird way?

"We English aren't too popular around here. Oh, it's not too bad now, but there still is some deep-rooted resentment and animosity from the locals. So, if you are down the Pub or at the festival then I thought it might be wise for you to understand a little."

Mark looked at the man. "By showing us some ruins."

Tom laughed at the apparent disdain for history. "There are under ninety thousand people living on the islands of Scotland."

Charlie threw a damp piece of broken gorse for Keegan to chase, only it wasn't heavy enough and fell limply in the grass just a few metres away. "That seems quite a lot."

"That's across all the islands and is a significantly fewer number than used to be the case. Some islands have more folk on than others. There is only 248 people on this island."

Jimmy stood inspecting one of the crumbling walls, "Isn't that nice though...to have a bit of space. Escape from all the manic chaos, all the bullshit."

"You would think, wouldn't you? I mean that's part of the reason I came here. I think that's why your friend Gully came too. That and the surf. But I listen to people always saying that they want to escape to the country, that they want a quiet village life and a bit of privacy to go about their lives. But that's just not the case in a small community. It's a misconception. If you want a private life, full of anonymity, then head to a city with millions of people - a small community is not the place to be. Everyone knows your business."

Mark pursed his lips and nodded his head. He had never really thought about it like that before. "I can see that; everyone seems to know exactly who we are and where we're staying."

"Exactly."

A flood of panic began to fill Jimmy's gut. Perhaps he hadn't escaped. If anyone found out where he had gone, he would be a sitting duck on this island.

"So, there used to be a lot of people living on the islands. A lot more than now. And this is the ruins of one of the oldest settlements on the island. There are others, but this one is probably the most complete. It was a village that was 'cleared'".

Jimmy snapped out of his rising panic. "What do you mean 'cleared'".

"You've not heard that term before?"

The three friends shook their heads.

"It started in the 1700's, as an attempt by the English to break up the clan system in Scotland. It happened all over the islands and the highlands. Houses were burned and pulled down, hundreds of people were packed up and shipped off to the new world. They outlawed tartan and dispersed the communities, replacing humans with livestock. And that went on for a lot of years."

"And they still hate the English three hundred years later?" Charlie pulled out his sunglasses and put them on so that he didn't have to squint at the scenery that was bathed in beautiful sunshine.

"Some events happen that scar communities for centuries. I

don't know why. I don't think the locals know why, but there is still some deep resentment towards outsiders and especially the English in these islands. I don't think they have ever really recovered, and it is why this part of Scotland remains one of the most sparsely populated areas in Europe."

They spent the next twenty minutes looking at the ruins, with Jimmy throwing rocks and sticks for Keegan to chase and Tom explaining the history of the settlers and how they would have lived, with up to ten people in a small cottage along with their livestock. They tried to listen to the history lesson and politely pay attention, but their gaze continually drifted towards the ocean, constantly assessing the promise of an incoming swell, willing the waves to suddenly stand up and start marching. Like all surfers who are swell starved, their anticipation at the prospect of a decent swell of significant size meant that they had the nervous butterflies fluttering in the pits of their stomachs, leaving a residue that made them feel a little sick with nerves. After half an hour they were back at the cars and pulling away to continue their tour.

The rest of the morning saw the two cars take in most of the north of the island, with Tom pointing out the offshore reef break which a small band of hardened local surfers tended to surf when conditions were right. The four of them sat for some time on some boulders in a small bay looking out at the horizon to where Tom was pointing, yearning for the ocean to reveal its hidden, secret reef break, whilst they sipped hot coffee from the thermos that Tom had packed.

"Did Gully surf the reef?" Jimmy was looking through the binoculars.

"Oh Aye. He fucking loved that wave. Said he'd been wanting to surf it since he was a kid.

Suddenly it all clicked. This was the wave that Gully had been bringing them up to surf that fateful summer. And now he was dead. This was why he had brought them all up here - to surf this reef.

"Do you think it will break with this incoming swell?" Jimmy looked at Tom and held his gaze.

"Oh Aye! It's going to be as good as it gets in a day or two. You're in for a treat."

Tom began packing up the thermos and called Keegan back to heel.

"I think it's time we went and found some lunch, don't you? I can take you up to the distillery and we can grab a sandwich and you can sample some of the local produce."

SNAKED

Neil Aldridge could hear the phone in reception ringing. Where was Stacey? Probably nipped off for some lunch. She was always disappearing. He would have to have a word. But right now, that was the least of his problems. Billy, his nephew was stood in the doorway looking sheepish and weak. One thing Neil Aldridge couldn't abide and that was weakness. He needed to find a way to get the lad to grow a pair of bollocks. The phone in reception continued to ring. Neil Aldridge could feel his blood pressure rising and actually boiling in his veins, as he glared at his nephew.

"I don't care what he says, you get round there and tell that fucking prick that he owes me money. You get me?"

Ring. Ring. Neil looked to the ceiling, breathed deeply and bellowed out to reception. "Where the fuck is Stacey?"

He fixed his nephew with a serious expression. "Listen, you smash his door in, and you take him to the bank for all I care. Break some fucking bones if you have to. Just get me that money."

Ring. Ring.

Billy turned on his heel and disappeared. Neil swivelled on his office chair and looked out of the internal window at the distribution centre on the warehouse floor below him. The warehouse doors were open, and he could see the haulage trucks parked in the yard outside. He could make out the familiar loping gait of Geoff making his way across the warehouse floor. Good. He was on time. He didn't want the goods on site for long, and they had enough time to unload and distribute the drugs tonight. He continued to watch as men on forklift trucks moved around like ants below him. It reminded him of that children's tv program when he was younger...what was it called? ... Fraggle Rock.

There was a knock on the door behind him just as his mobile phone on the desk began to vibrate. He spun around and indicated to Geoff that he should come in and close the door. He picked up the phone and pressed the green answer button.

"What?"

"It's Andy."

"Oh hi boss. Sorry. Stressful day."

"Don't give me something else to worry about."

Neil pointed Geoff towards the small fridge in the corner of the office. "No. Nothing for you to worry about Andy. All going like clockwork on the real business to be done."

"Good."

Geoff handed Neil an ice cold can of lager and then stood behind Neil looking out across the warehouse floor.

"Listen Neil, I need you to do something. I've just sent you a message. You remember that lad who played poker at the pub the other day. Jimmy Mac."

"Yeah. I remember him. Cocky bastard. You fucked him right over."

"Yeah, well, I've just sent you his picture. I need you to get some of your boys to find him. He's in Manchester. We've tracked his phone. He owes 20K."

Neil leaned forward and clicked the mouse, opening up the attachment on his computer. A screen grab from CCTV footage filled the screen - Jimmy's face clear as day.

"Ok. Leave it with us. If he's in Manchester, we'll find him."

Geoff was looking over his shoulder at the screen and began to gesticulate with his beer bottle. Neil looked up at him quizzically.

"Andy, hold on." Neil put his phone on mute. And looked at Geoff. "What?"

Geoff took a slug of his beer. God, it felt good after that drive. "That lad isn't in Manchester. I've seen him."

Neil was gobsmacked. How could Geoff know who Jimmy Mac was, let alone where he was. "What you on about?"

"I recognize him. I was on the dock the other day, giving Gordon his cut and that lad drove off the ferry. I remember him 'cos he was in a fucking ice cream van with some other lads. I was standing right behind Gordon when he took their ticket. Remember him because Gordo then banged on about how it was no wonder the Scots hated the English. He was in the pub later that night too. He's at the source. He's on the island."

Neil unmuted his phone. "Andy, you're not going to believe this. It seems your boy's pulled a fast one on you. He has taken a trip to Scotland."

DISTILLERY

The ice cream van followed Tom's truck as it made its way back south across the island, past the cluster of buildings they referred to as 'town', past the pub and up over another headland and down into a shallow bay where a series of connected, white-washed buildings sat proudly behind a crumbling asphalt car park. A creaking sign lamented in the strengthening breeze, the faded and peeling symbol of the distillery looking weatherbeaten and aged as the clouds began to roll in from the west. The two cars followed a large distribution lorry into the car park, where a handful of cars indicated a small number of visitors to the distillery. Jimmy switched off the engine and the three friends climbed out of the car and followed Tom in through the double doors of the entrance. The first thing that struck them was the smell inside the building, a strange mixture of apples, baking bread and ethanol. Through the entrance, doors took them into a reception area, which was dark and warming in atmosphere, with wood panelled walls, soaked in the history of the building. Wooden whiskey barrels were stacked against one wall and distillery merchandise lined the shelves on the remaining walls, alluringly backlit by cleverly hidden lighting. An old couple were perusing the various bottles of differently aged Whiskeys on one side of the room and a younger couple were chatting to one of the distillery employees at the reception desk as they entered. A barely distinguishable nod passed between Tom and the employee behind the reception desk, before he led his three fellow countrymen through an archway to the right, which took them into a small bar lined with multiple bottles of rich amber liquid and half a dozen small, round tables with low cushioned stools. Selected bottles of whiskey sat invitingly on the bar surrounded by crystal cut glasses. Mark was tempted to go and help himself, but social etiquette and the presence of a relative stranger checked his enthusiasm.

After a short while a man who looked like an aging rock star, with a long silver ponytail and a pockmarked and stubbled face appeared. He was wearing the same navy-blue polo shirt emblazoned with the distillery logo they had seen the person on reception also wearing. He took their order for a couple of cheese ploughman's and a beef sandwich and disappeared out the back.

"Doesn't say much." Charlie nodded towards the disappearing back of the barman.

"Pete Flannagan. He pretty much runs the distillery. No...you won't get much out of him."

Charlie and Mark both disappeared to the toilet next to the bar, and in the silence that hung over the empty room Jimmy reached for his mobile phone, before remembering that he had tossed it into that van on the M5. He pulled out the crumpled and creased ordinance survey map he had in his jacket pocket and began to study it. Tom watched him.

"So. you're ex forces aren't you?"

Jimmy briefly looked up from the map. "That obvious?"

"Takes one to know one."

Jimmy looked at the man opposite him, assessing this mysterious Geordie.

"Yeah?"

"Six years in the Paras. You?" Tom took a sip of his drink.

"Ten years. Marines."

"How are you finding it?"

"What do you mean?" Jimmy shifted in his seat and sat up a little straighter, feeling a little under the spotlight.

"Life after the forces? Pretty difficult for most. The adjustment to civie life."

"Yeah."

Jimmy looked back down at the map, unwilling to expand. Opening up to a complete stranger was not something he was comfortable doing. Tom watched Jimmy from across the table, happy to sit out the stalemate. He got it. He'd been there. He understood damaged goods when he saw it - he had seen it too many times among his friends from his previous life. He wasn't going to push.

The silence hung ominously.

"Here let me show you." Tom indicated the map and Jimmy placed it on the table. "It'll be mostly blown out tomorrow. The swell is coming, but so is the wind to start with. But if you check out this bay here." Tom pointed a thick weathered finger at a small hook of land on the south of the island. "This might be worth having a look at. The headland should provide a little shelter from the south westerlies. When you get to about here, there is a little track that leads out onto the top of some cliffs here." Jimmy leaned closer, his forehead crinkled in concentration, like the lines of swell he was dreaming of. "Park up on the cliffs and you'll find a little goat track down the face of the cliffs. It's a bit sketchy, but it's not too bad." Jimmy looked at the map again and made a mental note of Tom's tip.

"Thanks."

"As I say, it might work. But it's not an exact science."

Jimmy folded the map up and stuffed it back into the pocket of his coat.

"So, you've been on the islands long?"

"A couple of years. Didn't cope very well in the real world. Running away seemed like a good option."

Tom held his gaze. Jimmy felt like there was more to come, but this verbal game of chess was a strategic give and take. Jimmy smirked, playing the game.

"And you've been surfing this island on your own."

"Mostly. Until Your pal Gully turned up. But I didn't mind. It was nice to have some company to be honest. There are a couple of local lads that surf a little, and a few travelling surfers, but most of the travellers stick to the better-known spots on the islands in the north. Not many folk make it down here. It's a pretty well-kept secret. I guess the locals are trying to keep it that way."

"And what about you?"

"I'm not a local."

At that moment Charlie and Mark appeared from the toilet, just as their lunch emerged from behind the bar. Over their light lunch and a pot of coffee, the four men mainly exchanged stories of their surfing adventures, comparing notes and discussing options for future trips. It turned out that Tom was very well travelled. Having served in the Paratrooper regiment for a number of years he had surfed some pretty remote, out of the way surf breaks which were well off the beaten track, and as far from any surf guidebook you could find. He was generous with his knowledge, revealing just enough to the three surfers without being too precise - if they wanted to find any of these breaks they would have to go looking.

As they were draining their mugs of the thick black coffee, they heard the clang of a bell in reception.

"That's it. Time for the tour. You'll like it. You get to sample some of the produce at the end. But go easy, mind! I'm gonna head off and leave you to it."

The four of them stood up amongst the scraping of bar stools across the wooden floor. Charlie dug in his pocket to find his wallet but Tom stopped him.

"I've got it. You get into reception. You don't want to get left behind. You can buy me a drink or two at the festival."

They thanked Tom and made their way back into the reception area, where the two couples they had seen on their arrivals were standing huddled in the middle of the room listening to a female distillery employee who stood with her back to them.

As she turned around Charlie's heart skipped a beat. It was Maggie - the woman from the loch.

"Oh hi." She beamed a smile at their small group.

"Hi again." Mark grinned at her before looking at the rising red in Charlie's cheeks.

"Twice in two days." Maggie smiled at Charlie.

"I'm not stalking you." Charlie squirmed.

"It's a small island. It was only a matter of time before you found your way here." With a coquettish smile she turned back to the group. "Right, folks, if you'd like to listen up, we'll get going with the tour. The whole thing will take about an hour. I'll take you around the distillery and explain the process of how the malt whiskey is made before we'll head back there to the bar where you can sample a few complimentary wee drams of what we produce here on this small island before it gets shipped all over the world."

There were nods of approval and guilty smiles at this announcement. The scientist in Charlie ensured he watched and listened as Maggie launched into her script.

"So to start with, I'm just going to give you a little context to the Whiskey distilling industry. Around 85% of Scotland's whiskey is produced in the Highlands and islands - this covers Eilean Siar or the western islands, Orkney, the Highlands, Moray and most of the Argyll and Bute area. 77 of the 99 active and licensed distilleries are located in this region and it is home to a set of seven specialist malters. Scotch whiskey accounts for about 25% of the UK food and drinks exports."

Great, another history lesson. Mark looked around the room. He wasn't big on these sorts of things. He had spent a childhood being dragged around various tourist hotspots by two culturally over enthusiastic parents. He felt a vibration in his pocket and pulled out his phone. There was a message from Kelsie. Who the fuck was Kelsie? He clicked on it.

'R U stayin for the festival? X'

Suddenly it came together in his brain, and he made the connection. Kelsie. Kelsie was that girl behind the bar at the pub. He must have given her his number. He didn't remember. He quickly typed a message in reply.

'Looks like it.'

He thought about adding a kiss, but then deleted it. He didn't want to lead her on. She was just a girl. She was young enough to be one of his students.

"I'm sure many of you have visited Islay already, or that you will be at some point. Well in Whiskey terms, Islay, located off the west coast of Scotland has long since been a specialised whisky producing region famous across the world for its characteristic whiskies. The island itself is home to 8 individual distilleries. Whisky is also produced on other Scottish islands of Skye, Mull, Arran, Jura, Lewis, Orkney, and of course the lovely island we are on here." Maggie beamed a smile at her audience. "Ok, so, if you would like to follow me, I'll take you through to the heart of the distillery and we can have a look at how the whole process starts." Maggie turned her back and began to make her way past the reception desk and out towards the back of the building. The two other couples eagerly followed, whilst the three friends paused slightly before casually following the tour.

"Mate, don't be rude." Charlie raised his eyebrows at Mark.

"What?"

"She's talking. You're on the phone."

"Alright Romeo. I had a text. I think she's probably used to it."

"This was the girl who came by the house yesterday?" Jimmy lowered his voice as they passed the reception desk.

"Yeah. You should have seen my brother, man. Like a lovestruck puppy." Mark sniggered.

"Shut up." Charlie gave Mark a gentle jab in the arm.

They were walking down a narrow corridor, and the smell was growing in strength with every step they took. They turned off through some industrial swing doors and found themselves in a pristine room, reminiscent of a laboratory, at the rear of the building.

"So, this is the mashing room. To make malt whiskey, you need to start with barley. The barley is wet, warmed, germinated, heated and dried on a concrete floor to produce the starting material for the fermentation process. This used to happen on site, but due to economic constraints, these days this process now happens off site at a specialist 'Malter' company. Germination of the barley takes anywhere between eight to twelve days and the process basically prepares the barley for conversion into sugar. The dried malt is then transported here where it is ground down and the 'grist' is put into the mash tun. With a load of hot water" Maggie pointed at a large, copper domed, circular tank in the middle of the room. "This process converts the soluble starch into a sugary liquid known as 'wort'. That is then drawn off from the mash tun and the remaining solids at the bottom, known as 'draff', are distributed about the island and used for cattle feed."

"Lucky cows!" The man from the older couple chuckled at his own joke and looked at the others in the group who all politely smiled.

"Right. Follow me." Maggie walked back past the group and out of the door. Charlie and the others dutifully followed. As they made their way out of the 'mashing room' and back into the corridor, Charlie extended his stride to catch up with Maggie.

"I hope this isn't too boring. Your friends look like they'd rather be somewhere else."

"No, it's….I think it's fascinating."

Maggie looked over her shoulder at him. She wasn't sure if his tone was genuine or not. He wasn't her usual type, but there was something about this one that she couldn't put her finger on. Gully had been right - she liked him.

"Have you worked here a long time."

"Since I was eighteen. Most people on the island are connected to the distillery in some way or other. Either they work the land, or they work for the distillery." They turned off the corridor into another larger room, which was crammed full of equipment. Four large circular wooden tanks dominated the space, like four enormous Scandinavian hot tubs. As the doors swung closed behind them, Maggie launched into her script again.

"This is the fermentation room. You will notice the smell. Believe me, when you've worked here for a while it's pretty hard to get that smell out of your nostrils!"

Polite chuckles from the group reverberated around the claustrophobic room.

"So, after the 'wort' is cooled it is put into these tanks with some yeast, and the yeast attacks the sugar and converts it into crude alcohol. The fermentation process takes about forty-eight hours and produces a liquid we call 'wash'. Have a good look but don't get your nose too close!"

Maggie lifted off part of the lid from one of the tanks and stepped back revealing a small lake of brown froth. General chatter and laughter broke out as the tour group inspected the scummy looking brown liquid. As the others moved to the edge of the open tank, Charlie held his ground shifting from foot to foot and desperately racking his brain to find a conversation starter.

"So, I've heard a lot about this festival."

"Yeah? Not that many people know about it outside of these islands. It's like a hidden secret."

"But you do get people visiting from outside the islands for the festival?"

"Aye. But only really people in the know. If you love whiskey, you might have heard of it. But we like to try to keep it local. It's not meant to be a tourist event, but a local tradition. So, you're lucky. To have visited when you have."

"So how many people come?"

"I don't know, probably about five maybe six hundred. I doubt you will have ever seen anything like it."

There was that laughter again; not loud enough to echo around the cavernous room, it felt personal and intimate, like it was just for him. She looked at him and there was a flirtatious spark in her eye.

"So, presumably your whiskey gets shipped all over the world?" The guy from the younger couple was looking at them. Maggie reframed the features of her face, like a blanket being pulled down, the spark disappeared and a friendly but business-like smile turned on the man.

"Yes. We ship the whiskey all over the world. Currently we are distributing to over forty countries. The whiskey industry is a multinational model and is in demand across the world. It is big business. Right…" Maggie replaced the lid on the tank and the group took a step back. "Follow me and I will show you where the real magic happens!"

She turned and walked to the end of the room and through another set of swing doors.

"Don't try too hard mate." Mark leant in close to Charlie's ear, in a conspiratorial way, as he and Jimmy flanked Charlie and they followed the tour party through into the next room. "You don't want to seem too desperate."

As they walked through the double doors, they entered what appeared to be a high ceilinged, light and sterile warehouse. Copper 'Stills' lined the room in uniformed order. Copper pipes curled and spiralled, giving the sense they were in the laboratory of some crazed scientist. Maggie stood in the middle of the room facing them.

"The whiskey is fermented and then distilled twice. The 'wash' is taken from those tanks and put into these copper Pot Stills, where it is heated to a point where the alcohol becomes vapour. This then rises up and passes through the cooling plant, which is essentially these coiled pipes or 'worms'. These pipes have cold water pumping through them and this condenses the vapour back into liquid form. This creates what we call 'low wines'. This is then distilled a second time where the spirit falls off in strength and we end up with the whiskey that ultimately ends up in the bottles that the consumer drinks."

The final part of the tour took them through a low ceilinged, bare brick corridor which was lined with wooden barrels on racks. Maggie explained how the whiskey was left in the barrels to mellow for up to fifteen years. The tour party eventually emerged out of a door at the end of the corridor and into the bar area that they had had lunch in previously.

"And you bottle all the whiskey here?" The woman from the

older couple was standing by the bar next to Maggie.

"Aye. And then it is loaded on the lorries and distributed across the country and all over the world. Right. Now the part I know you've all been waiting for - the tasting! It is at this point that I am going to leave you as we have a lorry in at the moment that is being loaded up and I have to go and oversee that. So, I am going to leave you in the very capable hands of the distillery manager, Pete."

As if on cue, Peter Flannagan appeared behind the bar, his pock marked face twitching into a barely perceptible smile. The small tour party made their way to the bar as Flannagan began to pour seven small drams into crystal cut glasses.

"We are going to start with the ten year, which is more of an everyday single malt."

"Everyday?!" Jimmy leaned into Mark. "Every day and you'll end up like that."

Charlie's eyes followed Maggie as she left the bar area and headed back to reception, willing her to look over her shoulder, looking for confirmation of their connection. His heart was beginning to deflate, but then, just as she was about to disappear from sight she turned and there was that smile. And then she was gone.

DAY 4

(THURSDAY)

WAITING IT OUT

Dokes sat on the rigid plastic chair of the terminal, sipping the acrid machine-made coffee out of a polystyrene cup. He was tired. He could sleep for a million years. He felt his eyes get heavy. He allowed them to close momentarily. He had had enough of running around doing the dirty work for Andy, but he didn't have much choice. He was an illegal. He'd arrived in the country with no money, no passport and no visa. He took what work he could find, and being built like he was, that inevitably ended up doing something violent. He'd worked on the doors of a few night clubs before venturing into the shady world of debt collection. Andy had taken him under his wing and recognised a loyal and effective henchman when he saw one. Dokes was an intimidating figure at six foot five and nineteen stone of muscle. There weren't many people who would argue with him. But at the heart of it, Dokes was not a violent man. He'd been a teacher in the Ituri province of Congo before the violence started and he had fled. He missed teaching.

He sat back against the moulded plastic and opened his eyes. Rain was lashing the big windows of the ferry terminal, and he could hear the wind whipping around the edges of the building. The sterile, fluorescent lights cast a dim and depressing light over miserable looking passengers sheltering in the building. Niko moved across the room with a purpose. Dokes noted that he looked totally out of place in his dark suit, Italian leather shoes and slicked back jet black hair. It made him think of John Travolta in Pulp Fiction. He made a note that they needed to buy some clothes that made them a little more discreet.

"Cancelled. Storm here for a few hours. They reckon the first ferry might be tomorrow."

Dokes blew on the steaming cup of coffee, a mixture of relief and frustration rippling through him; he hated the sea - it brought back memories of the small, overcrowded boat he had fled to Europe in. Rough seas had filled his nightmares for years. So he was glad not to be venturing onto the ferry in this weather. Yet, he also knew they needed to get to the island and find the Englishman or Andy would 'rip them a whole new orifice' - he'd had to ask Niko what this meant. Still, maybe it gave them some time to find a new wardrobe.

CLIFFS AND DREAMS 1

Day four of their Scottish adventure saw the early morning light pierce the thin embroidered curtains and Jimmy rolled over on the lumpy single mattress, the cheap pine frame creaking under his weight. His eyes were heavy and felt crusted together from the thick fog off another whiskey hangover. After the initial free tasting at the distillery, they had ended up buying a couple of bottles of the local single malt and had continued sampling the produce back at the cottage, their increasingly drunken conversation turning nostalgic and, sharing stories of their adolescence, which had inevitably turned the conversation to Gully and why he had sent them up here. Obviously, part of it was to spread some of his ashes in a place that was important to him, but there was more to it than that. It was clear that it was an attempt at an apology and in some way a final gift to his friends. They had discussed the cottage and what they would do with it. Gully had said it was theirs, but until they heard the will they wouldn't get too carried away. Certainly, it was a nice bolt hole for all of them, but how it would all work out they weren't quite sure. They just needed to decide on where to spread the ashes - overlooking the reef break that Tom had taken them too seemed a good place - it was clearly the wave that Gully had come here for, and Gully had only ever been about the waves. He would like it there.

Jimmy didn't want to open his eyes, but he knew that he

was awake and that no matter what he did he wouldn't be able to drift off back to sleep - years of early morning alarms and a rigid and disciplined existence meant that his body was programmed in a particular pattern. But he couldn't put it off any longer and with great effort he ventured to open his eyes. He could hear the gulls outside, squawking and squabbling. He lay there listening to the sounds of the ocean and the seabirds. Dust motes flittered and floated across the room, caught in a brief searchlight of the morning sunshine, exposed and guilty in their presence. He knew that if he moved he would invariably suffer, his head rattling his brain in a form of self-flagellation.

Jimmy swung his legs out from under the covers and picked up his watch off the bedside table. 6.45am. He got up and walked to the door of the small, whitewashed room, pulling on a sweater as he went. He found Mark already up, sitting in the wing backed chair by a still roaring fire, hunched over a computer on his lap.

"Get any sleep?"

"Sleep's for pussies. There's a tight little onion of a low sitting just off the west coast of Ireland. It's moving north. That priest was right. This could go off."

CLIFFS AND DREAMS 2

The rumble of Mark's flatulence reverberated off the faux leather seat of the van.

"Jesus Mark." Charlie furiously wound-down the passenger window.

"Now, now. No blasphemy please. What would your new friend say?"

The ice-cream van pulled out of the rough gravel driveway, Jimmy swinging the wheel to avoid the now notorious pothole. Charlie stared at the ordinance survey map in his lap as Jimmy pulled up at the crossroads at the top of the lane.

"It looks like…."

"We've got to head south, to that bay there." said Mark, leaning over from the back seat and jabbing his finger at the map. "There's a rock shelf jutting out that could work as a tasty little slab. I had a look at your map last night after all of you slinked off to bed."

"Well, Tom said that we should check here," Jimmy pointed to a small bay on the west coast. "Said, there is a really good point and it'll be protected from the southerly."

"Listen, I'm a fucking professor of geography."

"Fine, we can check it out. We're in no hurry."

Mark lay down on the bench seat in the back, a sudden pang

of nausea washing over him. Jimmy pulled out onto the main road which seemed to dissect the island, and they began their journey across the desolate landscape, passing row upon row of peat trenches, like shallow mass graves that were waiting to be filled, the piles of peat slung up and stacked on the side. The early morning sunshine had moved on and now air was filled with static, the electricity of an impending storm crackling the atmosphere with a dangerous energy. Grey clouds darted across the sky as the strong jet streams ushered them along at altitude. The rumble of the tyres hummed and throbbed below them, filling the silence of their hangovers. A feint waft of petrol fumes filled the small interior as Mark tried to close his eyes and concentrated on not throwing up. Jimmy flicked on the radio and then turned the tuning dial, eventually finding the melodic tones of the shipping forecast.

Mark's agitated tone piped up from the back seat. "Are you trying to send me to sleep?"

"Thought you could do with some!"

"Hey, I've looked at the charts, I've checked the swell heights and the wind. I'm a lecturer in Geography."

"So you've said."

"This fucking dimpity dompety whale song isn't going to tell you anything I haven't already said."

"Dimpety, Dompety?"

"The best I can do. My mind is a little slow this morning."

Charlie and Jimmy smirked at each other. Charlie offered a gentle suggestion, "You reckon it's safe for you to get in the water, Mark? I'm on holiday, I could do without having to perform CPR!"

When they pulled up at the bay on the south of the island they didnt even bother getting out of the van. Onshore winds were whipping in horizontal sheets of rain which hammered the windscreen of the van. From their elevated position in the car park above the beach they could see that there was certainly swell, but it was huge and blown out by the wind.

"Good call, professor." Charlie turned and grinned at Mark.

Pursing his lips and holding his hands up, Mark reclined in the back seat retreating into an acceptance of bad judgement. Jimmy crunched the gears into reverse and the search for surf continued.

After two wrong turnings, one which led them down a rutted track and into a brief confrontation with a less than friendly famers wife, they finally found a narrow lane which took them out to a grassy headland overlooking a deep, wide bay with towering cliffs at either end. The rain was still heavy, and the wind was still blowing from the south as they exited the van and walked towards the edge of the cliff. Further across the bay, they could see that lines of whitewater were filling the bay and the sea looked wild and untamed. However, as they neared the edge of the precipice, they could see that the tall cliffs they were standing on created an element of protection from the worst of the wind, and the swell was wrapping around the headland and forming solid, rideable walls which were breaking beneath them in the lee of the cliff and unfurling into the middle of the bay. There seemed to be a lot of water moving around and the currents looked strong, but the longer they stood there, the more their minds convinced them that the waves below them looked appealing.

"With this wind, I don't think it is going to get much better than this." Jimmy and Charlie turned back to the van, Mark was more hesitant, his hangover and the lack of sleep becoming a raw reality as he contemplated the inhospitable ocean in front of him.

Jimmy giggled in nervous anticipation at the squeals and squawks of Charlie as he pulled on his still damp wetsuit.

Suited and booted, Jimmy threw the keys to Mark as he and Charlie picked up their boards and turned towards the rough goat track cut into the edge of the cliff, which they hoped would help them descend to sea level. Mark sat hunched in the back of the van looking out of the service hatch, his hood pulled up over his head and his damp, cold wetsuit in his hands. Mark caught the keys and lay down on his back with a mournful howl. He quickly sat straight back up and lurched out of the vehicle and, holding the back door to steady himself, he promptly threw up on the grass in front of him.

"See you in there buddy!" Jimmy cackled with laughter as Mark stood bent double with spittle dangling from his chin and being buffeted in the wind. Jimmy turned and disappeared down the goat track, eagerly followed by Charlie.

The track cut a sharp zig zag down the cliff face, with a mixture of roughly cut steps and stoney goat track. The rock was slippery in the rain and a couple of times Charlie almost lost his footing, but after five minutes, the two friends had managed to descend to the lichen covered boulders at the bottom of the cliff. At sea level the swell was much bigger than it had looked from the top of the cliffs, and they could hear a rumble and grind with every passing wave, as their raw power shifted the large boulders beneath them. Like two mountain goats the friends cautiously hopped from rock to rock as they searched for a good entry spot, aware that a slip could be costly in this remote location.

Their descent down the cliff meant that they would have very little paddle out and they were already standing level with what appeared to be the take-off spot furthest up the point. However, as with all point breaks, they had collectively surfed, they were aware that the jump off could be disastrous if timed wrong and even though neither of them voiced their fears, both felt nervous as they ventured into this unknown spot. Jimmy watched a set of waves roll down the point, his senses going into critical mode as he began to appreciate the size of the swell. The set was four waves and two of them had been close to double overhead. Neither of them had been in surf this size or critical in a good few years. As the final set wave passed, there was a lull of energy and Jimmy launched himself off the rock he was standing on, his board skimming across the water. The ocean below him suddenly seemed to sink as the energy of the passing wave left a void, sucking any remaining water back out towards the open ocean. Jimmy felt his fin clip a rock below him. He began to paddle furiously for the middle of the bay and felt the strong current pick him up and take him away from the rocks.

Charlie saw Jimmy launch himself into the water as the final wave passed. After taking a deep breath, he followed suit, using the foam of the passing wave to cushion his landing on the water and keep him floating above the fingers of rock below. He hadn't been in surf this sketchy in a long time, and he could feel his heart racing. The current quickly picked him up and swept him out into the line-up. As he paddled away from the headland and the rocks, he could see another wall of water suddenly stand up as it bent around the headland and began to march towards them. It was getting bigger by the second and he saw Jimmy paddling hard to get over the shoulder before it exploded and potentially throw him back into the rocks. The current was taking Charlie wider across the bay, and he felt comfortable enough to look up and watch Jimmy, who was scratching hard against the water being sucked up the face of the approaching wave. Then suddenly he disappeared up and over the mound of water, missing the white frothing foam ball by a matter of feet. The anger of the ocean seemed to momentarily abate, and Charlie paddled hard to catch up with his friend.

Jimmy sat up on his board to catch his breath.

"Whoo!"

"Wasn't sure you were going to make it.

"Me neither."

The rain was intensifying, falling in heavy drops, flattening out the water and creating a wild and wet playground that was exciting and invigorating - their senses suddenly kicking into overdrive and pushing away any fog of a hangover left from the night before. There was no room for error here and their bodies knew it and responded by going on high alert. Whilst the incoming humps of swell rolled underneath them, the two friends took a moment to look around them, take in the view - the drama of the imposing cliffs and the incredible scenery. Their initial nerves began to subside, and it was replaced with the realisation and thrill of being out in solid surf with no one to share the waves with but each other. They unconsciously sat in silence for a moment and savoured this little slice of time when all the elements came together. The cliffs certainly held off the worst of the wind and the waves were much cleaner in the shadow of the headland, breaking off the point with mechanical consistency. When waves came through, they were large walls of water with a foam ball breaking off the rocks on the point. It didn't look like a steep wave, but the waves were certainly big and powerful and looked like they were offering up clean walls of water to carve out the arcing curves of their chosen pattern.

An explosion of white water further up the headland identified an incoming set. Both men began to paddle deeper, adjusting their position to ensure they weren't caught out in this unknown spot. Jimmy suddenly turned on his board and began paddling towards the rocks. A wall of water rose in front of him and within seconds he was up and screaming down the clean face of a solid overhead wave. Jimmy leant in towards the oncoming wave, finding the rail of his board and letting his speed take him through a graceful bottom turn, bringing him back up towards the feathering lip of the wave.

Jimmy slammed on the breaks, twisting his body and pushing his back foot through to slide the back end of his board out of the lip of the wave, He straightened, arching his back like the surfing idols of his youth and let out a roar of approval that was swallowed but the boom of the crashing waves.

Charlie caught a fleeting sight of Jimmy and a plume of spray before he disappeared back down into the depths of the wave. He turned his attention back to the next set wave. It looked too heavy and sections further down the line were already breaking. What was he doing out here? These waves were monstrous. Maybe there was a time when he wouldn't have thought twice about paddling out here, but the longer he sat here, the more out of shape he felt. Charlie paddled for the safety of the outside and went over a clean section. From the summit of the wave, he could see the third wave of the set approaching. It had good shape and was slightly smaller. For a split second he wasn't sure if he was relieved or disappointed. He paddled towards the breaking wave and felt the wave pick up the tail of his board. Despite the size and power of the wave, it was a mellow and gentle take off, but that was quickly followed by a screaming rollercoaster ride as he tipped into the apex of the wave and he suddenly began to accelerate, chasing his friend towards the shore.

They lasted just over an hour, catching a dozen or so waves and taking a couple of wipeouts too. Jimmy was really going for it, like a man possessed and it reminded Charlie of the boy he had grown up with, fearful of nothing and charging like a man with a death wish. Eventually he pushed a little too hard, taking off very late on a monster of a wave and getting pitched over the falls. Charlie was momentarily worried that his friend wasn't coming back up after quite a long hold down; relief flooded his veins when he saw Jimmys head pop up out of the foam, but his leash had snapped, and his board was being tossed unceremoniously towards the flotsam strewn beach. Jimmy waved at Charlie and began to swim and body surf towards shore and to hopefully rescue his board. The wind and the rain didn't let off and were still very much present by the time Charlie and Jimmy exited the water with a strange mixture of exhaustion and energy. Jimmy's board had miraculously made it to shore in one piece, a small crease on the nose, but no damage of any real significance. The rising tide meant that they were unable to traverse the rocks that lined the base of the headland to the goat track they had climbed down, and they settled for the steps that wound their way up from the beach, and a longer walk back down the headland to the van. The rain and the cold meant that the chat between them was minimal, their sole focus being to get back to the van and to get warm, but they would occasionally stop and look out at the bay and the playground of waves they had just come from, a buzz of energy and satisfaction that they had gone toe to toe with an angry ocean and had come out on top.

Mark had pretty quickly come to the decision that he was not going in the water. He had tried to watch his friends surf, but looking down from the top of the cliffs in the wind and rain on a heavy hangover and severe lack of sleep was too much for him and was making his already fragile stomach cry out in objection. He had retreated to the safety of the van, found an old board sock and curled up on the back seat. It was soothing, listening to the rhythmic patter of the rain on the metal and glass of the van. The rain was hammering the van and the wind was gently rocking the high sided van as it sat on the exposed cliff top. The sound of nature's fury had the desired effect of sending Mark quickly off into a deep sleep full of restless dreams about angry sea Gods and vengeful mermaids. He had seen Gully kissing the girl that Charlie had met….what was her name? Maggie. Gully was kissing Maggie, who was a mermaid, and then she bared her fangs and looked at Mark. She picked up a huge boulder from the bottom of the sea and hurled it at Mark.

BANG. BANG

Mark sat up like a startled hare, his head swivelling maniacally as he tried to locate the sound of the banging. The metal of the side door banged. Mark half let out a scream. Cackling laughter seeped into the van. Through the condensation on the windows of the old van Mark could see two blurred, dark figures dressed in black standing outside. He pulled the rough cloth of the board sock up close to his chest in a cartoonish cower.

The door opened and Charlie's freckled face was grinning from ear to ear.

"Bailed then mate? Probably a good thing. It was fooking massive!"

Charlie turned around and continued talking to Jimmy, exchanging replays of waves they had just ridden, animated and laughing on the adrenaline of the experience they had just had. Mark lowered the board sock and let out a deep breath. The hairs on his arms were standing up and his body was mildly shaking throughout. He took a moment to try to control the panicked beating of his heart. Slowly he began to regain control. His mouth was dry, and he felt unsettled by the dream he had just been having.

The wind was backing off by the time the other two were changed and packed up. They were all keen to make their way back to the cottage for some food, but the rain had intensified, and the ancient wipers of the old van were struggling to win the battle, squeaking a mournful lament with every journey across the misted-up windscreen. It wasn't designed for this weather. Visibility was tricky and Jimmy was hunched over, his nose inches above the wheel as he looked through the demisted bottom half of the windscreen. They turned north off the dirt road which led out to the end of the headland and joined the coastal road. Rain was hitting the dark tarmac and exploding into a million tiny droplets. The van began to accelerate a little before suddenly there was a jolt and a bang Jimmy felt the car become very heavy and lopsided. He swung over to the side of the road, He pulled his hood up and stepped out into the heavy rain to inspect the problem. Immediately he saw the nearside front wheel was in tatters. He glanced back along the road and saw an innocent looking pothole filled with water.

"Shit"

He got back into the van, the damp smell of wet wetsuits making the air inside the car thick and cloying. "Tyre's gone"

"Great". Like a petulant teenager, Mark threw his hands up and slumped back in his seat. "Have we got a spare?

"No."

"No? Why not?"

"We left it so that we could fit all our shit in!"

"Great. Well, have we got a phone?"

"Haven't got mine." Visions of his phone sailing out of the window on the motorway slip-road flashed through his mind. Charlie pulled his own phone out of his jeans pocket.

"No signal."

"Walk up the road. See if you can get a signal." Mark snarled.

"Alright!". Charlie turned on Mark and met his stare. "And if I get any signal, who am I calling?"

They heard the engine before they saw it. A muffled throaty roar coming from the north.

"Think the cavalry has arrived." Jimmy slunk out of the car and pulled his hood up. The other two could just make out his blurred outline through the misted-up windows, standing on the side of the road. A white shape emerged over the brow of the hill and was moving quickly towards them. As it got closer, they realised that the car had markings all over it. It was a police car. Jimmy began waving his arms frantically, and the police car began to slow, before pulling over in front of them. The door opened and black hooded figure appeared.

It turned out that they had flagged down the only policeman on the island, Stuart Ferguson. He phoned the mechanic at the local garage and assured Jimmy that he would come out and change the tyre as soon as possible.

"As you can imagine, he's not that busy." Ferguson stood at the window of the van, the rain cascading down his waterproof kagool. "He'll have it changed in no time and then you boys can head back down to 'nowhere'."

"How do you…?" Charlie began. "Of course. Everyone knows everything around here!"

"Something like that." Ferguson gave a brief chuckle. "Well, I best be off. Got a few things to do."

Mark gave a snort of laughter. "I can't imagine you're too busy around here."

Ferguson fixed him with a stern glare, which caught Mark by surprise as it felt so misplaced. "You'd be surprised." With that he turned his back and was gone, his sleek white police car kicking up an arc of spray as it accelerated off down the empty road. Billy, the bearded local mechanic, turned up twenty minutes later and as promised, changed the tyre and had them on their way with barely three sentences exchanged between them. Jimmy promised to drop into the garage and settle the debt with him before the festival the next day.

DAY 5

(FRIDAY)

REEF

Sleep was sparse for Jimmy that night. Twisted nightmares echoed through his brain in vivid technicolour; the unsettling threat of Deaf Andy ever present in the anxiety that filled his mind. He was overdue the payment now. Well overdue. He was beyond the point of no return. Jimmy rolled onto his back and stared at the white artex ceiling and listened to the growing swell pounding the nearby shore. It sounded big. Tom had been spot-on with his forecast. Jimmy let his mind wander and he visualized perfectly peeling waves, before a surge of anxiety sent a shudder through his body and he turned over onto his side. His body was aching and sore after a week of surfing every day. His muscles had become soft since leaving the marines, and his shoulders and back were seizing up. He got up and began to stretch. He had to find a solution to the problem with Andy. He came to the conclusion that he had two options; he either, made a run for it; escape and evade. Get out of England. Maybe New Zealand. Yeah, New Zealand. Or somehow… he miraculously finds the money, faces the threat head on, begs forgiveness from Andy, lean on their history, ask for some leniency for an old friend… friend was probably pushing it, but something along those lines. Maybe he should talk to Charlie and Mark, explain the situation and sell the cottage? Or they could buy him out of his share of the cottage? What was the cottage worth?

He looked at the figure of a porcelain sheep dog sat on the chest of drawers under the window; the break in the curtains casting a thin shaft of moonlight onto the characterful face of the dog, tongue wagging, not a care in the world. It was the festival tonight and then they would be leaving the next day, Jimmy needed to come up with a plan. He looked at the dog.

"What do you recken eh? Got any bright ideas?"

It didn't offer any advice.

Tom hammered his hand on the door again. Part of him wondered what he was doing, inviting these strangers to surf his secret spot - it could blow up in his face and by next summer he could have half of the British surfing community crawling all over it. But he rarely had company in the water and these lads were friends with Gully and seemed like good folk, so he was willing to take a risk. He would just have to hope that they could keep a secret. He raised his fist one more time, but just as he was about to give one final knock before giving up, the door opened. Jimmy stood in the doorway in just a pair of shorts and a tatty old jumper, one eye was still scrunched shut as he battled to find focus in the first light of the day.

"The reefs on. First light in twenty minutes. Just wondered if any of yous fancied in?"

Jimmy closed his eyes and audibly exhaled as if he had completely forgotten an important meeting. He had barely slept, so the idea of a dawny on a heavy reef in sizable surf did not sound immensely appealing at this moment in time. He opened both eyes and squinted at Tom standing on the threshold.

"So, we've got five minutes? You want a coffee first? For the road?"

Ten minutes later Tom's truck was pulling away from 'Nowhere', with his three new surfing buddies following in the van, furiously fuelling their bodies with bananas and coffee. Gully's ashes sat on the dashboard, front and centre. He was going to witness them surf 'Gully's reef' and then they would lay him to rest overlooking the break.

The ocean looked nothing like it had when they had sat eating sandwiches and sipping coffee a couple of days before, its mood had completely changed. Under the weak, pale white light of the early morning, the water sat like a slate-grey slab of concrete, mirroring the early morning clouds above. Tom silently passed a small pair of binoculars to Jimmy, like they were on some sort of military exercise. Through the binoculars Jimmy could see a wave exploding over the reef, reeling, snapping and spitting like some sort of angry cobra. Light offshore winds were grooming the waves and allowing the odd set wave to barrel across the reef below. With a smile, he passed the binoculars down the line, and as Charlie raised them to his eyes Jimmy and Tom were already turning to the cars to get suited up. After missing out on the surf the day before, Mark was amped and frothing to go.

"Fucking hell!" Charlie brought the binoculars down from his face. "I'm not paddling out in that!" He scrambled to catch up with the others.

The paddle was about a mile out to the reef, and the four of them stuck close together, chatting in excited tones as the adrenaline coursed through their veins. Charlie was visibly anxious, his face pale in the dawn light. As they drew closer Tom gave them a brief overview of the wave, where to take off, the two rocks that became exposed as the tide dropped, the different sections. As they paddled through the channel and looked into the eye of the barrel the jovial banter and camaraderie disappeared and was replaced by a steely focus that came with the realisation that they were about to surf a critical wave a mile offshore.

It was big, there was no doubt about that. It wasn't the height of the wave as such but the thickness of the lip and the heaviness of the wave. There was a hell of a lot of water in that lip, and if you got caught it would be like having Mike Tyson land a hook right into your temple. The butterflies in their stomachs were going berserk, the adrenaline spiking.

Tom paddled confidently towards the peak and the others filed in behind him, Charlie coming last, nervous and apprehensive. A set reared up in the open ocean and began heading towards them. Tom hooted. "See that, boys! Now we're talking. I've not seen it like this for a long time." He turned and began paddling with long deep strokes. The wave began to stand tall, like a mountain of water and Tom began to paddle more furiously, scratching to get into the wave, and then he was gone. The others could feel the raw power of the ocean as the wave passed underneath them. Jimmy watched Tom fly down the face of the wave, crouching low and leaning into the curved face of the wave, grabbing his rail to help him hold his line on his backhand side. If yesterday had been intense, it was clearly just a warmup for this, the main event. Jimmy clenched his jaw and moved into position. He had priority next. He had never been one to back down, but seeds of doubt were creeping in and he felt nervous. The next wave approached, and a calm settled on him - it was as if he could hear Gully's voice in the line-up calling him in and hooting him. A smile split his face and he began paddling for the wave. It was moving too fast though and tipped him vertical, pitching him over the front of his board and into a freefall to the flat water beneath. He hit the water hard, and then got sucked into the vortex of the wave, as the water swept him back up into the lip and pitched him with all its might into the reef. He felt the rocks at the bottom as he was bounced, but just about managed to right himself and swim to the surface. He quickly looked around for his board and saw it was just a few feet away, but the next wave was breaking just a few metres away and so he dived as deep as he could and felt the fingers of the wave reach down to catch him. He could feel his leash stretch and groan as the wave passed over him and he came back up spluttering and gasping. He pulled his board towards him and shuffled on and immediately began paddling for the shoulder. As he slipped over an open face, Tom passed him, paddling back out to the line-up, a huge grin beaming across his face.

"Gully said you were a kamikaze motherfucker. And he was right. That one was a monster." His laughter cackled across the water. Jimmy smiled. That sounded so like Gully. But as he watched Tom paddle away towards the peak a knot twisted in his stomach - years of training and instinct were telling him that something wasn't quite sitting right. He couldn't put his finger on what it was, and with the heaviness of the surf he was in, now was not the time to try and think about that - he needed to concentrate, so that he did not get pummelled by another wave. He would come back to it later. He paddled after Tom and the knot in his stomach began to fade.

Mark was stroking into a solid sized wave as Jimmy reached the line up. It had good shape to it, and as he slid down the face of the wave, he arched his back as he leaned into his bottom turn. Jimmy had always admired Mark's style on a board. Mark had style in everything he did - it was one of the reasons that all the girls fancied him and all the boys envied him. As a goofy footer (left foot at the back of the board), this wave was perfect for him - breaking from right to left and reeling along the reef. He cut soulful arcs into the face of the wave, making it look lazy and casual, when it was anything but. Where Jimmy was aggressive and violent in the way he surfed, with harsh snapbacks and always looking to get his fins through the lip of the wave, Mark was poetic and graceful in the lines he drew on the wave. Jimmy was level with Charlie and Tom now, and he could see Charlie looking nervous and hesitant. He had never been that keen for big surf; yesterday had probably been as big as he was comfortable in, and the power of this wave was making him nervous and hesitant - something you could not afford to be in this sort of situation. It was something that Gully had always ridiculed Charlie for and caused some tension between them. Tom was egging him on and encouraging him to have a go at the approaching wave, but Charlie pulled back, letting the wave pass under him. He paddled for the next wave, looking down into the gaping jaws of the monster, the vertiginous drop before him, again he pulled back. He splashed his hands in the water before moving out of the take-off zone and paddling towards the shoulder.

Jimmy shouted over to him. "Charlie? You ok?"

Charlie pulled up and sat on his board on the safety of the shoulder and put on a brave face. "Yeah, just gonna sit here for a sec and get a feel for it. It's fucking intense."

Tom, Jimmy and Mark traded waves for the next half an hour, each of them taking off deeper and deeper as they began to dial into the wave and how it worked. Jimmy managed to get into a deep barrel and got spat out into the channel to the hoots of the others. Not to be out done, Tom paddled a little further inside. Another mountain of a wave approached, and Tom stroked hard into it. It jacked up and Tom was a little late in his take off, catching air before somehow managing to land the board and setting a line down the wave. The wave curled and hollowed; sitting on the shoulder, Charlie had the perfect view as Tom tucked low and stalled his acceleration by dipping his hand into the face of the wave, acting as a brake and slowing him down. The lip of the wave cascaded over him, enveloping him in the eye of the curl before Tom released the break and accelerated down the line and out from behind the curtain of water. The boys hooted. This was turning into one of the best sessions they had ever had.

The waves continued. The period was high, and the power of the wave was both intimidating and exhilarating. Charlie was just plucking up the courage to have another go, when Tom paddled into a wave that was so big it seemed to block out the light of the morning sun. The guy was a lunatic and was clearly revelling in showing these tourists how it was done.

But this wave was morphing and shifting in its shape, and Tom miscalculated the take-off; the lip pitched him, and his board flew out from beneath him. Tom free-falled into the pit of the wave and was immediately swallowed by a booming ball of white water. There was an eerie moment of silence as they searched for signs that he was ok. The foam ball passed, and Tom popped up in the boiling froth of the impact zone. His board was snapped in two and he was waving his arm to indicate that something was wrong. Fortunately, it was the last wave of the set and Jimmy reacted first, paddling into the impact zone and pulling Tom onto his own board and clear of the danger. In the channel They assessed the damage; as Tom had fallen, the board had flipped, and he had landed on the fins on the underside of the board. The impact had opened a deep gash on the left side of Tom's ribs, the wetsuit was sliced open, and blood was streaming out of his side. Despite the obvious pain he must have been in, Tom was smiling. He tried to laugh, but the probability of a broken rib or two curtailed the laughter and the noise that erupted from him was more like the howl of a wolf.

Between the three of them, they managed to paddle, drag, pull him ashore - taking it in turns to swim whilst Tom lay on their boards. It was a long paddle back to the shore, but fortunately the reef took out most of the power of the breaking waves and the water became relatively calm the closer they got to shore.

They stumbled onto the narrow strip of sand and Tom collapsed onto his back. Mark and Jimmy lay down and sucked in the air, exhausted from the exertion of the paddle. Charlie unstrapped his board and moved over to where Tom was lying, a crimson stain already spreading across the white sand.

"Here, let me have a look."

"I'll be alright!" Tom gave a less than convincing chuckle and tipped his head back and he gritted his teeth as a stab of pain ripped through his torso.

"I'm an A and E doctor. Let me have a look." Tom didn't resist again and let Charlie assess the damage. "Let's get you up to the van. I have a medical kit up there." They gently pulled Tom to his feet and helped him up the path to where the cars were parked. They cut his ripped wetsuit away to reveal a deep laceration about five inches long running parallel to his ribs.

"Nasty." Mark was glugging some water as he watched his brother do what he did best. He'd always been envious of how calm Charlie was in critical situations like this.

Charlie gently prodded and pressed around the wound, Tom grimacing and groaning every now and then. "I think you may have busted a few ribs, but it doesn't look too bad. Cut is pretty clean. But you should probably go to hospital."

"Hospital is on the mainland. I can't go there. It's the festival!" Tom tried another chuckle and ended up coughing. The convulsion of his torso sent a ripple of excruciating pain through him, and he howled again.

"Well, it will need stitching. I can do it here, but I don't have any anaesthetic, so it's going to hurt like hell."

"I was in the paras. I've had worse."

Jimmy poured iodine on the wound as Tom took a healthy swig of whiskey they had found in his truck, before Charlie carefully stitched the cut closed. Mark and Jimmy got changed and brought a towel and dry clothes for Tom. Charlie gave Tom some painkillers and then they lay on the grass over-looking the reef and let the sun warm them, giving Tom some time for the painkillers to kick in. The three friends had been in situations like this before but admired the toughness of the priest. He was a tough man, there was no doubt and as they lay in silence in the sunshine, listening to the crashing waves on the reef, the knot in Jimmy's stomach began to emerge again. He was a strange one, this priest. An ex-para, who had run away to a remote Scottish island to become a priest. What was he hiding? What was he running from? Jimmy felt like it was a familiar story. There was something Tom wasn't telling them. He had secrets for sure, but something wasn't quite sitting right with him. And that comment about Gully when they were in the surf, and how he had talked about Jimmy surfing.... Did he know Gully better than he was letting on? Maybe he was just being paranoid.

Mark drove Tom's truck back to the chapel before they said their farewells. Charlie assured Tom that he would pop in later that day, before the festival, and check on his injury. It was still early, and the three friends were exhausted but feeling alive from the intense morning they had just had. They needed food and some sleep if they were going to make it to the festival that night.

As they climbed out of the van Jimmy noticed Gully's ashes still sitting on the dashboard. In their euphoria of the surf and the emergency of Tom's injury, they had forgotten to scatter them. He picked up the tube and carried it inside. They would do it tomorrow.

FIRE AND WHISKEY

It was already dark by the time the three friends set off for the town. They could feel that something had changed in the atmosphere; there was a pulse of electricity throbbing in the air, and Maggie had been right in her warning not to drive - the side of the road approaching the high street was bumper to bumper with vehicles of all kinds. People had clearly come from the surrounding islands and the mainland - there was no way that there was this many people on the island. A dense blackness sat heavily over the surrounding fields and the ocean beyond the town. The little light being emitted from the cluster of houses danced across the windshields and the metallic sides of the vehicles they passed.

They could hear shouts and cheers from the area surrounding the pub, and as they came around the final bend in the road, they could see that there were hundreds of people filling the narrow street of the town. It seemed that most of those people were carrying paraffin torches, densely packed together and laughing jovially and uninhibitedly. It was at this moment that Jimmy came to the realisation that this was not the atmosphere of just some whiskey festival put on by the islanders to drum up some tourism and trade, this had a densely ritualistic feel, it was almost threatening, and he felt the hairs on the back of his neck stand up.

Charlie pulled out the bottle of local whiskey he had stashed in the deep pockets of his parka jacket. The cork popped with the familiar, warming sound.

"When in Rome and all that."

Charlie took a glug of the amber liquid before passing it to Jimmy. The strong peaty odour of the whiskey filled Jimmy's nostrils as he brought it up to his lips. He took a generous dram out of the bottle and held it in his mouth. He liked to let it sit there, letting the burn of the liquor fill his mouth before swallowing it and letting the warmth spread to the core of his body. The core of his body still felt cold from the surf that morning and he could feel the whiskey radiating warmth within. As he passed the bottle to Mark a horn sounded further down the street; like the hounds being called for the hunt, heads turned and there was a sudden murmur in the crowd. There was a surge of movement in the densely packed street, people beginning to stumble and stride towards the sound of the horn, like a dam opening, the movement gathered momentum as people broke from their revelry and began to flow like the ocean that surrounded them, moving purposefully down the street to the fires beyond.

The three friends were pressed in, shoulder to shoulder with the revellers and with no choice but to move with the crowd. The atmosphere was jovial, but since the horn had sounded there seemed to be an intensity in the air - a sudden focus. There was lots of shouting and cheering, with snippets of conversations being caught on the light sea breeze.

"A big one this year"

"Ay, don't you ken it?"

"Pass us a dram!"

"Sing us a song!"

The man on Jimmy's left was jostling and joking with someone on his other side, his elbow catching Jimmy in the shoulder. The man turned to him and apologised, "Oh, sorry wee man." The hood of his jacket was pulled up and as Jimmy looked into the darkness beneath, he could see the man's face was covered in Celtic patterns of paint. Despite his jovial nature and the wide smile he gave Jimmy, it was an intimidating site - full of menace and mystery.

"What's that?" Charlie was pointing up ahead where a dark shadow loomed.

"That is our ship to valhalla my friend!"

Somewhere in the crowd ahead, a drumbeat began, a determined rhythm which the crowd began to march to in step. The crowd around them began to chorally shout a deep guttural "Hah" at regular intervals within the drum's rhythm. A shiver spread up Jimmy's spine as the sounds reverberated through his body, his friends grinning at him with the excitement that began to infectiously spread through the swarming crowd. Charlie joined in the tribal shouts that accompanied the drumbeat, and Mark whooped, raising the bottle of whiskey in his hand, spraying those around him with the fire water. As the crowd began to reach the end of the street, they crossed a tarmac road and through a five-bar gate in the stone wall to a grassy field that led down to the dunes and the north Atlantic ocean.

They could clearly see the 'ship' now, a hulking replica of an old Viking longboat hewn from scraps of wood, giving it a rough and jagged profile. It stood erect and proud, propped up by long planks of wood which jutted out, wedging into the muddied ground and giving the impression of ghostly oars being pulled by the spirits of the islander's ancestors. The islanders surrounded the ship creating a circle of paraffin torches, the drum beat continued, and the crowd swayed back and forth in a relentless pulse, chanting the tribal call to the spirits of the island. The effect was both intimidating and mesmerising, and the three English friends found themselves in the midst of the crowd moving and chanting with those around them. They passed the bottle of whiskey and felt the fire burning within them.

Suddenly the drum beat quickened before abruptly stopping.

The crowd stilled and parted at the bow end of the ship. The silhouette of a man emerged. Backlit by the moon, he wore a headdress of what looked like shells and driftwood. Two curled rams' horns protruded from the sides of his head. As he moved forward, the light from the torches picked out the features of his heavily painted face, and the three friends recognised Stuart Ferguson - the policeman they had met in the pub earlier in the week and then again on the side of the road. A hush descended as Ferguson climbed aboard the make-shift boat.

"The sun has set, sinking into the ocean. Fire and water colliding and leaving us in darkness. And now the time has come to pay our respects to the spirits of our home and light the fires to the world beyond ours. Feel the earth beneath you, the earth our ancestors delivered to us. Breath the air around you and taste the salt of the ocean on your lips. See the fires that light the night sky and fill your hearts. Swallow the spell of the whiskey in your hands - the product of *our* earth, *our* air, *our* ocean and *our* fire. The water of life. The uisge-beatha. Let us unite as a clan and make our offering to the spirits of the islands, paying homage to those who guide us, protect us and lead us into the next life."

The crowd erupted into a deafening roar. Not taking his eyes off the spectacle before him, Mark leant across and whispered to Jimmy.

"What do you reckon mate?"

Jimmy looked at his friend, raised his eyebrows in a confounded gesture.

"What the fuck is going on?!"

Mark smirked. A brief connection. For a moment they were teenagers again. He missed that. Then it was gone; the moment broken, and they were standing there in a crowd of drunk and pent up celts, out of their depth and it felt like they were treading water.

Ferguson stepped down from the boat and a group of burly local men moved towards it, removing the planks which were propping the boat up. The mournful wail of some bagpipes filled the air; haunting and comforting at the same time. With surprising ease, the boat was lifted into the air and began to move across a sea of people, as the crowd turned towards the sand dunes at the bottom of the field and began to move slowly towards the beach and the ocean beyond.

******

Duncan watched from the back of the crowd as Ferguson made his little speech to the islanders. He mused how Ferguson had always loved the whole performance of it all, but Duncan had never bought into the mystique of the Teine Uisge-beatha offering, seeing it as just a load of bullshit for small minded insular communities stuck in a load of dead history. He was here now. He had bigger plans, he was living in the modern world and looking to the future. But the festival did serve a purpose - it kept the community together, tight knit and protective of its own with a shared sense of commonality.

Perhaps he just didn't have it in his blood, only being of a second-generation family in the islands. Those whose families had lived in the islands for many generations were wary of accepting outsiders, and a family was never really considered a local until it had lived on the islands for at least five generations. But it didn't bother Duncan - he had made his mark and found his role on the island. The locals had learned to accept him once he began to put systems in place to earn them bucket loads of money; working the land was a hard life and although the export of local whiskey brought in money to the island, there was only so much to go around, meaning that many of the younger generations had been forced to leave the islands and move to the mainland in search of work. So, the community had gradually accepted that they were willing to overlook their localism if it meant that they didn't have to worry about money for the rest of their lives, and their children could remain close to the family home. But many of them wondered if they had sold their souls to the devil when they had signed up to the plans of Duncan MacFarlane.

Duncan caught sight of Maggie across the other side of the circle. Her face casting in and out of shadow in the flickering light of the torches. An uncomfortable knot twisted in his stomach. The knot of rejection. He tried to suppress the bubbles of anger floating up through his body; anger was an unhealthy emotion which clouded judgement. Firstly, the Englishman, Gully, had come between them and now he watched as Christian MacIntosh stood next to her along with some of the boys from the distillery. He was probably smarming all over her with a hand on her arm here, an arm around her shoulders there, a press of his cock against pert arse as the crowd surged. The knot in his stomach twisted a little tighter. Christian would try it on with anything in a skirt, but he'd always had a thing for Maggie. It had never bothered Duncan before; when Duncan had been with Maggie, she had been in love with him. He knew it. She had never had eyes for anyone else. Then Gully had turned up and it had all disintegrated. Now Maggie hated him and the thought of someone else.... Christian's hands all over her filled him with an irrational rage which manifested itself in a malicious sneer. His thoughts jumped to the other Englishmen on the island - Gully's friends, and a burning inferno of hatred began to boil and bubble inside of him. But what had they done? Nothing. It was hatred through association. He buried the irrational emotion. Christian however....Perhaps there might come a time when he might deal with Christian, but right now Duncan had other things to deal with - once the next shipment had been shifted Christian would get his full attention.

GHOSTS

They could hear the shouts and laughter mingling with the amplified trance music further down the beach, the traditional sounds of the bagpipes and the sprightly jigs of local musicians having long since been drowned out as the younger crowd gradually took hold of the festivities; the rich amber glow of the beach fire lighting up the centre of the party like an ancient beacon.

As Charlie, Mark and Jimmy mingled on the beach they each began to have recollections of that night ten years ago when Charlie had disappeared, and their world had imploded. The beach party, the fires, the music and the drink all seemed a little too familiar, and it was like Gully had done this deliberately. None of them mentioned how they were feeling, but each of them felt the same way, and it was uncomfortable. Charlie sat on the sand as the other two went off to find some more drinks.

"Here." Maggie appeared out of the darkness like a ghost and sat down next to Charlie on the dune. He could feel the nerves seeping through every pore in his body; self-doubt filling every cavity, as she sat familiarly close to him.

"Oh, Hey!" Charli fractionally shifted his position on the sand, just enough to create a sheaf of air between their bodies; even though she had sat down next to him, he felt rude being so close to her. She pulled out a small half bottle of whiskey from the inside of her jacket and handed it to him whilst she dug around in her other pockets and managed to produce two small glass tumblers. Charlie looked at her, amazed at her resourcefulness.

"I've been looking for you for ages. This....now, this you've got to drink this out of a proper glass. Always come prepared." She handed him a glass and took the bottle back from him. "Now this, this is special. I don't just pull this out for anyone you know. This is a Teaninich forty three year old ... rare."

Charlie looked at her, amused by her mildly drunk enthusiasm. She was flirting with him, which felt good - it felt more than good. But there was a nagging feeling lingering in his heart; an irrational feeling of guilt and deceit. He needed to put those thoughts aside. He was a free man. Sarah had gone. She had left him. But there was something else, and he couldn't quite put his finger on it. Maybe it was the feeling of the ghost of Gully lingering. Maybe he was just paranoid, but something didn't feel quite right.

Maggie uncorked the stopper on the bottle, took the glass from his hand and poured a generous dram before handing it back to him and pouring her own.

"You seem very passionate about it."

Her eyes twinkled with mischief. Maggie looked at him and let her face settle into an authoritative and serious expression. "This isn't just any whiskey. This was distilled in 1975 by my friend's father. It was bottled by his daughter, my friend, last year."

"And you're sharing it with me because...?"

"Because....you're fit and sexy and I want to sleep with you." Maggie fixed him with a serious stare. A momentary silence hung in the air as Charlie struggled to articulate some sort of response. Her bluntness catching him off guard. Maggie's deadpan broke into a lopsided grin, and she let out a confident peal of laughter, before taking control again. She pointed at his glass.

"Ok take a whiff. Get your nose in there."

Charlie tentatively lowered his nose into the glass and inhaled. He quickly withdrew from the glass, coughing and spluttering as he tried to keep the glass level and not spill any. Maggie laughed - a musical sound that filled Charlie with warmth.

"So, what am I meant to smell?"

"Don't be so tough with it. Be gentle." Maggie grinned and looked at him with her big brown eyes. "Like you're caressing a woman!"

"This really is a seduction." Charlie was finding it hard not to fall under this girl's spell.

She took a light delicate whiff of the whiskey. "Gentle. See. Give it a swirl and gentle again." She briefly held it to her nose again. "And you should get hints of oranges and caramel."

Charlie copied her actions, feeling clumsy and awkward. "Smells a bit herby."

"Yeah. Right. That's good. That's right. Now take a sip. Just a small one and hold it in your mouth."

Charlie let the pungent whiskey swill around before he held it at the back of his mouth, the warmth of the liquor seeping into the taste buds of his tongue, a temporary anaesthesia before the rich peaty tang of the firewater flooded his senses.

"Now swallow. "Maggie gave a soft giggle of delight and lay down on the sand next to him.

The muted sounds of revelry wafted over the dunes towards them, mixing in with the regular beat of the crashing waves and offering a comforting soundtrack to the intimacy of the moment.

The sky was peppered with stars, just like how Charlie always imagined a planetarium would be. It reminded him of home and the days growing up with his friends in Cornwall. He thought of Gully and wondered what his friend would have made of this adventure. He lowered himself onto the sand and lay down next to Maggie. He could feel the warmth of her body pressing against his and he felt a wave of euphoria wash over him, a giddiness that brought back memories of the early, clumsy courting of teenage lust.

"Pretty amazing."

"Aye."

"People always say, don't they, that we all look at the same sky. But we don't really do we? I mean….I don't think I have ever seen so many stars."

"People just say that in old soppy rom-coms don't they?"

"Probably."

Suddenly Maggie was on top of him, and he could feel her hot whiskey breath as she leaned in and kissed him. Her full lips, soft and spicey from the whisky, found his, and lingered momentarily before her teeth gently clamped his bottom lip and gave it a playful tug. She pulled away, hair framing her elfin features, and looked at him.

"You're a dark horse, Charlie Watson from England."

Charlie was caught off guard. 'Watson'? How did she know his surname? He looked at her a little confused. "How do you know my name?"

Without any hesitation, Maggie took the empty glass out of his hand and stood up. "We know everything around here! Come on!"

Charlie lay on the sand looking up at her, her long dark hair gently blowing away from her face in the light offshore wind.

"Where are we going?"

"I want to show you something."

Charlie watched Maggie's retreating form as she climbed the headland path at the end of the beach, silhouetted against the light of the moon to the north. Island life had bred a built-in fitness into her and Charlie was feeling like an old man - the last few days of surfing had taken out most of the energy in his legs.

"Come on! We're almost there."

He began to run, chasing her like two teenagers at a beach party.

"I feel like I'm in 'Jaws'".

"I'm not skinny dipping in there. It's fucking freezing!"

Maggie stopped. They were at the top of the headland, standing on an exposed bluff, looking out at the expanse of the northern Atlantic Ocean. The mood of the sea was calm with a small swell creating corduroy lines as far as the eye could see. The moonlight twinkling off the rippled surface - it was incredibly beautiful.

"Wow."

"I know. Amazing, isn't it? On a night like this, when there's no wind or rain, it's my favourite place in the whole world. Not that I've seen much of the rest of the world."

"I'd say this is pretty special by any standards. You bring all the boys here do you?!"

"What are you saying? That I'm a slut?"

Charlie was taken aback by the way she responded to what he thought was a jovial tone. "What? No. I just…"

"I'm only teasing you. I've only ever brought one boy up here."

"Oh?"

A moment lingered. Neither of them sure who would speak

next.

"Gully."

Charlie's head whipped around, and he looked at her profile as she looked out at the sea. "You and he…?"

"For a while. Yeah. But it didn't work out."

"Oh." Charlie could feel the hairs on the back of his neck standing up. The ghost of Gully making his presence felt again. Was that why Gully sent him up here? Was he trying to make amends for Charlotte Westley? Maggie quickly changed the subject.

"And look, see that?"

Maggie was pointing out to the northwest. Charlie could just make out a rhythmic, pulsing light, flicking in the middle of the ocean.

"That's Eilean Mor. The lighthouse there is…..well, the people around here are scared shitless of it. No one goes out there anymore. No one lives in the lighthouse. It's all done electronically these days. Remotely, you know?"

"Why? Why are people so scared of it?"

"Legend has it that, around the turn of the century, the three lighthouse keepers that lived there just disappeared. Poof. Gone"

"Shit."

"Yeah. Apparently, when people turned up at the lighthouse, because no one could get hold of them, their dinner was sat half eaten on the table, their coats were still on their hooks, and people were like….what the fuck? Where the fuck are they?"

"Maybe they just got washed off the island in a big storm?"

"Maybe. The logbook at the lighthouse said the sea was dead

calm that night though."

"Maybe it was vampires…..like the Lost Boys!"

"Don't fucking joke. Everyone thinks it was the spirits. The spirits of Celtic seamen lost at sea. Anyway, people stay away from this part of the coast - gives them the heebie jeebies. That's why no one but Gully wanted my Grans cottage. That's why the church was built on the headland - to keep the spirits at bay."

Charlie looked about, taking in the magical vista under the light of the moon. He had been fortunate enough to travel to some incredible places in the world, but it always surprised him how magnificent Britain could be when all the elements came together - it didn't happen often, which is perhaps why it made it all the more special. And, as if on cue Charlie felt a gust of wind on his back and a few specks of rain. He turned and looked to the sky to see a dark, angry mass rolling towards them from the mainland.

"Think we are going to get caught out."

Bigger raindrops began to fall and there was the distant rumble of thunder. Charlie looked down at the cove below them and saw the outline of a building set back from the beach. It wasn't much, but it would perhaps keep them dry.

"Come on, down here."

Maggie turned to look at where Charlie was heading, but before she could stop him he was off down the path.

"Wait, Charlie….You can't…"

As ever in the Outer Hebrides, the weather was as volatile and unpredictable as it gets. By the time Charlie had reached what turned out to be a small stone outbuilding with a corrugated iron roof, the rain was hammering down. Maggie was just a few metres behind him.

"Charlie, you can't go in there."

There was another angry growl of thunder, closer this time.

"You want to stand out here?"

A sudden flash of lightning illuminated the sky, lighting up the front of the building. It was like the festival had truly summoned the spirits. They could hear squeals of the revellers further up the beach as the rain began to fall. There was a large garage style double door made of corrugated iron facing the sea. A rusted padlock stopped any intruders entering the building. Charlie moved around to the back of the building. A small, weather-beaten wooden door provided an alternative entrance. Charlie tried the door handle. It was locked. The rain was coming down very heavily now and the wind was picking up swirling around them with ever increasing power. His clothes were soaked, and he was having to plant his feet in the sand and earth beneath him in an effort not to be blown over. He took off his parka and gave it to Maggie in an effort to keep her warm and dry. Charlie looked at the ground around him,

Maggie shouted from beneath the parka, "What are you doing?"

"We have to get out of this weather." Charlie picked up a stone from beside the path and approached the door, before smashing one of the small, painted out window frames on the door with a single well directed blow.

"Charlie, no!"

Charlie pulled up his sleeve and reached inside, being careful not to cut himself on the remaining shards of glass protruding from the frame of the window. He found the latch and opened the door. He turned to Maggie and ushered her inside. She hesitated, looking decidedly against the idea of breaking and entering, despite the ferocity of the weather. A roar of thunder overhead, followed by another violent crack of lightning, made her decision for her and she hurried inside. Charlie followed her and closed the door. Despite the thick stone walls, Charlie could feel the force of the wind slamming into the small building like a physical object. Inside, the noise of the wind was muted, but the corrugated sheets amplified the splatter of the rain creating a cacophony of sound, and the wind whistled through the joints and cracks of the building, threatening to split it open and whisk it away.

It was dark inside and Charlie looked for a light switch.

"We shouldn't be here."

"I can pay to replace the window. We're too far from anywhere. We need to find shelter, sit it out and then we can leave and sort it all out with whoever owns this place. Who owns this place?"

Just as he finished the sentence, he found a light switch and turned it on. A single, bare bulb hung suspended from the ceiling in the middle of the room. It's pale, white light illuminating the damp, dank, whitewashed room. Around the edge, on the bare concrete floor were stacked metal drums, like beer kegs. The lids were sealed with what looked like some sort of moulded plastic.

Maggie looked about, anxiety oozing out of every pore in her body. "We shouldn't be here. Shit."

The deluge of rain was hammering against the corrugated iron roof giving the impression that it was going to cave in at any minute. It was almost deafening and made it hard to hear.

"What? What's wrong? What's in these do you reckon?"

Maggie moved to the door and opened it to see if the weather had abated at all, and to check to see if anyone was coming. Without a second invitation the wind flung the door open and smashed it against the wall, the few remaining shards of glass in the already broken pane exploding out in a glittering spray.

The intensity of the storm seemed substantially less than moments ago, but it sounded ten times worse under the iron sheets on the roof. It still looked raging and violent. Maggie closed the door.

"Listen, Charlie, we've got to get out of here. I don't think being in a building with a metal roof in a thunderstorm is a great idea. And, besides, the guy that owns this….he will not be happy at all that we're here. Especially you."

"I'll speak to him. I'm sure he'll understand. I can pay for the windowpane."

"Please, Charlie. We need to leave. Now."

He looked at her. There was a fear in her eyes which was unmistakable. He hesitated, unsure of where this reaction had come from.

"Sure. Ok….. Let's go."

Maggie moved towards the exit, turned off the light and opened the door. She stopped on the threshold and looked out into the darkness. Charlie was curious about what had spooked her, but now was clearly not the time to ask. Satisfied that they weren't being watched, she moved out of the building, Charlie following. She closed the door and moved swiftly off into the night. Her sudden anxiety was unsettling him, he could sense her panic and stayed silent. They came to a fork in the path and Charlie began to take the one leading up the hill towards the main road. Maggie grabbed the sleeve of his shirt.

"No. This way."

She led them off to the right. Down another path which appeared to drop down and hug the coastline.

"There's a beach path. It runs all up the coast, all the way to the distillery. It'll be safer."

A little confused and mildly alarmed, Charlie duly followed.

NAILED

The flames of the fire were flickering in and out of focus. Mark was finding it hard to bring his hand up to his mouth so that he could smoke the cigarette. The world tilted. He overcorrected and had to work overtime to remain sitting upright. The whiskey had hit him hard, and he realised he hadn't really eaten that day. That together with an intense surf on the reef meant he was struggling to hold the booze. Where was Jimmy and Charlie?

"Woah. You ok there?"

A blond girl. Appeared on the sand next him. She was familiar. The barmaid. Kelly. Kayleigh. K…

"Kelsie."

Mark raised his index finger in the sign language version of 'I knew that.'

"Wondered if I might pinch one of your fags?"

Kelsie tilted her head coquettishly and beamed at him in mock flirtation.

"Sure."

Mark managed to find the packet of cigarettes in his jacket pocket and passed them to her.

"Got a light."

Mark laughed and pointed at the fire. Kelsie chuckled at his childish drunken behaviour. She had seen a lot of drunks, what with growing up in a pub. It was part of life.

"Here."

Mark flicked his zippo lighter open and offered her the light. She cupped her hand around his. It was soft and delicate. As she leaned in, the sea breeze caught her light perfume, pushing tendrils of peach and citrus towards him. She inhaled deeply, and then again, letting the tip of the cigarette pulse in the darkness. She let out the smoke in a controlled manner, watching it being taken on the strong breeze.

"Are you ok?"

"Uh-huh."

Suddenly some thick globules of rain pattered the sand around them. The fire hissed, and Kelsie's cigarette was extinguished.

"Shit"

She looked up accusingly at the sky as the rain drops began to fall more heavily.

"Think it might be time to find some shelter. Follow me!"

Kelsie sprung to her feet and pulled Mark up onto his feet. Sher strained under his weight, and he staggered into her. Their faces were only inches away from each other, but he was finding it hard to bring her face into focus.

"Come to the pub. I'll get you some water."

All around them the melee of people was beginning to take flight from the beach. The wind was gusting, and the fire was hissing its discontent.

Mark turned and unsteadily followed Kelsie's lithe form along the path in the dunes that led back to the town.

******

"You're soaked to the bone. We should get you out of those wet clothes."

Mark was shaking. He couldn't tell whether that was because

he was cold or whether the whole building was shaking in the ferocity of the storm. Kelsie was leaning over one of the barrels in the cellar of the pub. With one practiced blow she hammered the tap into the fresh barrel. She stood up and looked at Mark.

Mark was drunk. He knew that. But he hadn't quite realised how drunk he was, and this overtly forward seduction routine was making him feel unsteady and a little nauseous. It was like he was in some uncontrollable dream.

Suddenly she was there. Her face millimetres from his. He could feel her soft breath and smell that peach and citrus. She pressed her lips hard against his, her tongue parting his mouth. It was powerful and hungry.

"I want you to fuck me. Here. Now."

She was a little young. But the drink was making his decisions now and the press of her perfectly formed breasts against his wet chest was beginning to pump his blood south. Mark's hand moved up the soft flesh of her back, it felt rippled and the small hairs on her skin were standing on end. He could sense her excitement. He unclipped her bra in one, swift, movement. Kelsie looked at him and bit her bottom lip. Suddenly Mark turned her round and pulled down her elasticated hareem trousers, the soft white flesh of her pert buttocks reflecting the harsh light of the single bulb. As she bent forward over one of the beer barrels, she groped behind her in search of Mark, desperate, like some withdrawing addict. He entered her. He could feel her wetness and it aroused him more. He thrust hard and she moaned like a cat purring. Mark began to rhythmically thrust her from behind, his gnarled hands clamped onto her bare hips. His head swirled but he could feel himself winning the war with the alcohol coursing through his veins. They settled into a frantic and desperate rhythm, before Mark pulled away, aware that he didn't have a condom on; his heart rate was high and his breathing heavy. She pulled him towards her and raised her leg around his waist, pressing him towards her with a vice like grip. Her mouth found his and her teeth clamped his bottom lip. He lifted her, but in his drunken state he had overcorrected and stumbled, his body weight slammed her into the wall. She let out a squeal and Mark responded, thrusting harder and faster, pounding with relentless, drunken determination. His body was desperately trying to fight the effect of the drink, but he could feel his erection fading and his energy began to wane. After a minute or two the rhythm slowed, the muscles in his arms and legs were tiring and she was becoming a dead weight in his grip.

"I can't."

Mark stopped. He pulled his face away from the crook of her neck and looked at her. Her mouth was open, and her eyes were bulging. She looked unnatural - a grimace of cartoon surprise. For a moment Mark was motionless, holding her limp body in his arms. He began to feel something wet pooling where his hand was pressed in the small of her back. It was sticky. Mark pulled away and looked at his hand. A metallic odour filled his nostrils as he stared at the dark red smear of blood. He looked at Kelsie. She hadn't moved. She was stood against the wall, her expression unchanged.

"Kelsie?"

Mark moved closer and then suddenly recoiled. The back of Kelsie's head was attached to the wall by a large, rusted nail - a thin trickle of blood was snaking its way down the rough, whitewashed wall. Mark looked again. He recoiled again.

"Fuck. Fuck."

A surge of adrenaline ran through his body, sobering him in an instant. Vomit exploded from his mouth and splattered on the cold stone floor. Tendrils of spittle hung from his chin. He looked around the room, at a loss of what to do and struggling with an inability to process what had just happened. A paralysis of realisation was setting in and he was finding it hard to move, hard to process, hard to even think- the shock was spreading through his body. The door to the cellar opened.

"Kels? You down here?"

Sam stood on the top of the three wooden steps into the cellar. She immediately caught sight of her daughter, half naked, pinned to a wall with blood pooling at her feet. Her gaze shifted to Mark, standing with his jeans half way down his legs, motionless, with vomit and saliva hanging from his chin and a half crazed look in his eye. Her gaze morphed into a mask of rage and tragedy. Mark snapped into the moment. He tried to speak but no words came.

Sam was gone and the key to the door of the cellar turned in the lock.

BACKDOORING

Christian turned off the engine and stepped down from the cab of the truck. He hated the way that Duncan always gave him the shit jobs - "Go check this", "Go pack that", "Drive this here." He was always telling him that it was because he could trust him. That was bullshit. He knew they all took the piss out of him behind his back. Well, he would show Duncan MacFarlane, walking around thinking he was the big boss man. His time would come. He approached the backdoor of the beach hut. The moon was bright and he could see one of the panes of glass in the door was smashed in. He could see boot prints in the mud outside the door. He turned on his Maglite torch. The weight of the torch in his hand suddenly giving him a sense that he was holding a weapon and that he might need it any second.

"Hello? Anyone there?"

TAKING IT ON THE HEAD

Mark was kneeling on the floor of the cellar. The acrid stink of the vomit in front of him mixing with the yeasty fust of beer, ale and mould. Tears were pouring down his face as his body convulsed with silent sobs. Stuart Ferguson stood towering above him, his menacing bulk casting imposing shadows across the walls.

"Well? What are you gonna do?" Sam stood at the bottom of the steps staring at Ferguson, her jaw clenched in barely controlled rage. Dark rivers of mascara now lined her cheeks and tears welled in her eyes, threatening to cascade down her face at any moment. A cigarette shaking in her hand. She unsteadily raised the cigarette to her mouth and pulled ferociously on it.

"Well, I'm gonnae take him down the station and lock him up. Then we can deal with it in the morning."

Just at that moment Duncan burst through the cellar door. Slamming it behind him. He took in the room, his movements slowing down as he absorbed the tragedy of the scene.

"You're gonnae lock him up?! He's jus killed mae daughter."

"What's going on?" Duncan moved cautiously into the room, looking from Mark to Ferguson to Sam.

"What the fuck does it look like? This English cunt has killed Kelsie, and Stuart here just wants to lock him up and deal with it in the morning when his hangover has gone eh?! ARE YOU FUCKING KIDDING ME?"

Sam launched herself at Ferguson, but Duncan got there first, taking hold of Sam's flailing arms and pulling her close to his chest. The thick winter coat muffled the wailing of the grief-stricken mother as Duncan looked over her shoulder at the prone form of Kelsie pinned to the dank and mouldy wall of the cellar. He turned to Ferguson.

"You want to lock him up. And then what tomorrow, eh? Call the mainland and get the island swarming with pigs? We've got two tonnes of gear moving into the distillery in the morning. Do you think that might be something you want to think about?"

"I was just…"

"You were just what?" Duncan fixed him with a commanding stare. Ferguson may have been physically intimidating but he knew which of them was the more dangerous.

"What are we to do?"

"Get this prick up and get him out of here. Take him up to the distillery, away from the crowds. Take him out through the back."

Just at that moment the door to the cellar opened once more and Christian MacIntosh came in. He closed the door in slow motion as he looked around the room.

"Jesus Christ."

"Christian?"

"Jesus…."

"Christian! I thought I told you to go and check the barrels."

"I did. I did. I…" Christian suddenly snapped back into focus and looked at Duncan, still holding Sam close to his chest. "That's why I'm here. Someone has broken in."

"What?" Duncan relaxed his tender hold of Sam, his body becoming tensed and coiled.

"Door's been smashed in. Doesn't look like anything's missing. I checked and counted."

"Go find the other English surfers. Round them up. And find Maggie too. She looked pretty cosy with them. Take Flannagan and meet us at the distillery."

Ferguson looked at Duncan. "What are you going to do?"

"I'm going to tidy up here."

Duncan pulled a Colt 45 pistol from the depths of his winter coat. Mark looked up and saw the gun glinting in the harsh light of the bare bulb and then everything went black.

CAUGHT ON THE INSIDE

Mark could hear sounds, but they were muffled and muted like he was underwater. His head felt foggy and confused, and then a searing pain exploded at the back of his skull. The man must have hit him with the gun. Mark kept his eyes shut. He could sense the voices were in the room with him - they felt like they were far away but somehow close at the same time.

"What're we going to do? Eh? Duncan?"

"Just be patient."

"I think I am being fucking patient. Kelsie's dead."

The image of Kelsie pinned against the wall like some apocalyptic zombie filled his brain and a helpless sense of guilt and desperation flooded Mark's body. He was not a bad person. He was not a murderer. It had been a mistake. A stupid drunken mistake. He could feel an ache in the muscles of his shoulders and he realised his hands were tied behind his back - he could feel the hard plastic ties digging into his wrists.

"And someone is going to pay."

"Ay. Him". Mark could hear that these words were spat with venom in his direction. A sudden guttural scream filled the cavernous room. He opened his eyes to see Kelsie's mother only feet away from him, charging at him with a screwdriver in her hand. Instinct made him sit up just as she brought the screwdriver down, and it narrowly missed his head, but it sank deep into his thigh as his legs swung around, counterbalancing the movement of his body upwards. Mark let out a gut-wrenching wail of pain which echoed and bounced off the hard industrial surfaces of the distilling room. Suddenly there were hands pulling her away.

"You cunt. You're gonna pay for this. You hear me?"

The policeman and the other man both had an arm each and were dragging her backwards, her face contorted in rage and anguish. They placed her down on a wooden stool and the policemen held her still whilst the other man whispered urgently into her ear. Mark couldn't make out what he said but it seemed to have the desired effect- after a moment her body visibly relaxed, but her eyes never left Mark, a stare full of hatred and vengeance. The pain in Mark's leg was like a fire burning. Blood was seeping from the wound. The plastic cut into his wrists and his shoulders screamed for mercy as instinct made his body try to move his hands to help stem the flow of blood. A whimpering sound fluttered out of his mouth as he began to try to deal with the pain, and he realised that he was going to have to suffer it.

He heard the clunk of a door opening behind him. He could hear voices. Was that Charlie?

In his peripheral vision he caught movement. There was Charlie and Maggie, and behind them there was another man, prodding Charlie in the back with a sawn off shotgun.

"What the fuck?" Charlie ran over to him. "What have they done? What's going on?" He took hold of Mark's shirt, tore a strip from the bottom and immediately began tying the fabric around his leg and compressing the wound. Charlie began to tighten the knot and Mark let out a howl of pain.

Maggie looked at Duncan and Duncan looked at her. The room was charged as Duncan waited, and Maggie searched for the right words to resolve the suddenly very dangerous situation she found herself in. He looked at her, challenging her.

"Listen Duncan." Maggie raised her hands in a placatory gesture, "we were up on the Mor Rubha, and the squall came in and we just had to find somewhere to shelter. So, I smashed the window and we went in. Mark had nothing to do with it. And Charlie….well….", Maggie took a step closer to Duncan. She felt like he was softening. Perhaps. Maybe. If she couldn't save this situation, she didn't like to think what Duncan was capable of. He was dangerous, and ambitious - an evil cocktail of a combination, and Maggie knew him well. She feared for her new friend's safety. And her own. Her next words came out in a conspiratorial whisper. "…..he doesn't know any of it. It was just barrels in a hut".

The silence in the room screamed as Duncan looked at her with a blank expression. Maggie stood motionless, uncertain at what was to come next. Suddenly Duncan erupted into peals of laughter. Maggie looked at him with a mild sense of relief being masked by a more dominant sense of confusion and concern.

"Christian! You were right!"

Maggie turned to Christian who was nodding his head like a pathetic puppy dog.

"We were wondering who had broken into the store."

"Well, it was just so we didn't get blown off the cliffs or die of hyperthermia" she offered tentatively, hoping to lighten the severity of her misdemeanour. "I don't think you need to torture anyone." Maggie attempted a laugh and briefly looked at Mark. His eyes were glazed and Charlie was staring back at her with a look of trepidation.

"Maggie, this isn't torture. This is an execution." Duncan puffed up his chest and pulled out the gun from his waistband.

Charlie and Maggie looked at each other, confusion contorting their faces. Mark writhed and groaned. Charlie looked at his brother before turning to the man in the black jacket.

"Can someone explain to me what the fuck is going on?"

"With pleasure. Your friend here has just fucked and killed this poor woman's daughter. She is a dear friend of ours....part of the community, part of the family. As is this man here - Chief of police, Stuart Ferguson. And we just think that on this island, when we feel the law might not do justice for the crime committed, we take the law into our own hands."

"Have you gone fucking mental?" Maggie's outburst propelled her towards Duncan. He backed up, keeping his distance and raising the pistol between them.

"Whoah, Whoah. There are a lot of things to consider here Maggie. I'd like to give you the benefit of the doubt, so I'm gonna give you the opportunity to choose where your loyalties lie. You've got a lot invested in this. And you've known this lot for what.....all of five minutes?"

"They're Gully's friends." Maggie's voice began to crack.

"Ah yes. Gully." A sinister sneer spread across Duncan's face. "You don't think I know about you and Gully, eh? You'd fucking open your legs to anyone wouldn't you? You told him about our little operation."

A tear rolled down Maggie's cheek.

Another silence drifted through the room as all eyes looked at Maggie. Duncan turned to Christian. "Where's the other one?"

"Couldn't find him."

"Well, you better go and find him unless you want to end up in a fucking barrel as well." Duncan stuffed the gun into the waistband in the small of his back and gestured to Christian to get going.

With some reluctance, Christian turned and exited back through the distillery.

THE LIGHT AT THE END OF THE TUNNEL

The car park at the front of the distillery was deserted and eerily quiet after the clamour and activity of the last few hours. Large puddles dotted the tarmac, reflecting the yellow hue cast by the lone security light affixed to the front of the distillery. Jimmy killed the engine of the old Peugeot 205 and ghosted into the shadows to the side of the main building. He sat in the silence for a moment, whilst he assessed his options. He listened for any movement or voices in case his approach had alerted anyone. The only sound he could hear was the rhythmical, metallic creak of the old sign at the entrance gate, swaying in the wind.

He had been on his way to the pub to find shelter and hopefully catch up with the other two when he had seen the policeman carrying Mark out of the pub and bundling him into the police car. He had been about to cross the road to question what was going on when he had seen the man in the black jacket and the landlady come out of the pub and cross to the police car, all the while having an animated conversation. His jacket had slipped open, and Jimmy had caught a glimpse of a pistol in his waistband. Something was amiss. Mark had been a limp dead weight on the shoulder of the big policeman, and there was something about the urgency and aggression in the conversation between the other two which had alerted Jimmy's sixth sense. Once the police car had pulled away, Jimmy had run to the nearest vehicle - it had been unlocked, such is the way of island life. Despite there being no keys, a misspent youth followed by years in the marines meant he had little trouble jump-starting the old, classic Peugeot. He had tailed the police car at a safe distance, keeping his headlights off so as not to arouse suspicion; but it was difficult to drive at any speed with so little light on unknown island roads, and he had lost sight of them after a while. However, the road was a dead end, he recognised it - it was the one leading out to the distillery on the East side of the island, and as Jimmy had crested a hill he had caught sight of the police car sitting in the car park of the distillery, the reflective strips on the side of the car lighting up under the glare of the security light.

And now, here he was sitting in silence and wondering what to do. He needed to get inside the building, but his gut was telling him that walking through the front door was not the most sensible approach. Something was wrong here and he needed to find out what was going on. As he reached for the door handle, he heard the rumble of an engine behind him. He immediately slipped down in the seat and tried to keep his head as low as possible and out of sight. The glare of headlights passed through the interior of the car and then were gone as the vehicle entered the car park and swung around into one of the spaces at the front of the building. He heard doors opening and slamming, the sound of a muffled voice barking an order. The gentle sound of footfall retreating towards the main entrance prompted Jimmy to take a chance and peer over the edge of the door and out of the window. He could see the unmistakable figure of Charlie, silhouetted in the light. The woman, Maggie was next to him, and they were being marshalled towards the building by two of the locals he had seen in the pub. As they disappeared inside, Jimmy caught sight of a sawn-off shotgun being pressed into Charlie's back. The situation was escalating, and Jimmy could feel himself slipping into military mode. The door closed behind them, and he let out a breath that he didn't realise he was holding.

He counted to three before inching across the front seat and silently letting himself out of the passenger door. He pushed the door closed behind him and stealthily crept around to the front end of the car, staying low and using the car as cover. In the silence he could hear his heart beating out of his chest - memories of his last covert operation in Afghanistan flooding back to him. He was part of a team of highly trained professionals then - here, he was unarmed, slightly drunk and on his own.

He took a breath and tried to clear his mind. With a sudden movement he was off, moving at a crouch into the darkness that shrouded the back of the building. He stuck to the shadows of the building, moving swiftly and silently, keeping an eye out for security cameras or movement sensors for lights. He reached an old stable door and suddenly froze as he heard the door at the front of the building bang shut, footsteps and then the slamming of a car door. The throaty cough of a diesel engine filled the silence of the night and then disappeared into the distance. Jimmy let out the air that he was holding in his lungs. He once again focused on the door in front of him. He turned the handle and discovered that it was unlocked. He moved into a dark corridor and closed the door behind him, not wanting a draft to alert anyone to his presence. He crouched, motionless for a minute, allowing his eyes to adjust to the inky blackness of the corridor. He followed the whitewashed brick walls for twenty feet where he could see some light spill as the corridor turned ninety degrees. He cautiously looked around the corner. A number of doors led off the corridor, but all were shut. Another corridor led off to the right and seemed to be the source of the light spill. He could hear the muffled grunts of angry voices and followed them down the corridor and towards the light. The light spilling into the corridor was coming from the reception area at the front of the building. Jimmy looked through the security-glass panel in the door and could see the reception was lit up but was empty of people. The voices were coming from somewhere on the other side. He pushed open the door just wide enough for him to slip into the reception area and winced as the hinges gave a disgruntled squeak. He moved at a crouch, slipping in behind the large reception desk made up of stacked wooden, whiskey barrels. He took a moment to work out his bearings, trying to recall the tour they had taken just two days ago, and listened again for the voices he had heard. It was only a few seconds and then there they were again, louder this time - angry voices followed by a howl of pain. Jimmy instinctively reacted and moved around from behind the counter and over to one of the doors on the other side of the reception. He held his ear to the door, feeling exposed in the bright light of the reception area. He deduced that the sounds were coming from further back in the building and he began to move towards them, following the green arrows on the floor that indicated the tourist route through the distillery. Two round windows in some double doors to the left were projecting a cold wash of sterile light across the hallway, and if Jimmy remembered correctly, this was the Distilling room. The murmur of voices was louder and clearer - they were coming from behind these doors. Jimmy took a moment to remember that room, the layout, the materials, the exits and entrances, trying to find anything that might give him an edge.

GETTING BARRELLED

Duncan fingered the Colt in his hand, feeling its weight, its power. He stood behind three wooden barrels in the middle of the room with their lids off. He felt the surge of adrenaline. He had always been on the wrong side of the law, but this was different - this was real gangster business, and he was getting a taste for it. He motioned towards Mark.

"Bring him over here." No one moved. Duncan maniacally waved the gun in the air. "Fucking bring him over here!"

Charlie tried to help Mark to his feet, but Mark slipped in the pool of his own blood as his good leg found a footing, and Charlie fell back onto him. Mark let out a howl of pain. Charlie scrambled off his brother, slipping in the blood and spreading it in a bigger arc across the painted concrete floor. Stuart Ferguson suddenly appeared and with one deft move lifted Mark to his feet and forcibly dragged him towards the barrels.

"Get in." Duncan indicated the barrel in front of Mark.

"What?" Mark's throat was dry and sore, and his words sounded more like a croak. "I can't."

Duncan turned to Ferguson. "Put him in the barrel."

Ferguson scooped Mark off his feet and placed him into the central barrel, feet first. Mark stood there in the harsh white light of the distillery room, visibly shaking as the realisation of the situation began to dawn on him. This *was* an execution - he hadn't been joking.

"It's ok if you pish yourself. I probably would if I was in your situation." Duncan walked over to Sam and offered her the handle of the pistol. He turned back to Mark. He hated the English. "Any last words?"

Maggie was standing by one of the copper distillery tanks, watching. She could see the smirk spreading across Duncan's smug features. He was enjoying this, puffing up in barely concealed relish and it repulsed her. She could feel the bile rising in her throat. Turning a blind eye to shifting cocaine as part of a third-party chain was one thing, but cold blooded murder was not something she would ever agree to.

"Duncan?"

"Shut up, Maggie."

Sam was weighing the pistol in her hand. She looked at Mark through a contorted mask of rage and hatred. Mark was losing control of his body - his body was spasming, shaking in the barrel, a mixture of snot, dribble and blood staining his once handsome face.

"Please. There must be some mistake." Charlie looked pleadingly at Sam.

"No mistake." Duncan cut in.

"Please. We must be able to work something out. It was an accident." Charlie took a step towards Sam, the blood he was standing in making a sticky squelching noise as he lifted his foot. Sam took a step closer to Mark so that they were only an arms width apart. Charlie began to shout, "Mark would never hurt anyone." She raised the gun to Mark's eye level. "Yes, he can be a bit of a..."

"You killed my girl."

BANG. Everyone's head turned to the double doors as one side of the door swung open and crashed into the wall. The door swung back violently and then abruptly stopped as the rubber seals caught. Everyone stared at the empty doorway. Duncan stepped between Sam and Mark and removed the gun from her grip and pointed it at the door, the agitation making his jaw pulse. Ferguson glanced at Duncan before removing his own weapon from his waistband and approaching the door with caution.

"I thought there was no one here." Duncan jaw clenched.

"Me too. We swept the building." Ferguson reached the door, both arms extended to hold his own Glock steady. He cautiously pushed open one side of the double doors. As he began to move through the doors, a figure emerged from behind the other door, wrapped his arm over Fergusons and with practiced precision, disarmed him. Before he knew what was happening Stuart Ferguson found himself standing back in the distillery room with his left arm pressed in a firm grip behind his back, and his own gun pointing at the back of his head.

Jimmy steadily moved into the room behind the policeman, keeping him as a human shield. He could see the man in the black jacket holding a gun and pointing it towards him. A stillness settled. Suddenly Duncan switched focus and pointed the gun at Mark. A grin spread across Duncan's face.

"I wouldn't do that." Jimmy shouted out from behind the bulk of the policeman.

Duncan laughed. "Oh Yeah? Why's that?"

Without hesitation Jimmy shifted the aim of the Glock from behind Ferguson's massive head and BANG. An explosion of sound reverberated around the distilling room as if a thousand hammers were hitting the metal tanks at the same time. The gun Duncan was holding shot out of his hand and skidded across the floor to the other side of the room. Blood spurted from his hand as he screamed and cursed. At the same time Stuart Ferguson buckled and fell to the floor clutching his right ear, deafened by his own gun's discharge. As Ferguson went down, Jimmy raised the gun and clubbed him behind the ear, putting him out cold, before bringing the gun back up and moving it from Duncan to Sam. A mixture of fear and rage filled Sam's face as she stared at Jimmy stepping over the prone figure of Ferguson. Duncan's whimpering filled the room as he clutched the stump of his right hand.

Jimmy approached them with the gun extended. "I don't know what's going on here. But I don't like the look of it". Jimmy noticed some plastic ties on the floor and indicated to Charlie. "Tie them up. Wrists and ankles."

Within five minutes they had Duncan, Ferguson and Sam tied to the pipes of the distillery tanks. As Jimmy patted down Ferguson and Duncan for any other weapons, Charlie turned to Maggie.

"I don't know how you fit into all of this, but I need to know, are you with us or them?"

"Charlie, I'm not a bad person. I've done some bad things in my life, but I would never kill someone." Jimmy's gut believed her.

"Good."

He stood up, satisfied they were secure. "Let's move. We've got to get out of here. Now."

They marched down the corridors towards the front of the building, only pausing once they got to the main reception area.

Jimmy turned on his friend, "What the fuck?"

Charlie raised his eyebrows. "Long story."

"Give me the headlines." Jimmy pulled out the magazine of the pistol to check the ammunition. Force of habit.

"Mark shagged the barmaid from the pub and accidentally...."

"Accidentally what?"

"Well, she's..."

Mark, leaning heavily on Charlie, blood oozing from the wound on his leg, suddenly burst into life, snot and tears streaming down his face, "She's dead. I killed her."

"It was an accident." Charlie looked pleadingly at his brother.

There was a void of silence that filled the room.

Jimmy slammed the magazine back in. "We've got to get as far away from here as possible."

Mark's head lolled from side to side, his face twisted in pain. Charlie looked at the steely determination on his friend's face - his game face. Charlie broke the momentary silence. "I hate to point this out, but we are on a fucking island."

"I've got to go back. To the house." Maggie looked edgy. Frightened but with a fire burning in her eyes. "To Nowhere. The croft you're staying in. There are things there. Things of Gully's and mine. I need to get them. It won't take a second."

Jimmy shook his head. "No fucking way."

"I've got a boat." she fixed him with a stare.

Jimmy looked at her, his mind fizzing as he tried to assess the situation, the dangers.

All three men were looking at Maggie.

"Just take me with you."

Jimmy looked at his two friends.

Maggie suddenly straightened, "You've got to get off this island - you don't understand, the whole island is in on this. You're dead if you don't leave. And I'm dead too. That big guy in there....he's our policeman. As far as they're concerned, I'm one of them; and I've just fucking betrayed them." Jimmy set his cold steel eyes on her.

Maggie pleaded, "But this isn't for me. I didn't sign up for this.

For murder. I just wanted some extra cash. I've got to get off this island too."

"Was Gully in on this?" Jimmy gave her a cold, hard stare.

She reluctantly nodded. "Sort of."

"Great." Jimmy began to pace, his mind desperately trying to piece together the options.

"But I have to get back to the croft. Trust me. It's important. Then we go straight to the boat, and we're gone. All of us. You need me."

"You're not just a pretty face are you, Maggie?" Jimmy turned on his heel with a grin on his face and made for the front door. "How do I know we can trust you?"

"You don't. But before Gully died, we were going to run away together." It all began to fall into place - why Gully had sent them here.

Charlie could feel the tension fizzing between his friend and the woman he was falling for. "But how are we going to get back to the house?"

Jimmy looked to the double doors, "I've got a car outside. I followed you from the pub."

The four of them burst out through the front door and into the glare of the security light that flooded the tarmac outside. Their frenzied movements suddenly slowed as they looked up to see Christian standing in the middle of the parking lot, a shotgun pointing directly at them.

"Well, well."

Jimmy cursed under his breath, "Shit." He raised the pistol and pointed at the lone man standing in front of his van.

"Maggie? Do you want to explain what the fuck is going on?". Christian looked disappointingly at Maggie.

"Christian...look...."

"Look pal, whatever is going on here, I think there has been a big misunderstanding; so if I were you I would put the shotgun down, get in your van, and go and sleep off that whiskey, eh?" Jimmy trained the pistol on the man's head, natural instinct telling him to go for the kill shot. Buck shot from the shotgun could take them all out.

"I don't think so. You see, your pal here killed one of ma friends. One of the local girls."

"It was an accident."

Jimmy kept focused on the tension and bare muscle of Christians right forearm, looking for any sign that he might pull the trigger, but all the while the conversation continued, he was slowly ushering the group towards the car he had left in the shadows at the edge of the car park. They were now only a metre or two away from a display of whiskey barrels at the front to the building.

Christian turned his glare on Maggie. "Where are your loyalties eh, Maggie? You're supposed to be ma friend."

Maggie met his stare, but her mouth stayed closed. She'd known him most of her life, but this was wrong. It was time to draw a line in the sand.

"We're not friends." Maggie was shaking her head, looking down at the black asphalt.

"I knew it. The whole island knew it. As soon as you started running around after that English bastard, Gully."

Jimmy saw it - a momentary scrunching of the man's eyes as the rage and anger Christian felt boiled momentarily to the surface. It was coming. It was now.

A resonant 'boom' shattered the night sky as the flash of the shotgun flared its nostrils and spat a volley of buck at the group. Jimmy instinctively hurled himself sideways, tackling the others so they fell behind the barrels. A searing pain ripped through the calf of his left leg. He scrambled back to his knees and turned to the others, fear rippling across each of their faces. "Go. Get out of here. I'll cover you. Take the car. Go to the cottage. I'll meet you there. No keys, just touch the wires together."

Charlie began to protest, "But…"

"Go. Now."

Charlie pulled Mark to his feet, getting ready to make a dash for the car that Jimmy had left in the darkness. Jimmy looked over one last time as he steadied himself at the other end of their makeshift cover. "Go!"

In one smooth motion he leant around the barrel and let off two confident shots. The explosion of gunfire in the quiet of the island night left the air ringing in its silence. The two brothers made a dash for the car, closely followed by Maggie. Suddenly a return volley from the shotgun forced Maggie to retreat and duck back down behind the barrels. Jimmy peered out - Christian had withdrawn behind the open door of his van. Suddenly the car in the shadows roared into life, the wheels squealed and sprayed loose gravel behind it, before eventually finding traction and propelling the car forwards. Jimmy used the momentary diversion to roll out from behind the barrels and let off three shots, the first one ripping into the front tyre and the other two embedding themselves into the van door with a metallic 'thunk'. The small hatchback careered across the car park, heading for the exit, and Christian made the amateurish mistake of stepping out from his hiding place and taking aim at the fleeing Englishmen. The lone security light presented him as the perfect silhouette, and as he raised the shotgun to his shoulder, Jimmy took aim and pulled the trigger. Christian's body collapsed on the tarmac, the shotgun clattering to the ground as the taillights of the car disappeared out of the car park and up the road.

Maggie looked up at Jimmy, a pleading and painful look on her face, "Is he…?"

Maggie scrambled to her feet. "Oh my God! Oh My God! No. Noooo…." Tears pouring down her face, she began to move towards the prone body of Christian Fletcher. Her childhood friend. A strong arm clasped her around her waist and pulled her up. It was Jimmy.

"We have to go. Now. I'm sorry." He looked at her with genuine hurt. She would always remember that look. It would haunt her for a very long time. Jimmy turned to pick up the shotgun, it was then that Maggie saw that half of Jimmy's calf was missing on his left leg, the material of his jeans shredded and a bloody pulp of flesh, muscle and sinew was clearly visible where Christian's initial shot must have found its mark. Maggie turned and took one last look at Christian Fletcher, the man she had played kiss chase with on the beach when they were kids, the man who had just tried to kill her, and then she followed Jimmy to Christian's van.

Jimmy paused at the open door of the van, "I think you're gonna need to drive."

GOING OVER THE FALLS

With one flat tyre, the van was heavy and sluggish as they meandered over the headland, back towards the pub and the croft beyond. It was made harder by Jimmy insisting that they drive without the headlights on. Fortunately, the moon was almost full and the earlier clouds had been blown out to sea, leaving a clear, bright, starlit sky that shone down on the desolate, dark asphalt road. The van began to accelerate down the wet tarmac on the hill towards the centre of the island. Maggie felt the van lurch and wrestled the steering wheel to hold it straight, but suddenly the front of the van tilted, and sparks began to fly out from underneath.

"Somethings' wrong."

Jimmy braced himself. "Tyre's gone. Brake. BRAKE!"

The front of the van skewed to the right, so that they were momentarily sliding down the hill sideways; the passenger wheels caught, and the van was suddenly airborne and rotating through the crisp night air, before crashing down and landing on its side. There was the screech of metal as it slid down the road, a hellish sound of the grinding metal that only stopped as the van abruptly came to a halt, the cab nestled in the ditch to the side of the road and the rear of the van poking out across the deserted island link road.

They clambered out of the crumbled and mangled van. Keeping low, Jimmy pulled Maggie across the road, and they slipped through a five-bar gate into the darkness of the field beyond.

"You ok?" Jimmy placed a hand on her chin and turned her face to look at him. There was panic and shock in her eyes. A trickle of blood was running down her face, but when he brushed her hair aside, he saw that it was only a superficial cut. She was shaken, that was clear, but they didn't have time to dither.

The undulating and boggy surface would have been hard at the best of times, but injured and in the dark it was ten times worse. After twenty minutes they had travelled about half a mile before Maggie suddenly stopped and fell to her knees.

"Come on!"

Jimmy's leg was bleeding, he could feel the blood running down his calf and pooling in his shoe. He didn't know how bad it was but he wasn't going to check now.

"Where's Charlie?" Maggie's voice was desperate and quivering with fear. She had stopped and was looking back across the field, the blackness refusing to reveal anything.

"I don't know," said Jimmy. "We can't stop. We have to get out of here. We have to keep moving. We have to get to the cottage."

"But…"

"Now!" Jimmy dug in his pocket to try and find his phone - natural instinct. But he quickly remembered that he no longer had a phone.

"Shit."

Suddenly something caught Jimmy's attention. His body tensed and without thinking he crouched and became statue-still, listening. He could just make out the gentle swoosh of the small waves breaking on the beach to the north of them. Then, there it was - a low rumble. He looked towards where the sound was coming from; it was getting louder, and without warning the road above them was suddenly flooded in light as a car came around the corner.

"Shit. Stay down."

Jimmy pushed Maggie to the floor and dived on top of her as the headlights of the car momentarily flooded the field they were in. Then the lights were gone, weaving and bobbing along the undulating, empty coastal road.

Jimmy pulled Maggie to her feet.

"Come on. We have to get back to the cottage." Jimmy could make out Maggie's silhouette in the moonlight. She wasn't moving. He moved towards her, his face now inches from hers. She was crying silent, desperate tears.

"I can't."

"You can. They will find us, they will find Charlie and then it will be a whole lot worse. You have to trust me. I've been in situations a lot worse than this. Trust me." She looked at him, the tears clouding her vision, but she could see this was a man who knew what he was doing and if she wanted to get off this island alive, she realised that she needed to follow him.

Jimmy put his arm around her waist, and they began to move again, slowly picking their way over tussocks of thick grass and towards the lights of the small crofters cottage at the bottom of the hill.

Within ten minutes Jimmy and Maggie were knelt behind the hedge that separated the cottage from the field bordering it on the southern side. From his position, Jimmy could see the front of the cottage and the rough and untended driveway. The Ice cream van was where they had left it. The hatchback Jimmy had used as their getaway car lay slung carelessly in front of the cottage, the two doors still open as if the occupants had been in a hurry to get inside. His sixth sense was kicking in and he felt like something was off. As an elite soldier he had always been taught to trust his instincts and right now something was screaming 'caution!'. He scanned the perimeter of the cottage and caught a shiny metallic glint poking out from behind the Ice cream van - there was another car.

Jimmy looked at Maggie's frightened form, crouching in a ditch, scratches cris-crossed her face and the blood from the cut on her face was now smeared across her cheek.

"Stay here. I'll be back in a minute or two."

"Don't...what if..."

"Just stay here and keep your head down. I won't be a minute. I'm just going to do a quick scout around the cottage - make sure there aren't any unwanted surprises." With that, Jimmy was off, keeping low as he moved around the perimeter of the building, keeping his eyes on the windows of the cottage, looking out for any signs of movement from within. He paused behind the dry-stone wall at the back of the cottage and watched the light from the living room and the kitchen that spilled out across the back garden. The windows were typically small and narrow for a building of this style, but he could just make out the bald black dome of a man's head in the living room. It wasn't moving. It was waiting.

THE CLEAN UP SET

Pete Flannagan pulled the old Ford Fiesta into the car park of the distillery - Christ, it wasn't even first light yet and he was already at work. In the old days he probably wouldn't even have gone to bed yet, and he certainly wouldn't have been going to work. But there were things to do. The new shipment needed packing and Christian would be here with the kegs from the bothy in a couple of hours. He needed to get everything sorted before the distillery opened up to the public for the day, although he wasn't sure they would be getting many early rising tourists today - not after the festival! He smiled at the thought of the festival - how much fun he used to have. But that was then, and this was now. Different times: when he was another man, full of anger and drink. People wondered whether working in a whiskey distillery was such a brilliant idea for an alcoholic, but he couldn't think of anything better. He was taking the battle head on - everyday reminding himself what he was fighting. Keep your friends close and your enemies closer was what his father used to tell him. It was keeping him on the right path for now, and that's all anyone needed to understand.

He could see lights on inside the building and he wondered who was already there. He was sure it was just him this morning. He couldn't see any cars, but then again, they may have parked out the back in the spaces reserved for the staff. Or maybe he had left the lights on when he locked up the night before? He was sure he hadn't, but then again, his memory was a little hazy these days and he often found himself realising that he had forgotten to do something - maybe it was a sign of age creeping up on him, or maybe it was just typical of a recovering alcoholic.

The headlights of the car swung across the cracked asphalt and Flannagan slammed on the brakes as he saw the dark figure of a body lying in the middle of the car park. He could feel his heart suddenly kick into overdrive, pounding the inside of his frail and withered chest. What the hell? His brain took a moment to process what he thought he could see in front of him. It was a little slow on the uptake these days after many decades spent pickled at the bottom of a bottle. His yellowed, nicotine-stained fingers drummed the rim of the steering wheel as he looked nervously around the car park and into the shadows that ran along the edges of the building, searching out any signs of danger. His breathing was wheezy and heavy, like an out of breath dog. His senses felt heightened to superhuman strength ever since he had given up the grog, but in reality, they were probably functioning just below what most would consider normal. Nothing appeared out of place, and he didn't sense any eyes watching him. He slowly lent on the accelerator and nudged the old car forward, the gravel crackling and crunching under the tyres.

The car drew closer to the prone figure on the floor, and Flanagan was continuously looking around for signs of what might have happened. He got out of the car, but left the engine running just in case, for whatever reason, he had to make a quick escape - his nerves were almost crippling him. He approached the figure and saw the pale and contorted face of Christian, lying on his back staring up at the dark pre-dawn sky. A pool of congealed, crimson blood encircled the body. He was dead, there was no doubt about that - he could see the dark circle of what looked like a gunshot in his forehead. A multitude of thoughts rippled through his brain about what might have happened; were their suppliers on the island? Unhappy with the operation? Were they here to shut them down and tie up any loose ends? Where was Duncan? Should he get in the car and drive? Escape? Take his money and run? Had something gone down at the festival?

Flannagan took a breath of the early morning salt air and gathered his thoughts. "Breathe", he told himself. He could feel wisps of the early morning breeze moving in off the ocean, like deathly fingers reaching out and caressing his paralysed form. A shiver rippled up his spine. He needed to find Ferguson. He turned away from the body, pulled out his phone and made the call. Nothing. Straight to voicemail. He was probably sleeping off his hangover.

Flannagan was sure someone was in the building as he pushed open the creaking front door of the distillery. He could hear voices. Curiosity kept him moving forward into the building; somewhere in the back of his brain, his instincts told him he wasn't in danger, that he wasn't walking into the middle of the battle, but rather walking over the bodies at the end. Christ, he wasn't sure he could deal with more bodies. The voices were growing louder.

"Help!"

"Oi! Who's there?"

The voices were coming from the Distilling room.

Duncan's face was contorted with rage, the veins in his temples pulsing with each word he spat out as he explained what had happened. Flannagan dutifully took his old fishing knife out and cut the plastic ties, freeing the three captives from the distillery tanks. Duncan exploded onto his feet, howling in pain as he waved his throbbing and mangled hand in the air. His bloodied hand seemed to be missing two fingers, shot off by one of the Englishmen apparently. Duncan's curses echoed through the building as Ferguson and Sam groggily moved after them, following Flannagan into the reception area to find the first aid kit so he could bandage Duncan's hand and hopefully shut him up a bit - he was giving Flannagan a headache.

As Duncan explained the course of the night's events, Flannagan looked over at Sam. He felt for her. Kelsie was a nice girl. He'd known her all her life - watched as she'd grown from little girl into a young woman. And now she was no more - what a waste, when there were so many people less deserving of the precious gift that is life. He should know - he was one of them. Hell, all of them were less deserving. Look at the mess they were in. Look at the wrongs they had done. But it wasn't them that had moved on from the earth, it was an innocent girl with so much life in front of her. An anger began to boil in the pit of Flannagan's stomach - a rage he hadn't felt in years. For the first time in a long time, he wanted a drink.

****

In the glare of the Fiesta's headlights, Ferguson disappeared behind the large, newly built, white-washed house. He had it built over the last year or so, and many of the locals had raised a few eyebrows. Not at the expense of it - they all knew where he had got the money, they just didn't like the 'modern' element of the house and thought it a little 'flash' for their island. The house sat proudly at the top of one of the hills, looking out across the north Atlantic. Unlike the more traditional houses on the island, which tried to hide themselves in the contours of the land, the position and design of this house stood out in every way, demanding to be looked at. The landscaping wasn't finished yet and brown earth surrounding the house hadn't softened its impact but simply added to its incongruous presence, like a rather uncouth guest at a cocktail party.

Minutes later, Ferguson appeared carrying two shotguns and a rifle slung over his shoulder. Flannagan could also see two handguns, one in a shoulder holster and one tucked into his belt. He felt like they were in a low budget Scottish version of

Rambo. How the hell had it come to this? The boot of the Fiesta slammed, and Ferguson squeezed into the front seat next to Flannagan like some sort of comedy sketch.

"Right, let's go find these fuckers." Flannagan glanced at Duncan through the rearview mirror. Duncan was almost salivating at the prospect of the hunt.

Despite her protestations, they had dropped Sam back at the Salty Dog - she needed some rest and some time to process the events of the night. They promised to let her know when they had found the English, and if possible, would bring her daughter's killer to her for justice. Flannagan swung the small car around and headed out into the dark lanes of the island on the hunt and heading for 'Nowhere'.

He drove as quickly as the small car would go; the engine labouring up the hill out of town under the weight of the three large men. As they crested the hill and slipped down the other side an obstruction in the road filled their view; in the amber glow of the ancient headlights, they could see the back end of what appeared to be Christian's van sticking out into the road. It was on its side, crumpled and dented, the bonnet buckled and half hidden in the ditch on the side of the road.

"Slow down." Ferguson commanded, slipping the gun out of his shoulder holster and fingering the trigger. His eyes were fully focused on the wreckage in front of them - the hunter stalking his prey. Ferguson was a proud and arrogant man, and Flannagan almost felt sorry for the Englishman who had dented that ego; an unrelenting desire for revenge was emanating from every pore of Ferguson - this wasn't about Kelsie for him, this was about his own pride and how it had been sorely damaged by the softly spoken Englishman.

"Stop." Ferguson climbed out of the car, keeping his gun trained on the wreckage of the van. Duncan cautiously followed.

"Stay here and keep the engine running." Duncan exited the car, letting his lap dog lead the way, his bravado having been dented and damaged along with his hand. In the light of the headlights Flannagan saw Ferguson pass Duncan the second handgun without looking at him and Duncan took it awkwardly with his left hand. They stepped cautiously as if stalking a deer, which Flannagan seemed to find funny - he found himself quietly chuckling to himself. Why was he laughing?

The doors slammed as both men climbed back into the car. "Nothing. They've scarpered. Let's head over to old Elsie's place."

IN THE PIT

Maggie felt the cold creeping into her bones, the shock and the fear filling every pore of her being. Alone in the dark, squatting behind a low stone wall gave her a moment to reflect as dark thoughts swirled through her mind - was she making the right decision? Were these really Gully's friends? Murder? Suddenly a face appeared above the wall line and Jimmy slithered over.

"Everything ok?"

"You need to stay here."

Maggie tensed with fear. "What's wrong?"

"It's nothing for you to worry about. Stay here and don't move unless I come and find you." Jimmy's mind was awash with questions - how had they found him? What was he going to do now? He was stranded on an isolated hostile island with two groups of people out for his blood. "I'll be back. Stay here." And with that he was gone.

Jimmy slid back over the wall, careful not to make a noise, even though the wind and the rhythmical pounding of the waves on the nearby shore was certain to muffle any sound he might make. He checked the magazine again, one in the chamber, one in the magazine. Two bullets. Not much to play with. He approached the front door of the house, careful to keep to the shadows. He pressed his ear to the door and could hear the odd muffled exchange of voices. He circled around to the back of the cottage, thinking that he could sneak in through the back door of the kitchen. Suddenly he heard the back door open and Jimmy pressed himself against the cold render of the cottage.

In the warm amber light emanating out of the kitchen he could make out the outline of the Eastern European thug from the Kings Head - Deaf Andy's henchman. The soft glow of a mobile phone cast his face in a fluorescent light as he held it up to his ear. From where he stood Jimmy could hear the persistent ringing at the other end of the line.

"We have two of them. One of them is in bad shape. No sign of Jimmy yet."

A gentle breeze took the rest of the brief conversation away from Jimmy, but he got the gist. They weren't going to let any of them walk away from this and he needed to be smart and ruthless. There was no space for being a nice guy here. The hired thug ended the call and took a final drag on the cigarette he was holding, flicking it nonchalantly into the darkness, sparks catching on the breeze and flickering in the darkness.

"Don't move. Don't speak. Or it will be the last time you do."

Nico could feel the cold of the steel pressed firmly against the bare skin at the base of his skull. He cursed himself for getting caught out - perhaps they had underestimated this Englishman.

******

Charlie looked over at his brother; he was sheet white. Despite using his belt to tourniquet the leg, Mark had lost a lot of blood and was now barely conscious. Both of them had their hands secured with plastic ties and were sat on the sofa. Charlie had hoped that he would be able to get back to the cottage and use his first aid kit to patch Mark up a little whilst they waited for Jimmy and Maggie. Jimmy and Maggie? Where were they? His friend was a highly trained soldier - behind the quiet, troubled kid was a lethal killing machine. If anyone was going to come to their rescue, it was him. Charlie was worried - this was not his world and he was filled with fear, as he sat restrained, with a gun pointing at him and watching his brother bleed out in front of him. How had he got here? He silently cursed Gully. He looked at the tube of Gully's ashes on the mantlepiece. Everything he had ever done had ended in tragedy and disaster. And even in death he was dragging them into his mess. He just wanted to go home. This wasn't turning out to be the trip he had hoped for.

"Where is your friend? Jimmy? Where is he?"

The mountain of a man in front of him hadn't moved for the last twenty minutes, he had just sat there, monotonally repeating the same question, glumly staring at them and resting his gun on his knee. The whites of his eyes looked weary, bloodshot and yellowed, but they never wavered from Charlie and Mark. The small brass carriage clock on the windowsill behind him provided a rhymical soundtrack to the hostile silence that filled the gaps between the repetition of the question - tick tock, tick tock. Charlie felt the draught on the back of his neck as the back door opened behind them - the other thug returning from outside. The yellow, bloodshot eyes lifted momentarily from Charlie, suddenly opening wide in surprise at whatever had just walked in and, in that moment, Charlie knew Jimmy had come to rescue them.

"I see you've made yourselves at home."

Just the sound of his voice was like someone wrapping a blanket around him - it filled him with warmth and made him momentarily feel like everything was going to be ok. Then his ears exploded as a gunshot reverberated around the confined space, the thick stone walls of the cottage acting like impenetrable sound barriers and allowing the deafening noise to continually ricochet around the room. Charlie saw the large Nigerian's head explode, bone shattering, brain and blood splattering the chimney breast behind him. His head snapped back and then slumped onto his chest, before his body went limp and toppled to the side, his large frame hit the floor, blood pooling on the heavily patterned carpet.

It took a moment for everyone to recover. A ringing sound seemed to linger in the air, like a permanent tinnitus. Everyone seemed to be moving in slow motion. The Eastern European was crouching on the floor clutching his right ear and howling in pain, the gun's discharge having burst his eardrum.

"Jimmy, what the....?"

"I can't explain now. We haven't got long. We've got to get out of here. Grab what you need."

Charlie stood in a daze, frozen in a fog of confusion, shock and fear.

"Now." The word momentarily cleared the fog and Charlie stumbled to his feet and moved towards the bedrooms. Jimmy pointed the gun at the Eastern European thug who was still crouching and clutching the side of his head. He had one round left - hopefully he wouldn't need it. "Get on your feet." He didn't move. "Up. Now!" his voice rising to a desperate shout. Nico slowly stood up and raised his hands above his head. Jimmy moved in and patted him down, removing the gun from the inside of Nico's jacket and putting it in the back of his jeans. His leg was now throbbing, and he needed something to take the edge off. His mind was getting a little fuzzy around the edges and he really needed to be able to think with clarity if he was going to get them out of this mess and off this island. "Sit." Jimmy indicated the wooden chair that Dokes had not long since vacated. He carefully backed up to the front door, keeping his gun trained on Deaf Andy's hired help. He opened the door and a cold breeze surged into the confined space, washing out the lingering stench of death. "Maggie!", Jimmy shouted into the darkness. Within seconds Maggie was at the door, fear creasing her normally beautiful face, as she gazed upon the scene inside what was once her grandmother's cottage. "Get whatever it is that you need. We don't have long."

As Maggie moved into the room, Charlie returned, his hands

now free of restraint and carrying a rucksack and a first aid kit. He set about cleaning and bandaging the messy wound on Mark's leg. He woke with a start and screamed as Charlie poured the dregs of a whiskey bottle onto the wound before irrigating it with the sterile water from the first aid kit and wrapping it in gauze and bandage. Iodine would have been preferable, but he had used it all on Tom's wound.

"What the fuck's happening? Who's he?". Sweat beaded his brow, but Mark was now awake, and his eyes were alert, searching the room in heightened panic as if waking from a hideous nightmare.

"Be calm mate. We're just getting a few things and then we are getting out of here." Jimmy looked out into the darkness, he thought he could hear the faint rumbles of an engine. He shut the door, turned off the light and peered through the crack in the curtain.

The sudden darkness made everyone in the room freeze and listen.

"What? What is it?". Four faces looked towards the front of the cottage. "Nothing. I just thought I heard a car. Get going - we don't have long."

The room was now bathed in the soft glow from the embers in the small grate in the fireplace, shadows dancing across the whitewashed walls. Jimmy stayed by the front door, keeping an eye out for anything approaching along the road. Maggie moved the small coffee table off the rug in front of the sofa and pulled the rug to the side, revealing a trap door in the floorboards with a padlock carefully nestled in a bespoke recess so that it would not show once the rug was on top. Nico, Charlie and Mark all looked on as she busily worked at the code on the heavy padlock.

Nico surreptitiously looked around the room. The darkness, since Jimmy had turned off the lights, had given him a window of opportunity, and with everyone distracted with the various things they were doing, he realised this was his chance and he needed to take it. Dokes was dead. His friend and colleague. He would avenge his friend's death and kill these English *gadovi* as Deaf Andy had wanted. They had not tied his hands, thinking he had no weapon - but Dokes was dead at his feet, his friend's blood was lapping the soles of his shoes, and he knew Doke's gun was trapped underneath his ample body - Jimmy had missed it. It was a gamble. If he could just roll his friend over, grab the gun and grab the girl or one of the Englishmen, then he could use them as a shield. But he knew Jimmy was a good shot, he had already shown that. He would have to be quick.

Just as Nico was about to make his move, Jimmy moved from the curtain. "Someone's coming." Maggie had undone the padlock and opened the trap door. In the dim light they could see a block of neatly stacked money. A lot of money. Jimmy leaned in and looked into the hidden recess. "Jesus!"

"Well, we couldn't put it in a bank, could I?"

"This is Gully's money?"

"Mine and Gully's. Like I said. We were saving to escape."

A moment of silence lingered as they stared at the money. Nico took his chance and grabbed for the gun in Jimmy's hand. The brief distraction was enough - in a practiced motion, Nico held the gun, twisted Jimmy's wrist and delivered a powerful kick to Jimmy's injured leg. Jimmy howled in pain and crumpled to the floor. Nico stood over him, the gun in his hand now, pointing straight between Jimmy's eyes.

"My boss, he is a generous man. He gave you time to pay. Your time is up."

"I can pay. Look." Jimmy spluttered and pointed at the money between them.

"Your time is up. You killed my friend. I kill your friend, then I kill you."

Nico turned the gun on Mark and another explosion erupted inside the confined space. Mark's body spun in a pirouette as it rolled off the sofa onto the floor, taking out the coffee table as he fell. Maggie screamed. Jimmy roared. Charlie whimpered in fear. Nico immediately turned the gun back on Jimmy. They could hear the engine of an approaching car now. "A good day's work. I get the money and I kill you. A very happy boss." He pulled the trigger and there was an empty metallic click. A look of panic filled Nico's face as his eyes met Jimmys. One of the embers flickered to life and cast an angry glow across the scene. Jimmy pulled out the gun from the small of his back - Nico's gun, and aimed it at the Serbian's head.

"First rule of poker - know what's in the other man's hand". Jimmy lowered the gun and fired. Nico's right kneecap shattered, and he fell to the floor, writhing in pain. " I don't like killing people unless I have to." He picked up a bundle of the money, glancing at the high denomination of bills as he threw a stack at Nico. "Here, this covers the debt. Tell Andy we're done."

Charlie rushed to Mark's prone body and felt for a pulse. Nothing. A simple look at his friend communicated that his brother was gone. There was no time for anything else as the rumble of a car engine outside and crunch of stones told them that their time was rapidly running out. The headlights broke through the threadbare curtains and flooded the dark room with shafts of artificial light. They heard car doors slam and orders barked in aggressive tones.

"Here, quick." Jimmy's voice had moved into a low and urgent whisper as he threw Maggie the rucksack Charlie had brought. "Fill it and let's go." Meanwhile Jimmy took the now empty wooden chair and in just a few painful strides was at the front door. Charlie could see the grimace on his friend's face, and he glanced at the open wound in Jimmy's calf. Jimmy chair-locked the door with practiced precision, before pressing himself against the solid stone wall and tentatively glancing through a crack in the curtain. He could see the silhouettes of four or five men standing in front of the cottage, back lit by the glare of the headlights. He tried to focus his mind and to think clearly. Charlie was sobbing, and whimpering over Mark's prone figure, trying to be quiet but unable to control the emotion of losing his brother so brutally. This was all Jimmy's fault. But he couldn't think about that now, he had to try and get them out of there alive.

He hissed at Charlie to be silent and then signalled to Maggie and Charlie to stay low, stay quiet and follow him. Maggie put the rucksack on her back and could feel the weight of the money. She unconsciously reached for Charlie's hand. Jimmy picked up the tube of Gully's ashes from the mantelpiece, a half empty bottle of whisky from the floor next to the sofa and grabbed Charlie by the back of his coat, dragging him away from his brother and towards the galley kitchen at the back of the cottage, Maggie crawling after them. He stuffed Gully into the top of the rucksack on Maggie's back. "You stay in there mate." He found a dishcloth hanging off a hook in the kitchen, took a swig of the whiskey to try and stem the searing pain in his leg. He soaked the cloth in some of the whiskey and stuffed the sodden rag into the open neck of the bottle.

"They'll want to kill you for wasting the whiskey!" Maggie's half-hearted attempt at humour came as a surprise to her, but Jimmy smirked - it was exactly what he needed and brought back memories of the macabre humour he so often heard in his previous life. They heard the rattle of the front door, a moments pause, and then the shattering of wood as it was kicked in. Maggie and Charlie crouched by the back door like two children playing hide and seek. Jimmy stood in the darkness at the threshold to the living room; he had a plan, but it was a long shot to try and get the three of them out of there alive. Like a family of foxes being hunted down by a hungry pack of dogs, they were down a hole with nowhere to go.

The headlights made them sitting targets as the dogs closed in, creeping into the living room. He let them come.

THE DOGS ARE COMING

The lights in the cottage turned off as they approached. The fiesta pulled up outside the cottage and Flannagan could have sworn that he saw the curtains on the front window twitch. Ferguson and Duncan were straight out of the car and popped the boot. The driver's door was pulled open and Ferguson roughly pulled Flannagan out and thrust a rifle into his hand. "Stay away from the windows and keep your head down. Try not to shoot one of us eh?!" There was a maniacal glint in Ferguson's eye, and Flannagan thought that he seemed to be enjoying this a little too much. Flannagan's hands were shaking, like those early days when he gave up the booze and the cravings crippled his body. Only this time, it wasn't cravings - it was fear. This had spiralled out of control and Flannagan didn't like it. He was an ex-alcoholic, dabbling a little illegally on the side to try and make a few extra quid so that he could escape and live out the twilight of his years in relative comfort somewhere where the sun shines - he wasn't cut out for guns, gangsters and shooting each other. He sheepishly followed Ferguson, as Duncan casually wafted his handgun and indicated that he should get ready to kick open the door.

The three men stood outside the front door and listened for any noises from inside the cottage. The sky was beginning to lighten and the chirrups and squawks of the dawn chorus, together with the rhythmical pounding of the nearby surf muffled any other sounds. Ferguson gave Duncan a determined nod and held up his hand doing a silent countdown with his fingers before Flannagan raised his foot and kicked the old front door as hard as he could. The door was flung back, and Ferguson moved into the darkness of the cottage as if he was some sort of special forces soldier, shotgun raised to his shoulder, scanning the room. The embers in the grate pulsed as the air from the open door fuelled the fire. The swinging door came to a halt and the three men stood and listened to the silence of the room. Their eyes slowly adjusted to the darkness and the faint orange glow from the hearth gave off just enough light for them to make out the three bodies lying in front of it and the slowly expanding pool of blood spreading across the floor. There seemed to be a hole in the floor where the rug had been pulled back - a trap door maybe? Ferguson approached the dark void cautiously, his shotgun raised, his body tense.

"Where the fuck are they?"

"I heard shots."

"Look."

Their torches illuminated the bodies on the floor, the beams of light reflecting off the pool of glistening blood that was spreading across the floor.

"Shut the door. Check the bedrooms." The front door closed, and the living room was once again bathed in the flickering light of the fire and the shafts of the cars headlights. The sound of a door creaking on its hinges cut the silence and before anyone could react a yellow flame was sailing across the room before suddenly exploding against the now closed front door. Flames erupted and ignited the curtains of the front windows. Flannagan screamed as hot liquid splattered and singed his face. He dropped his rifle and grabbed at his burning skin. The sound of a shot exploded and reverberated around the room as the rifle discharged on impact with the stone floor. Duncan screamed and Ferguson threw himself to the floor. Flames licked the ceiling and lit the room up like it was fireworks night. Fire and whiskey Flannagan thought.

"Now!" Jimmy shoved them ahead of himself.

Maggie burst out of the back door, closely followed by Charlie and Jimmy. They moved around the periphery of the cottage sticking to the shadows as screams of panic emerged from inside. They got to the front of the cottage and could hear the crackle of the flames; one of the front windows exploded as the fire took hold. Using the explosion as cover, they sprinted the short distance to the vehicles in the drive. Charlie instinctively headed to the Ice cream van, but Jimmy yanked him away and towards the stolen Peugeot. "Too slow and stands out like a sore thumb." They squashed into the Peugeot and within seconds Jimmy had the engine started and was swinging the car around and accelerating up the rough driveway, stones spraying out as the wheels fought to find traction.

"Where to now?" Charlie's wide-eyed expression communicated his panic. Tears were streaming down his face. His voice was hoarse and broken with emotion. "What the fuck Jimmy? What's happening?"

"To the harbour. We can use my boat." Maggie opened the rucksack and looked inside to check she still had her money.

"Not the harbour. They'll expect that. They'll have all exits off the island shut down by now. We need somewhere to hole up - to make a plan." Jimmy's face was scrunched in a grimace of determination and pain. "And Charlie? I need you to have a look at my leg." The engine whined as they climbed the incline to the main road in complete darkness. Charlie nodded through a steady stream of tears.

"Go to the church. The one on the headland." Charlie spoke in a jerky monotone, as he tried to control the overwhelming grief he was feeling. He looked out of the window at the passing darkness, lost in an empty void - replaying the violent death of his brother over and over in his mind. But the call to action from Jimmy had somehow got through to him and it had triggered something in Charlie; medical treatment - this was something he could do. Something he knew and something he could hold onto.

"To Tom's?" Maggie looked concerned.

"Yeah. He's an outsider. He's not one of you." Charlie checked himself. "…. them. Is he?"

Maggie caught Jimmy's eye in the rear-view mirror. "No. He's not involved. Jimmy held her gaze for a moment.

"Shit!" The car lurched across the road, swerving away from a sheer drop on the left-hand side. Jimmy regained control. He was sweating. The adrenaline was wearing off and his leg was pulsing with pain, sweat was pouring down his forehead despite the cold of the early morning.

"Who were those men?" Charlie spoke almost in a daze, the shock beginning to take over. "At the cottage?"

Jimmy took a moment before replying. He knew this question was coming. The blame for Mark's death was his. "They were after me. I owe money. A lot of money to a very bad guy in London. They tracked me down."

Charlie didn't respond. His silence was deafening and tore at Jimmy's heart. He didn't need to say anything. He knew that Charlie would now forever hold him responsible for his brother's death.

Maggie looked out at the island she had lived on for most of her life. "It'll be light soon. Once day breaks, we'll be screwed. The whole island will be hunting us down." Again, Maggie caught Jimmy's eye. This girl was fierce - a warrior - it must be her Celtic blood.

SANCTUARY

The church was dark, an ominous shadow on the headland. Jimmy pulled the car to a stop behind the building, hidden from view from the main road.

The door to the church creaked open as the three of them crept into the cavernous interior. A wall of stale air hit them. Jimmy heard the bolt of a rifle being rammed home - it echoed through the stillness of the air, bouncing off the hard walls of the building.

A deep voice seeped out of the blackness, "What do you want?"

"Tom?" Charlie's voice cracked like an adolescent choir boy, fear constricting his throat.

Jimmy and Maggie edged into the chapel behind him, closing the door. Jimmy lifted the old metal bar across the door to secure it.

Tom could see the state they were in and sense the tension and fear radiating off Charlie and Maggie. Jimmy was something else - this was a military man who had gone into battle mode. "What's going on?"

None of them knew where to start. Maggie spoke first. "We need your help."

Tom looked at them, taking in the mud, the blood and the cuts and bruises. "Where's Mark?"

Charlie looked at Jimmy, but Jimmy wasn't taking his eyes off the gun that was pointing at him. Jimmy set his jaw. "He's dead."

The moon shifted out from behind the cloud and a shaft of silvery light illuminated the scene. "Dead?" Concern crossed Tom's face as Jimmy nodded. "I heard gunshots. Put my head out and saw the flames at the cottage." He looked at Maggie. No one moved. "what's going on?"

Jimmy delicately raised his hands, palms open, like an ancient gesture of peace. "Tom, will you put the gun down? We can explain everything, but right now we need shelter and we need to hide and hole up for a bit."

The entrance to the crypt under the ancient church was barely noticeable, master stonemasons having crafted a secret door in one of the internal walls. The stone stairs down were narrow and well worn, a threadbare rope clung to the wall as a makeshift handrail.

"Here, take this." Tom handed Charlie a small metal torch. "Go on down. I'll lock up and bring some blankets down." Charlie led the way, Jimmy leaning on his shoulder for support and Maggie bringing up the rear. The air was musty and stale, an odour of death and damp emanating from below. It was eerily quiet the further they descended, the solid stone around them blocking out all sound. At the bottom of the stairs the crypt opened up to a room roughly half the size of the church itself. The feeble light of the torch only illuminating part of the space at any one moment. Fleeting glances of ghostly marble men lying on top of ancient tombs flickered past their eyes. None of them spoke. The door creaked shut behind them and Charlie swung the small beam to the top of the stairs like a scared kid in some Hollywood Halloween movie. Even in the blackness of the crypt Jimmy could sense Charlie going into shock, the torch shook and Charlie's usually olive skin was ghostly white in the darkness. Tom moved down the stairs towards them, carrying some blankets, a sleeping bag and what looked like a first aid kit. He handed the first aid kit to Charlie. "I thought you might need this."

Jimmy clasped his friend's shoulders. "I need you to focus. Can you do that?"

Charlie bit his bottom lip and managed to nod.

As Maggie sat on the bottom step and recounted the events that had led them to this point, Tom listened without interrupting. Jimmy lay on his front on one of the blankets and Charlie inspected the wound in his leg by torchlight.

"Sounds like Duncan's going all Al Pacino." Tom looked deep in thought, frown lines creasing his weathered face. "But Kelsie's dead?"

"It was an accident." Charlie's eyes burned fiercely.

"I've never seen him like that. But, Tom, this isn't good. You know what this place is. You know the people. By first light this island will be locked down and we won't stand a chance. This is fucking serious." Maggie winced at the choice of language as she realised where she was.

"I never realised. I knew something was never quite Kosha though." Tom looked at Maggie.

"You're not local."

"No."

"They'll come here. You know that."

Tom nodded and looked at the stone floor, his brain beginning to assess all the options before him.

Charlie put the torch down on the floor and lowered Jimmy's leg. "I'm going to have to try and close up the wound as best I can. Have you got a sewing kit?"

Jimmy bit down on the old piece of rope that Tom had given him, agonized and guttural moans desperately trying to be repressed as Charlie tried his best to stitch the ragged edges of the wound together. Tom had brought down some candles and, in the low amber glow, Maggie could see the perspiration dripping off the end of Jimmys nose and staining the dirt on the stone-cold floor.

"I think that's as good as I can do under the circumstances. I'll put a gauze on it and bandage it and it should hold and keep it clean until we can deal with it properly."

"I think yous should all get a little rest. The sun'll be up in an hour, and they'll be looking for you. You're best to stay down here and out of sight until nightfall. We'll make a plan. It'll be alright. Get some rest. I'll bring down some food and a cup of tea a little later." Tom got up and tied his dressing gown tighter. "I'll leave the rifle. Just in case."

"Thanks." Jimmy caught the eye of the Geordie priest and gave a small nod.

"I'd best cover your car. Keep it out of sight. I've got an old tarp I can throw over it, and I'll pile a few of the materials for the vestry against it. Should do the trick for the moment."

"We're gonna need to get to my boat." Maggie looked worried.

"All in good time. Get some rest. You're safe down here. There's only a few folk who know about this place. I'll be back." With that, Tom turned and quietly padded up the stone steps, the hidden door softly closing behind him as he disappeared into the blackness of the chapel above. The small orange flames of the three candles flickered and danced as the draft tried to blow them out, before resuming their determined and steady dance. Maggie moved off the bottom step and went to sit down next to Charlie who was leaning against the wall at the bottom of the stairs on one of the blankets. His head was in his hands and his body was convulsing with quiet sobs. The momentary respite had brought the opportunity for Charlie to reflect on what had happened and the realisation that Mark was gone.

His twin brother. He couldn't get the image of his body out of his head. He yearned for his brother. Maggie put her arm around his shoulders and nestled his head into the crook of her neck, whispering soothing sounds and gently kissing the top of his head.

Jimmy leant against the other side of the staircase, the rifle resting across his lap. He let his head fall back against the wall and closed his eyes. His mind popped and spluttered with flashing images of the last twelve hours, but within minutes he was asleep.

As the sound of Jimmy's breathing softened and became a regular metronome that filled the echoey crypt Charlie's crying subsided and he leant back, taking a deep breath. He was exhausted, scared and distraught. He had lost so much already - his parents, his wife and now his brother. All he had ever done in life was to try and do good, to help people. And this was his reward? He looked up at Maggie in the darkness, his eyes wet and raw from his outpouring of grief. He began to order his thoughts, he wanted to make sense of what had happened. He summoned the courage to ask Maggie the question that had been at the forefront of his mind since earlier that evening. "So, are you going to tell me about Gully?"

"What about Gully?" Maggie sat up, moving her head off his shoulder.

"Well, what was going on between you both?"

"Not much to tell."

"You said you and he were saving to run away together. Sounds like there is quite a lot to tell."

"And why do you want to know? Gully's dead." She shifted her position, closing herself off from him.

"Listen, Maggie. I've known you for less than a week. But Gully….Gully…" Charlie tried to find the words to explain the situation.

"He told me about you. Told me about you all. He loved you like long lost brothers."

"Did he tell you why we didn't speak anymore?"

"Yeah. He did."

Charlie wasn't quite sure how much she knew, but it was clear that Gully had given her some background. He let the silence hang. After a few moments she lay down on her side as if the conversation was over.

"You loved him?" Charlie spoke to the darkness.

"Yes."

Somehow, in the darkness of the crypt it felt like they were in confession - no eyes to judge them.

"He said he killed your girlfriend."

Charlie didn't respond, unsure of what to say.

"Did he?"

"I guess. He didn't kill her, but his actions led to her death."

Jimmy began to moan; a stream of incomprehensible words spilling out of his mouth before he turned his head and resumed his quiet rhythmical breathing.

"Have you ever forgiven him?"

Charlie weighed this up. He had never really dealt with the question head on. "No. I don't think I did. I don't think I have."

"And now?"

"Now? Even in death Gully is fucking up my life. My brothers dead. My friend has half a leg missing, I'm stuck on a remote Scottish island with some demented gangsters trying to kill me. Gully sent me here. How am I meant to feel?"

"He loved you."

"Sometimes love isn't enough."

Time passed without either of them speaking, and Charlie thought she might have fallen asleep. "I guess this whole trip feels a little like an echo of that summer. It's like his ghost is following us around and twisting the world around us. The beach party, the surf…you."

"He wanted to make things better. To say sorry. He wanted to leave you the cottage, the money."

"You?"

The word hung in the air, lost.

"No. I'm not a gift. I make mae own decisions. I like you. I like you for you. Not because of Gully or anyone else."

In the darkness, and despite the tragedy of their situation, Charlie smiled. It felt odd and uncomfortable, in light of everything that had happened, but he couldn't stop the muscles in his face. She liked him for him. Maybe….just maybe if they made it out of here alive something good could come out of all of this.

DAY 6

SMOKING

The wind had dropped off and the early morning sky was flecked with a dazzling array of pinks, golds and oranges. It created a stark and beautiful contrast to the acrid black smoke rising from the smouldering remnants of Old Elsie's cottage down in the bay. The thatch of the roof had completely burnt through and all that remained were the blackened stone walls and some charred timbers of the roof. The morning was crisp and clear with a chill in the air that suggested warmth and sunshine would dominate the rest of the day.

Like ghostly spectres rising from the graves, the steam from the hot tea warming his hands rose and swirled in the morning air, as Tom tried to piece together a plan of action for the mess that had landed in his lap. He had come to this remote island to escape - to lead a simple life. Fifteen years in the special forces had given him a life's worth of adventures and dramas; but this sort of trouble seemed to follow him wherever he ran. He was a magnet for danger it seemed.

He took a deep breath of the sea air and could smell the acrid smoke from the burnt out cottage - there must be a southerly breeze blowing. He could feel the cold of the stone through his tracksuit bottoms. Robert 'Duffy' Brown's final resting place provided the perfect viewing platform to overlook the bay and to think, and Tom often sat here in the mornings to gather his thoughts and to slow his mind.

He had always known that there was something about the community on this island that was a little amiss. He had never quite been able to put his finger on it, but he could always sense it. Yes, he was an outsider, and he had never been fully accepted, never quite been let in...never been fully trusted. He had always felt that the community were holding back on him and that there were a million unspoken secrets and stories that he was not kin to, that people were hiding something from him. He had tried to be their friend. He had tried to get involved in the community, but eventually, after a couple of years, he had withdrawn and stopped. He was tired of trying. He was here if people wanted him, or God. God? His relationship with God was becoming increasingly complicated as time went on and he had found the time to reflect and think. Tom glanced over his shoulder at the silhouette of the chapel on the headland and the flare of the sun burning behind it. How can God create such beauty one minute and such destruction and darkness the next. He looked back down into the bay at the charred remains of the cottage.

The noise of a car engine broke his reverie and he turned to see an old white panel van pull up on the road. Gordon Harris, 'the Ferryman', got out and walked over to where Tom was sitting.

"Nasty fire."

"Looks like it. What happened?" Tom tried to keep his voice even and casual.

"Not sure. Just heard it went up in flames in the night. Tourists, eh? Bunch of lads, wasn't it? Probably drunk and behaving stupid. Seems the thing these days. No respect and all that. Not sure if they got out. No one knows, what with the festival last night and all that. There is a meeting up at the distillery now - think everyone is trying to look for them - make sure no one died."

There was a brief pause. Sea birds squawked. Tom continued to look at the smouldering cottage.

"You didn't see or hear anything in the night, did you?"

"No. Slept like a baby."

"Didn't go to the festival, eh? I don't blame you. Those days are long gone for me now. Me and Rose would prefer a nice quiet night in front of the telly and leave the partying and drinking to the young folk."

"How is Rose?"

"Oh, grand. Taking her on a foreign holiday. It's a surprise you see. She's been banging on about it for years. FInally got the money so I'm taking her. Keep it quiet, mind. I've not told her yet."

"Good on you."

Both men continued to look out across the bay, the calm sea glinting in the early morning sun.

"We're lucky aren't we? To live in such a beautiful place."

Gordon turned his back to make his way back to the van. "Ay, storms coming though. You know how it is. Weather's always changing. Cancelled the ferries for the rest of the day. Going to be a nasty one it seems. See you at the meeting."

With that Gordon turned and was gone, hobbling back to his van. Tom watched him go, his mind spinning - a storm, no ferries - the escape routes were narrowing.

THE PACK

The car park of the distillery was full when Tom arrived. He recognised a number of the cars. It looked like half the island was here. The sign on the door said it was closed but he could hear the hubbub of voices inside.

He followed the muffled voices as he entered the distillery, which took him to the bar area. About forty or fifty people sat on chairs or stood around the room looking towards the bar where Duncan was talking. He looked agitated. His hand was heavily bandaged and dark circles surrounded his eyes. Ferguson, the policeman was propped on a stool next to him. He had never liked Ferguson - he was an arrogant man, and that was a quality that Tom disliked more than anything else. For the first time, Tom thought that Ferguson looked like he had had the wind knocked out of him - his head was bowed, and he looked defeated. Tom walked further into the room and Duncan abruptly stopped midsentence. All eyes turned to the island's priest.

"It's ok Duncan. I told him about the meeting. Thought he might be able to help. What with his background and everything." Gordon was squashed around a table on the far side with a few familiar faces from the harbour.

"It's a little sensitive Gordon." Duncan growled. Murmurs and whispered conversations began to ripple around the room. The community had always had their secrets and never enjoyed involving an outsider.

Tom held up his hands. "It's ok. No dramas. I can leave. Was just willing to help. Missing tourists is not good for the island, is it?" Tom tried to keep his tone innocent but tuned in to the gravitas of the situation. He looked directly at Duncan. "Not good for business." Duncan held his gaze, and the room went deathly quiet. The ambiguity of what Tom had said was deliberate, but he suddenly felt that he may have pushed his luck.

Without breaking eye contact, Duncan enunciated his next question with over exaggerated diction. "And what is it that you know about *the situation*?"

"How have you hurt your hand?" Tom felt the butterflies in his stomach as he tried to hold his nerve. He needed to be let in here. He needed to be accepted and taken into the confidence of the island if he was to get any information and be able to help Charlie, Maggie and Jimmy. But he was having fun - he was enjoying this game of cat and mouse.

Duncan ignored the question. "What do you know about what has happened?"

"Just that some of the tourists have gone missing at the festival." Tom turned to Gordon. "And that the cottage has burnt down. Old Elsie's place. The English lads staying there. Could see the smoke from the chapel this morning." He turned back to Duncan. "Has anyone been inside…checked if their bodies are in there, if they were trapped in the fire?"

Without moving a muscle, Ferguson's deep, cigarette scarred voice resonated around the room. "They aren't in there."

Duncan continued to stare at Tom. "You were all friendly with them. People saw you surfing with them yesterday." Tom subconsciously touched his throbbing ribs and the bandage beneath his shirt.

"That's right. Gully's friends. They came up for the surf, so I offered to show them a few spots."

"Any idea where they might have gone?"

"Have they left? Left the island I mean. I know they were planning on leaving after the festival."

"They weren't on the ferry this morning." Gordon chipped in.

"What would you do in their situation?" Duncan's eyes were fixed on Tom.

"I don't know." Tom pursed his lips, choosing his words carefully. "What do you mean by 'situation'? What's happened?"

Gordon's voice piped up again but with less confidence this time. "Just tell him what's going on."

Suddenly, Ferguson snarled at the old ferryman, spitting the words across the room. "Keep your trap shut, Gordon."

Duncan took a sip of a tumbler of whiskey on the bar before turning back to Tom. "One of them killed Kelsie last night."

Sam suddenly erupted from the side of the room. "And we need to find the cunt who murdered mae daughter." Flannagan was standing next to Sam and gently put his hand on her arm.

"I need to find them so I can put them under lock and key and contact the mainland. But I can't do it on my own. It will be quicker and easier if the community come together to find them. They can't have gone far. They can't hide on an island forever." Ferguson stood up from his stool, seemingly taking charge.

"Why not call the mainland now. Get some police over here to help search for them?" Tom retained his feigned innocence.

"This is island business. And besides, the island is full of tourists. What's it going to look like if we have every copper from the mainland coming over?" Duncan took another slug of whiskey. "So? Any ideas?"

Tom took his time. He looked at his shoes as if thinking through the problem. All eyes in the room were on the priest.

He needed some misdirection here if he was to help his countrymen in the crypt. Mark had killed an innocent girl. That was wrong, accident or not. On the other hand, he had an opportunity to bed himself into this community now, earn their trust and become a local. Did he give up his little slice of paradise - uncrowded waves and a quiet life? For what, for some people he barely knew? Or did he entangle and entwine himself in a community twisted in a dark cloud of drug smuggling and criminality so that he could live out his days surfing perfect waves with no one around? He needed to choose his words carefully. He looked up and addressed the room.

SITTING DUCKS

When Maggie opened her eyes, she felt disoriented in the darkness, unable to fathom what time of day it was. A faint light was filtering down the stairs and she could see that Jimmy was no longer in the crypt. She gently lowered Charlie's head onto the blanket and stood up, her muscles aching and taught from the exertions of the night before and then sleeping in an awkward position on a stone-cold floor. She cautiously made her way up the stairs and peered out into the gloom of the chapel. Jimmy was hobbling up and down the central aisle, his footsteps rhythmically echoing around the cavernous interior. The rifle was slung over his shoulder and his head was down, inaudibly murmuring to the floor.

"Hey." Her voice sounded uncomfortably loud in the silence.

Jimmy startled and pulled the rifle to his shoulder, paranoia etched all over his face. When he saw the source of the noise and the momentary fear on Maggie's face, he lowered the rifle.

"Hey."

"What time is it?"

Jimmy looked at his simple black diver's watch. "About midday."

"Did you sleep?" Maggie looked concerned.

"On and off. You?"

He was a closed book; Jimmy was not like Charlie and Mark. Or even Gully. He was a hard one to warm to. But she knew he had been Gully's best friend and Gully had told her to trust him with her life.

"Yeah. A bit. How's your leg?

"Ok." There was a fire burning in his eyes. Something a little unhinged that unsettled Maggie.

"Have you got a plan?"

"I'm trying to work that out now. But I don't like sitting here. We're sitting ducks. We are putting a lot of trust in Tom. We barely know him."

Charlie appeared behind Maggie, woken by their voices, his eyes swollen and puffy from lack of sleep and the emotionally rollercoaster of the previous night.

"How's your leg?" His tone was cold and unfriendly, but Jimmy wasn't surprised, and he didn't blame him. This was his mess. Mark carried some blame too, but the complication of Dokes and the Eastern European thug was all Jimmy. And in Charlie's eyes, they were the ones that had pulled the trigger and ended Mark's life. And that was Jimmy's fault.

"Fine. We need to move. Get out of here. I don't like it."

"We should wait for Tom." Charlie fixed him with a stern look and began to head to the vestry to see if he could find some water or any form of liquid to quench his parched throat.

"We don't know him. How can we trust him?" Jimmy began to follow Charlie.

"He's all we've got at the moment."

"I don't like it. We're taking a big risk."

"Jimmy's right." Maggie's voice cut through the tension. Charlie whipped around and looked at Maggie and then at Jimmy.

"What choice do we have? This is your mess. You brought them here…those thugs and now what? Mark's dead. I'm not sure I want to trust you, Jimmy. " Charlie felt groggy and exhausted, the death of Mark still sitting over him like a heavy dark cloud. He could barely think.

"I get it, Charlie. I do. And I take responsibility for my actions. And I am sorry. I never wanted this to happen. But It's more complicated than that isn't it? And we can't just sit here and keep our fingers crossed. All I'm saying is that we don't know Tom. Where is he? He could be rounding up the cavalry right now and be about to burst through those doors with the entire island ready to lynch us. I don't fancy fighting the Alamo. Maggie, you said you had a boat?"

"Yeah. It's at the harbour."

"They'll be expecting that, especially if Tom has opened his trap."

"Why would he do that?"

"Why wouldn't he do that? He's got no loyalty to us."

"He was Gully's friend."

Jimmy sat down heavily on a pew. He was backed into a corner. The options were limited. His mind desperately searched for a solution. Charlie returned from the vestry with a bottle of water and handed it around. Jimmy began to order his thoughts. "The only way off this island is by boat, yes?"

Maggie took a glug of water. "Yes."

"They're going to expect us to head for Maggie's boat. The harbour is a no go. They'll have it locked down. Are there any other moorings around the island?"

"No. It's all too exposed."

Jimmy began to play with the bolt of the rifle. "We need to create a diversion."

"Wait. There is something." Maggie looked like she had discovered the cure for cancer.

"What?" Jimmy looked up from the rifle.

"What about the lighthouse?"

"The lighthouse?" Jimmy was looking at her eagerly.

Maggie briefly explained the story of the lighthouse and the disappearing lighthouse keepers.

"There's a wave that breaks there. It's heavy. Tom told me about it." Charlie went and grabbed the photo of Tom off the wall. "He said it's a long paddle - just over a mile."

"But we could paddle it." There was a glimmer of hope in Jimmy's eyes.

"If we had boards. All our boards were in the cottage." Charlie crushed the hope.

Jimmy spoke quickly at the thought of this option. "But what about the boards in the crypt. There are guns and long boards. Better than what we had."

Maggie nodded her head. "They won't suspect that. Everyone stays clear of the lighthouse."

Jimmy stood up. "Come on. We need to get moving. I've got an idea. They could find us any moment."

As Jimmy hurried back down to the crypt, Charlie placed the photograph carefully on the altar. Maybe they had got this wrong. Maybe Tom was on their side. He liked to look for the best in people.

CLOSING THE NET

Duncan was twitchy. This was all getting out of control and needed wrapping up as quickly as possible. The distillery was meant to be open for business in half an hour and they needed to start moving the goods. With Christian out of the picture they needed to shift the goods as soon as possible, then he could turn his attention to the Englishmen. He didn't trust the priest, but maybe he needed to take a chance on him. Something else was nagging him too - the two men in the cottage. Dead. Who were they? Where had they come from? Was there a third party involved here?

"Right, we need to get moving. The doors to this place need to open as usual and we all need to get back to our jobs and keep everything normal. Got it?" There were nods all around the room. "Let me know if anyone sees the English surfers. Pete, You go to the bothy. Shift the goods back here. We're on the clock."

"But..." Flannagan didn't like it.

"Just do it. And be quick about it." Duncan turned back to the room as Flannagan disappeared out of the back door. "Gordon? Keep an eye on the harbour. Let me know if anything is going down. Everyone else go back to your business, but keep your eyes peeled for anything out of the ordinary. Stuart?" he looked at Ferguson as the sound of chairs scraping the stone floor filled the air. "Grab the priest and meet me out front. Let's go hunting."

CUT BACK

They had parked on the road so as not to alert them of their approach. "You say they are in the chapel?" Ferguson was checking the firing mechanism on his hand gun.

"Yeah. they're in the crypt. Below the chapel." Tom was beginning to regret his decision to give up the two Englishmen and Maggie. He could clearly see that the justice they were going to deal out was going to be brutal and deadly. But they were amateurs at this, and Tom had a sense that Jimmy on his own would be a hell of a match for these two. Even so, his decision was made. He wanted a quiet life.

"And the only entrance is in the chapel?"

"That's right."

"I didn't know there was a crypt." Duncan was downing some pain killers for his hand.

"Not many people do. Not many people come to church anymore." Duncan looked at him in the mirror on the back of the sun visor.

"Right, let's go." Ferguson exited the car and the others followed. "You let me lead alright? Stay back and don't get involved. Are we clear? You get in my way and I'll put you down." Ferguson was wild eyed and agitated, like he was running on speed.

"Rightio boss." Tom smiled, intending to portray a submissive demeanour, but internally he was mildly amused at the puffed-up policeman. He could kill the both of them in a heartbeat if he had wanted to. But those days were over for him. He wasn't a soldier anymore.

Tom squinted as they walked cautiously up the gravel path. The sun was shining and the day was calm, with barely a breath of wind. Gordon had said a storm was coming but he couldn't see any signs of it yet. Ferguson nudged open the heavy wooden door and it creaked on its hinges. A shaft of light from the open door stretched out across the stone floor and Ferguson inched forward, his gun raised in front of him, finger poised on the trigger. Bad technique, Tom thought. Ferguson had obviously been watching too many movies. Duncan followed the policeman in, his damaged hand hanging limply by his side and his other hand struggling to hold the unfamiliar weight of the pistol steady.

Ferguson turned to Tom and whispered, "Where?" Even his hushed volume was enough for Keegan to pick up in the eerie silence of the chapel and suddenly barking filled the space, loud and rebounding around the room. Keegan bounded along the central aisle, eager to greet his returning master. Ferguson recoiled and batted the dog away as it jumped up in its enthusiasm. "Shut that fucking dog up."

Tom glared at Ferguson, disgusted at the way he had pushed Keegan aside with his heavy paw of a hand. "Keegan, here boy." The dog immediately came to heel, sitting on its haunches at Toms feet and rubbing his head against the priest's thigh.

"Where's the crypt?"

Tom pointed to the other side of the chapel, and watched as Ferguson stealthily made his way across the flagstone floor, surprisingly light-footed for such a big man. He found the hidden handle in the stonework and pulled open the door before stepping back and pointing the gun at Tom. He raised his eyebrows, indicating that Tom should speak.

Tom went along with it. "Charlie? Jimmy? It's me. Tom." They were greeted with a deafening silence, the only sound being the panting of the dog.

Ferguson looked at Duncan and nodded before slowly descending the steps into the crypt. Duncan raised his gun and pointed it at Tom's head, but he was too close. It would be so easy to disarm him. Keegan could sense the tension and began to softly whine. Tom tried to placate him by rubbing his ears.

"Nothing. It's empty." Ferguson emerged from the darkness of the stairwell.

"You said they were here." Duncan was almost beside himself with rage. He was losing his grip.

"They were here when I left. They must have woken up and gone elsewhere. Maybe they didn't trust me. I wouldn't blame them all things considered." Tom let out a brief chuckle as he began regretting his deceit immediately. He knew he had chosen badly. It was clear he had opted for the wrong side.

Duncan reacted explosively to the apparent nonchalance of the priest. "This isn't a fucking game priest. They killed one of us. They killed Christian. They shot mae hand off. They killed Kelsie. Eh? I don't find it a fucking joke!" The shouting and the aggressive tone of Duncan was too much for Keegan - he didn't like people attacking his master and he began barking at Duncan incessantly, filling the room with a cacophony of noise. The barking was loud, and Duncan and Ferguson's patience was thin with no sleep and their pride in tatters.

"Shut the fucking dog up." Ferguson was searching the rest of the chapel.

"Maybe you should stop shouting at me then."

"You shut that dog up or I will." Duncan pointed the gun at Keegan, who was growling now, his fangs bared, a drool of saliva hanging from his exposed gums.

Tom held Duncans gaze for a moment. He didn't like Duncan's

tone, and he didn't like it when people threatened his dog. "Here boy." He held Keegans collar and stroked his head. The dog quietened a little, but he could feel that Keegan was tense and his hackles were raised.

Ferguson came back from the vestry. "Where are they?"

"I don't know."

"Well, think Priest." Ferguson moved forward aggressively waving his gun in Tom's face. Keegan immediately reacted and launched himself at Ferguson, mauling his extended arm that held the gun. Ferguson screamed and went down, wrestling the dog and trying to prise its jaws off his wrist. Instinct kicked in and Tom immediately spun around, grabbing Duncans wrist and twisting it into an unnatural position and locking it out. Duncan screamed and dropped the gun. Tom moved in behind him and wrapped his arm around Duncans neck, pressing his head forward with his other hand and increasing the pressure on the sides of Duncan's neck. Within moments Duncan fell to the floor unconscious. The crack of a gun reverberated around the room and the whimper of Keegan sang over the top. Tom watched as his dogs body went limp and Ferguson pushed the dog off him, a gaping hole in the belly of his loyal companion. Ferguson was breathing hard and holding his wrist where Keegan had sunk his teeth into the soft flesh. Tom was momentarily paralysed at the realisation that Ferguson had killed his dog. They locked eyes before Ferguson saw that Duncan was lying unconscious on the floor. He quickly scrambled for his gun, which had fallen under one of the pews. Tom took one step towards him and kicked him in the face with all his might. Fergusons head whipped back, teeth shattering and scattering across the stone floor. Tom reached down and picked up the gun. It felt familiar, like a long lost friend. Rage was burning inside him. He pointed the gun at Ferguson.

"You killed my dog."

The policeman's mouth was bloodied and swollen from the impact of the kick, and spittle and bits of broken teeth bubbled out of his mouth as he spoke. "He bit my hand."

"You're an embarrassment to your profession." Tom pulled the trigger and Fergusons head exploded back against the solid flagstone, a dark hole smoked from the centre of his forehead. Tom was shaking, shock kicking in. He looked up at the cross above the altar and a tear rolled down his weathered face. "Forgive me." He knelt by Keegan and cradled his soft head in his arms, but he was dead, his eyes lifeless and his body limp. "Thank-you. You were the best friend a man could ever have. I'll see you soon." he laid Keegan down on the ground and sprang up to his feet - he needed to get out of there. His life on the island was over.

He ran down into the crypt, scanning for any clues as to what had happened to the others. Even in the gloomy light he could see something was different. He methodically looked around the room. His boards. Three of his boards were missing.

He began to rack his mind as to what they had done, where they were going. What was he going to do? He bounded back up the stairs, his eyes searching for any clues, taking in every minor detail of the building. He looked at the cross again, hoping for some inspiration, some guidance. And then he saw it - the framed photograph of him surfing 'Lighthouses'. He moved over to the altar, his mind running through all the possibilities of what this meant. In a moment of crisis, he was naturally slipping into his mindset of old. And then he realised. That's where they had gone. The lighthouse. Good option. He turned and took one last look at the chapel before running down to the crypt and picking up his old Takayama longboard.

PADDLE OUT

The sea was cold without a wetsuit, but the sun was shining and the water was as flat as they had seen it. The boards glided over the glass like surface of the sea, but the paddling was brutal. They were physically, mentally and emotionally exhausted. Jimmy's leg was causing him a lot of pain now - the walk down to the sea with the boards had been difficult, but now he was lying prone on the board, it had taken some of the pressure off and he tried to focus his mind on rhythmically stroking towards the distant lighthouse. Even though they were a small target in the vastness of the Atlantic ocean, he was aware that in broad daylight, they were incredibly exposed out here. If anyone was on the cliffs, they would spot them. But they didn't have time to wait it out, they needed to take the risk and make a run for it whilst the conditions were as calm as this.

Their progress had been slow initially, as Maggie was unfamiliar with paddling a surfboard, but once beyond the breaking waves at the shoreline, where the water was flatter, she had begun to find her balance and her rhythm. They were making headway, and the lighthouse was getting bigger. They were now only about half a mile from the rocky outcrop. Jimmy arched his back and peered over the plastic bin liner perched on the front of his board stuffed with Maggie and Gully's cash. Thoughts of what he could do with that money began to spiral through his mind, thinking about what they would do if they ever did make it out of this mess. He looked across the water, trying to spy a landing point. Charlie hadn't spoken at all and Jimmy could sense that shock had taken hold of his lifelong friend, but there wasn't time to grieve right now, they needed to get to safety - time would heal the scars, maybe not completely but he would be there for his friend when this was all done, if he was willing to forgive him. But first and foremost they needed to get out of this mess.

OPEN WATER

Tom stood on the cliff and looked out to sea. The binoculars scanned the expanse of blue between him and the lighthouse. Nothing. He refocused the binoculars on the lighthouse, looking for any signs that he had been right and they had headed to Eilean Mor. He caught a glimpse of movements on the rocks below the lighthouse and saw the unmistakable outline of some surfboards lying on the rocks at the foot of the white obelisk. Tom lowered the binoculars. "Good on you." He bent down and picked up the longboard at his feet, checked the Glock pistol that was tucked into the waistband at the small of his back and began to make his way down to the shoreline. He was worried about whether his ribs would survive the long paddle, but taking the longboard was a good choice - he could always knee paddle.

EILEAN MOR

The rocky outcrop upon which the lighthouse stood was rugged and desolate. The idea of someone spending days here was dumbfounding. In the crisp afternoon sunshine, with the water glass like around it, it was picturesque, but Jimmy imagined in a storm or when the sea was rough, it would have been bleak and miserable. The lighthouse itself had seen better days; the whitewash paintwork was crumpling and peeling, the old wooden windows were rotting and on their last legs. A myriad of different seabirds had made the lighthouse and outcrop of rock their home, meaning that the entire ground was covered in their excrement. They had found an old landing stage on the far side of the island where presumably boats moored to drop off any visitors. The landing stage was crumbling and broken, battered by the relentless weather, but although it creaked and groaned in an audible protest at their weight, it held firm as they clambered ashore, exhausted and dehydrated. There was little vegetation they could see as they made their way over the jagged rocks towards the solitary door at the base of the lighthouse. They deposited their surfboards on the rocks and Jimmy tried the door. It was padlocked. Being a steel door, he didn't fancy his chances of kicking it in. He looked around for a rock and found one of suitable size just a few feet away. He glanced at Charlie who was standing shivering with his arms crossed staring at the floor. "We're safe buddy. Well done both of you. It'll be alright now." Maggie was clutching the black bin liner and staring back across the water to the island she had grown up on. He turned back to the door and smashed the padlock as hard as his tired limbs would let him. It took three solid blows before the rusty padlock gave way and they hurriedly pulled it off and opened the door.

The interior was much better than the outside. Broken panes of glass lay scattered over the wooden floorboards on the first level. Most of the furniture from the days when it had been manned by humans was gone now, but there were some old chairs and a dilapidated table with a tendril of ivy wrapping itself around the flimsy legs. They found some blankets in a cupboard - they had a strong musty odour, having clearly layed folded and unused for decades. Jimmy hobbled through the room, treading carefully over the broken shards of glass. He wrapped Charlie and Maggie in blankets and sat them down on the chairs. He tried the tap above a sink in the corner, but the water had clearly been turned off years ago. He continued to search through the building, trying to locate anything that might be of use. He was hoping there might be a telephone or a radio of some kind, although he was not sure who he could contact, but he found nothing of any real use. "Shit." The adrenalin that had kept him going for so long was now starting to ebb and he felt the hungry fingers of exhaustion begin to take a grip over his body and his mind. He needed to keep moving. If he stopped, he would pass out and they weren't out of the woods yet.

Suddenly he heard a shout. He hobbled as fast as he could down the stairs that hugged the outside wall, thinking that something had happened to Charlie or Maggie, but they were on their feet and looking startled, panic in their eyes.

"Outside" Charlie whispered to him.

"Stay here. Bolt the door." Jimmy picked up a shard of broken glass as a weapon and moved as quietly as he could to the porthole window on the side and peered out but the angle was all wrong and even when he craned his neck he could see nothing but a huge expanse of blue water. He moved over to the door and exited down the small set of steps to the outside door. He heard the bolt slam into place behind him as Maggie shut the door.

Once he heard the bolt ram home Jimmy centred himself, focusing on a box breath before he began to slowly prise the stiff metal door of the lighthouse open. The weight and degradation of the door made it difficult to open without making noise, but he just about managed it. He opened the door just a fraction and looked out. The bright sunshine was blocked by a figure standing on the threshold. Jimmy was about to slam the door shut and retreat when he recognised the face grinning at him.

"It's me. Come to get my boards back!"

Jimmy opened the door a fraction more and peered beyond Tom.

"I'm alone." Tom felt the pang of guilt in the knowledge that he had earlier betrayed them.

Not letting his guard down, and holding tight onto the shard of glass he was holding behind his back he opened the door and ushered Tom inside. He clocked the bulge of the pistol in the small of Toms back as he passed, and Jimmy tensed. Could he trust him? This could all just be a ruse, a Trojan horse. Jimmy closed the door.

"How'd you find us?" Jimmy's grip on the glass tightened.

"The picture on the altar. Then I noticed the boards were missing. I put two and two together."

What picture? Charlie must have left him a clue. His friend was always one to look for the best in people. He was too trusting.

"What happened? We woke up and you were gone."

"There was a meeting at the distillery. I went along, thinking I could get some inside info to help you."

"And?"

"Ferguson's dead. Duncan is out cold. But it won't be long before he wakes up and will be spitting blood."

"Dead? What happened?"

"They came at me. Didn't trust me as I'm an outsider. Killed my dog. I hate animal cruelty."

Jimmy was on edge. His answers were evasive and generalised. He was holding something back. "What's with the gun?"

"What?" Tom feigned innocence.

Jimmy didn't move a muscle but just fixed him with a searching look. Tom smirked. "Thought we might need it. Look, I'm in the same boat as you now. I need off that island. My life there is over. Here." Tom began to reach for the weapon.

"Whoah there." Jimmy reacted quickly and held up the shard of glass. Tom paused and held up his hands.

"Listen, Jimmy. I respect your caution. You're a military man and I get it. But I'm on your side. You're being paranoid."

"So, forgive me Father." Tom grinned at Jimmys wit. "Turn around." Tom followed the order, keeping his hands up in the air as Jimmy moved in and removed the Glock from Tom's waistband. He tucked it into his own trousers and pushed Tom towards the short flight of steps and the door that Maggie had bolted.

"Maggie? It's fine. Open the door." The sound of the bolt sliding back resonated through the small space and then the door swung open.

"Tom!" Maggie looked surprised but happy. She glanced over his shoulder at Jimmy and noted the frown lines, his expression full of concern. Charlie stiffly got to his feet and smiled broadly at the priest."

"You worked it out!" Charlie approached Tom and wrapped his arms around the Geordie. "Jimmy felt like we were sitting targets there and we couldn't risk it. But I knew you were good. I'm glad you're here."

Maggie sat back down. "What happened?"

"Let's just say I made the situation a little worse and I'm in as much danger as you now." Tom looked around the room, taking in the apocalyptic feel to a room that time had forgotten.

"Well, I reckon we're safe for a bit. But someone may have seen us, or you, paddling out here. We need to find a way to the mainland." Jimmy was leaning against the wall, lifting his leg and trying to take some of the pressure off it.

"I can't paddle anymore." Maggie looked at Jimmy pleadingly. He could see the strain on her face. She was on the edge and her emotions were rollercoasting, ok one minute, followed by a pit of exhaustion and desperation.

"It's too far anyway. Too many risks." Jimmy ejected the magazine of the pistol and inspected it.

"There's a storm coming too, I think. But I can't see any signs of it. It may have just been Gordon letting me know that the island was shut down."

"FUCK! What's happened, Jimmy? How have we got here? Huh?" We haven't got any food or water. Mark's dead." Charlie was spiralling, he had his head in his hands. His body began to quietly convulse as the emotion overcame him. Jimmy could see he was barely clinging on. Maggie moved to him and enveloped his crumpled form. The two ex-soldiers had seen people fall apart before and they needed to find a solution fast before it became unmanageable.

"Any radio equipment?" Tom looked over at Jimmy, who shook his head. "Phone?" Jimmy shook his head again. "Shall we have a look around?" Jimmy was about to tell him that he had already searched the whole building, but he picked up the subtext in Tom's tone - as the two calm heads, they needed a moment to work out they're next move, without the other two listening.

Tom exited the room and Jimmy followed. His leg was really hurting now the painkillers had worn off. If he didn't get it sorted soon, he knew it could become infected. Each step was agony as he followed Tom up to the next floor. He could feel each step draining valuable energy from his tired body.

Tom walked into what had clearly been the living quarters on the next floor and assessed the room. Jimmy sat down on the mouldy mattress on the old wooden bed frame and tried to clear his head.

"You don't need me to tell you that those two aren't going to last." Tom turned to Jimmy and watched his head sink. "And you don't look too bright yourself."

Jimmy raised his head and looked at the ex-paratrooper. "Got any ideas?"

"Jimmy! JIMMY!" It was Maggie shouting up the stairs. The urgency in Maggie's voice momentarily shut out the pain in his leg and Jimmy was out the door. Tom moved to the small window and looked out. He could see what he thought was a boat and it looked like it was heading this way. He pulled out the binoculars from his pocket and tried to find focus.

Jimmy was standing at the window on the south side of the lighthouse when Tom walked back into the room. Charlie was still slumped at the table and Maggie was behind Jimmy, craning her neck to see if she could see over his shoulder. Jimmy turned back to the room. "It's definitely a boat."

"It's a fishing boat by the looks of things. Irish name I think." Tom handed Jimmy the small set of binoculars.

"What are we going to do?" Maggie stumbled over the words in her desperate sense of hope.

Jimmy looked at Tom as he lowered the binoculars. "We try to get their attention somehow."

CATCH OF THE DAY

The boat cut through the still water like a hot knife through butter. When the weather was like this, there wasn't anything that Kieran O'Mahony liked more than being out on the ocean. His two sons, Sean and Simon were sitting up. Simon was rolling a cigarette and Sean was using his knife to cut away some of the plastic and rubbish that had got caught up in the nets. It was getting worse and worse every year. But Kieran put out the brief flare of anger towards the big corporate companies responsible for polluting his waters - the fair weather meant that they were heading to one of his most lucrative fishing grounds - the reef by Eilean Mor. Local folk were so scared of the place that no one ever really ventured out near the old lighthouse; but he wasn't superstitious, and with the weather set to be fine for a few more hours and no drops to make for their 'side business' he was chuckling to himself at the prospect of fishing the teeming reef. Perhaps they might make a good catch of cod or some Ling on the reef - it would make a nice change to the whiting and haddock they would normally go for around the islands. Yes, his daughter, Jemma, loved cod - she would be over the moon, and maybe she might cook up that cod and chorizo stew? He loved that, even though he would never tell her in so many words - he wouldn't admit to liking all these foreign flavours. He sang a few bars of an old Irish ditty his mother used to sing; he hadn't been in such a good mood in a long time.

He looked out of the wheelhouse window and thought he saw something glint and glare on the rocks at the base of the lighthouse. Perhaps it was just the sun reflecting off one of the windows. There it was again. Kieran put his binoculars to his eyes and pulled the focus to the bottom of the lighthouse.

"What the bleedin….?"

He could make out two figures hunched at the foot of the lighthouse with blankets wrapped around them. A couple of surfboards stood prominently against the white of the old building, their dark colours stark against the white background. One of them looked like he was holding a mirror and was using it to signal to them with the sun. Keiran spun the wheel and slightly altered his course. They must have seen the change in direction because one of them began jumping up and down and waving his arms. Kieran leaned out of the wheelhouse and shouted at his boys. "Oi! We've got company." He nodded towards the lighthouse and Sean and Simon stopped fiddling with the nets and squinted towards where their father was indicating. They dropped their nets and Sean sheathed his knife.

Kieran picked up the VHF radio. "Harbour master Harris, Harbour master Harris, Harbour master Harris. Shamrock, Shamrock, Shamrock." The crackle of the radio spluttered and fizzed.

"Shamrock, this is Harbour master. Over"

RESCUE

"Looks like they've seen us." Jimmy winced as a stabbing pain shot up his leg and began to pulse through his body. He could begin to smell the pungent waft of decay emanating from the wound on his leg. He looked down at the bandage wrapped around his calf - it was wet and pink from where the wound was still weeping through the makeshift stitches Charlie had sewn.

"Stay here. I'll get the other two."

By the time the boat pulled up to the crumbling jetty, the four of them were huddled on the rocks above, stripped to their underwear and wrapped in blankets, their boards lying on the jetty. A hefty fisherman nimbly jumped off the boat and the jetty groaned under his weight. He tied a rope around one of the posts, but the bearded man in the wheelhouse didn't cut the engine. Tom gave his best smile to them.

"Hi." Tom said. "Thanks. We were getting pretty worried. Didn't think anyone would pick us up."

"What the hell are you doing out here?" The bearded fisherman stepped out of the wheelhouse and looked at the four bedraggled surfers.

"We were surfing the reef yesterday evening and Jimmy here got a nasty cut on his leg. We couldn't make the paddle back and hoped someone would rescue us." Tom clenched his jaw, hoping they would buy the story.

"Not many folk come out here." The fisherman's beady eyes

narrowed. Jimmy noted the other two, who were significantly younger and more athletic, were unable to take their eyes off Maggie.

"Not from around here?"

"No. Just on holiday."

"You surfers are crazy folk."

Tom smiled. "I guess. Something like that. What about you? You sound a long way from home." Jimmy noted the look between the three fishermen.

"That's right. Just fishing these waters for a few days whilst the weather's good."

The conversation was stilted and cagey. Both groups could sense that the other was holding something back.

"Climb on board then. We'll take yous back ASAP. Can't have you stranded out here. Sean, grab the surfboards."

As they sat below deck it was hard to hear anything with the rumble of the big diesel engine, so none of them spoke. Jimmy could hear the crackle of the radio and the bearded man's thick Irish accent saying something. Suddenly the light filtering down through the open stairway up to the wheelhouse was blocked and they looked up to see the larger of the two young fishermen standing at the top of the four wooden steps. "We'll be there in about ten minutes or so." And then he was gone, and the light returned to the room.

Tom looked at Jimmy. "We've got five minutes."

Jimmy nodded. He looked at his brother and Maggie who were on their last legs. "Stay here."

Tom nodded to Jimmy and moved quietly to the four wooden steps leading up into the wheelhouse. The old fisherman had his back to them as he stood at the wheel. Tom was almost within reach when the top step creaked and the old man turned around, alerted by the sound.

Tom was below him but within easy striking distance and jabbed the old man on the inside of the thigh, buckling his leg. He moved above him pressing down on the old man's throat, but the old man was surprisingly strong and bucked and flayed, managing to land two blunt blows to Tom's head. Tom's hands gripped his throat and applied pressure. He knew just the amount of pressure he needed to apply to the carotid arteries to render the fisherman unconscious and within ten seconds, the old man's body went limp and his eyes closed. Jimmy pulled him down the steps and grabbed some twine lying on the side. He threw the nylon twine to Maggie.

"Tie him up." And then he was gone, up the steps and into the wheelhouse.

Sean and Simon were at the front of the boat, detangling the fishing nets when Jimmy and Tom emerged from the wheelhouse. The cold breeze brought goose bumps to their naked skin. Jimmy raised the pistol at the larger of the two men, but the boat lurched to the side with no one manning the wheel, and his leg gave way, causing him to fall and the gun clatter across the deck. The movement broke their focus and Sean reacted first, pulling out his knife and launching himself at Tom. Tom easily parried the swinging arm and delivered two accurate blows to the larger man's abdomen, knocking him back towards the front of the boat, winded and gasping for air.

With Jimmy sprawled on the deck of the boat, Simon saw his opportunity and threw the fishing net in his hands at Jimmy, ensnaring him like a wild animal. He pulled his knife from the sheaf and crossed the deck towards the Englishman, but Jimmy's legs were free from the net and, as soon as the Irishman was within distance , he managed to land a bone crunching kick to Simon's knee, buckling the man where he stood.

He fell across the deck and Tom stamped on Simon's hand, sending the serrated fishing knife across the deck and out through one of the wash holes and into the sea. Sean, the more muscular fisherman, was back on his feet now, his breathing heavy as he recovered from the savage blows. "You'll not escape this. They know we're bringing you in." Tom picked up a crate from the stack by the wheelhouse and, with a roar of effort, launched it at the approaching man who easily ducked, and the crate sailed over his head into the sea. At the same moment, Jimmy went for the gun that was lying just a foot away from him. Simon had seen the gun too and managed to grab Jimmy's leg and pressed hard on the bandaged calf, making Jimmy cry out in pain.

The noise of his scream momentarily distracted Tom and Sean swung again with the knife, but this time feinted and threw a powerful punch into Tom's ribs. Tom went down, hitting the deck hard and gasping for air, the laceration on his ribs from surfing the reef opening up, and he could feel the blood begin to seep between his fingers. He knelt on one knee clasping his injury with his elbow, trying to protect his weak spot.

As Simon attempted to crawl over Jimmy to reach the gun, Jimmy swung his elbow, connecting with Simon's jaw. He rolled off him, allowing Jimmy to stagger to his feet.. The big, muscular fisherman looked at Jimmy and then looked at the gun. The boat slewed to the side and the gun skidded closer to the fisherman. There was a moment of hesitation and then Sean turned his back to Jimmy and bent down for the pistol. Jimmy grabbed the fishing net and threw himself onto the man's back wrapping him in the net before stepping away and landing a solid kick to the lumbar region of his spine. Sean staggered towards the rail of the boat before his momentum hit the rail and flipped him over the edge, leaving him thrashing in the water, entangled in the net and being swallowed by the wake of the boat. Jimmy turned back to the smaller one. He was back on his feet, swaying with the motion of the boat and an animalistic snarl splitting his weathered face.

"This could have been a lot simpler." Jimmy could feel the salty spray on his back.

"You've picked a fight with the wrong people." A trickle of blood was running down the Irishman's chin.

"We'll take our chances."

"You don't know who you're dealing with." Simon steadied himself and felt around behind him for something, any kind of weapon. His hands came up holding an old rusted billhook that had lain discarded on the deck and looked at the two Englishman with a ferocity burning in his eyes. He grinned, delighted with his new weapon.

Jimmy moved towards him carefully, the rocking boat and slippery surface made it hard enough as it was to stand upright, let alone with a severely damaged leg. Jimmy could see past the man to where Tom was breathing in short sharp gasps. "Come on, we can find a solution. This doesn't need any more blood spilt."

Simon laughed. "I'm gonna gut you like a fish. And if I don't….*they* will"

He surged forward towards Jimmy, swinging the rusted claw of a hook. Jimmy ducked and weaved out of harm's way, circling back behind him. Simon was now caught between the two Englishman, snarling and spitting with rage.

He spun on his heel and went for Tom, seeing him as injured and weak, but Tom saw the move coming, it was amateurish and predictable, and although human instinct encouraged him to retreat from the heavy iron hook, Tom's training kicked in and he closed the space between them, coming in under

Simon's raised right arm and jabbing him in the windpipe. Simon stumbled back, clutching his throat and gasping for air, like a fish out of water. As he stumbled backwards, his heel caught on one of the stray fishing nets and he tripped - the billhook clanged on the metal deck and his head came down hard on the corner of the raised hatch to the hold. There was a sickening crack, before a pool of thick, dark blood began to seep from beneath the Irishman. He remained motionless. For a moment the only sounds were the seabirds' cries and the thrum of the engine. They picked the lifeless body up and dropped it over the side of the boat. Seagulls swooped down thinking the boat was chumming the water.

Tom and Jimmy turned to the wheelhouse to see Maggie holding the wheel steady, tears glistened in her eyes.

The old man had regained consciousness by the time they put a life jacket onto the him, cut his restraints and threw him overboard a few hundred meters from the beach of an isolated cove on the north side of the island, one that Maggie and Tom said was rarely visited by any of the islanders and would be sufficiently isolated that it would take him a good few hours to raise any sort of alarm.

Jimmy turned the wheel and pointed the fishing boat north, towards the open ocean. For the first time in what felt like days, he felt the tension in his shoulders abate, and he began to laugh to himself.

An hour later Jimmy found Maggie below deck counting out the money from the bin liner on the table. Charlie was asleep on one of the bunks and Tom was dressing his wound with an old first aid kit he had found.

"How much is there?!" Jimmy looked down the steps at the big pile of neatly stacked notes and thought back to the poker table at Deaf Andy's when his life had begun to fall apart.

Maggie put the last bundle of notes onto a stack. "Just shy of three hundred and fifty grand."

Tom whistled.

Jimmy looked at Maggie. "What does all of that mean?"

"What do you mean?" Maggie returned Jimmy's stare.

"Well, you say it was yours and Gully's. What did Gully want us to do with it?"

"He wanted you to take your share and use it to better your lives. To buy a house, chase the waves, start a business... whatever made you happy."

Charlie scoffed and everyone turned in his direction, unaware that he had woken. A sneer creeping across his face.

"He wanted to right his wrongs Charlie. None of this was meant to happen. But it did. He wanted to leave you something. He wanted to say sorry. However you felt, however you feel now, he was a good man. He may have wronged you. But you were young and...and stupid. He was trying to make it right."

"By leaving us his drug money." Charlie half turned his back on the pile of cash like it was infectious.

"Wherever it came from it's yours now. Give it to charity, spend it on the horses, buy a house or a car, do what you like with it, but he wanted you to have it, to make your life better."

"I don't have a life to go back to. I have no wife, I have no home, I have no brother, no parents. What the fuck am I meant to do with it eh?" Charlie's voice was full of anger and resentment, spittle forming at the edges of his mouth.

"Half of this mess is my fault, Charlie. Mark's death wasn't Gully's fault. It was mine. Those guys at the cottage were after me, because of the wrongs I'd done, not Gully. So, if you are going to hate, hate me. Forgive Gully. It's time." Jimmy looked at his friend with sorrow. He couldn't imagine how he was hurting. All he knew was that they could come back from this. They had to come back from this.

A silence stretched out and mingled with the thrum of the engine.

"Listen, there is nothing I can say to make this go away, but what now? We curl up and die?" Jimmy sat down on the top step and began to gently rub his throbbing calf.

"That might not be such a bad option." Charlie was staring at the wall, feeling empty and full of anger, conflicted and unsure of who to blame.

"For I will forgive their wickedness and remember their sins no more." Tom slurped at a cup of tea.

"I don't believe in God."

"Nor do I." Tom's response came quickly.

Maggie, Jimmy and Charlie all looked at Tom. He glanced up from his tea, catching their surprised looks. "I haven't for a while. The Bible has some good stuff in it, but in the end it doesn't matter does it? You can spend your whole life trying to do good, be a good person, make a difference. But in the end, it doesn't make any difference does it? Life's gone. Forgotten. And you are just a pile of ash. And who knows what happens then."

"It makes a difference to those you leave behind. Those who'll remember you." Charlie's eyes were brimming with moisture that glinted in the late afternoon light.

"I'm still here for you buddy. Maybe this is just the start of a new chapter. We can take the money and start again. Wherever you want. We can go to Australia, Indo, America, France. Surf warm waves in board shorts and build hospitals for sick kids if that's what you want. But we have a chance here.

Think about Mark. Think about what he would say." Jimmy gingerly got up onto his one good leg and turned back to the wheel in the wheelhouse.

Maggie began to put the money into a holdall she found under the seat. "Jimmy's right you know. This could just be the start of an adventure."

"I don't want another adventure."

"No. But Mark would have, wouldn't he? He would have jumped at the chance."

Maggie zipped up the holdall and threw it into the corner of the banquette. She looked at Charlie who didn't not return her gaze. She turned and climbed the stairs to the wheelhouse.

"Let your eyes look directly forward and your gaze be straight before you." Tom stands, his body aching from head to toe.

"And what is that supposed to mean?" Charlie mumbles.

"Exactly what I said. We can't live in the past Charlie. We all make mistakes, but we can only move forward and learn from them and become better and to love." Tom began to climb the steps to join the others. The sun was beginning to set, and the sky was cast in a luminous spectacle of oranges and pinks and blues.

"Tom?" Charlie shifted his position to look at Tom. "Where do you think Mark is now?"

Tom turned on the step "Out there." Tom nodded towards the carpet of colour in the sky outside. "Look."

The three of them stood in the wheelhouse and let the cool evening air flow through the cabin and ruffle their hair. They didn't speak but breathed the air of freedom…of possibility. They heard the steps behind them creek, but none of them turned.

"Should we scatter the ashes or take the fucker with us?"

Charlie stood holding the little tube of Gully's ashes.

Jimmy looked at his friend. "I think we should bring him with us."

"So….where are we going to go?"

AFTERWORD

Thanks for reading 'Finding Nowhere'. I hope you enjoyed it. Please note that all characters and locations are fictional; although inspired by real life people and places, like any real surfer, I would never reveal the location of a decent wave! Get out there and go searching.

If you have enjoyed this book, please leave a positive review - I would love to hear what you have to say.

If you didn't enjoy this book....I am sorry....thanks for giving it a go - please don't crush me in your review.....be a lover, not a hater!

ACKNOWLEDGEMENT

This book is dedicated to my wife, Lucy, who has stuck with me throughout the whole process, encouraging me, and giving me helpful ideas and advice. She is amazing and life's adventure would not be half as fun if I didn't have her in my life. Thank-you.

I also want to thank my parents, who have always believed in me, even when perhaps they shouldn't! This isn't really their bag, but I hope they enjoy it in some way. My children, Daisy, Ted and Barnaby are a constant source of entertainment and I love them more than anything....even the ocean. I hope one day they will get to read this and be proud of their Dad - you guys can do anything you want....just set your mind on it and do it.

Finally, I want to say thanks to my best friend, Chris - thanks for your feedback and your support. You are the brother I never had, and kindest, most generous man I know. I am lucky to have you in my life.

ABOUT THE AUTHOR

Js Brough

Jamie lives in Devon with his wife, three children and their dog, 'Claude'. He is an avid surfer and sportsman. He likes nothing more than walking coastal paths, paddling in the sea and enjoying adventures in the great outdoors. Jamie trained in sports science at Loughborough University, before going on to study acting at the London Academy of Music and Dramatic Art (LAMDA). He worked for many years as an actor, director and writer, before eventually realising that he needed a steadier income in order to raise his three children, and so he took the plunge and became a drama teacher. Now his children are getting older, he feels it is time to get back to doing what he really loves.

Jamie is an award winning playwright (fringe first winner), and has witten a screenplay that was commissioned and directed by David Morrissey and Tubedale films. This is his debut novel.

Jamie is combining his love of writing with his love of surfing and the ocean - he will be releasing a series of novels, 'the barefoot chronicles', based around surfing and the ocean. He loves reading and grew up being inspired by the surfing/crime fiction of Kem Nunn. This, together with being inspired by the amazing characters in books such as 'The Outsiders' by S.E Hinton, the 'Beartown' series by Fredrik Backmann and 'Malibu Rising' by Taylor Jenkins Reid has led him to attempt to bring a similar sort of vibe to a British based surf series.